Jesús began to creep along the stream. He had some trees for cover but he was exposed now and then.

"Keep your head down, Jesús," yelled Ethan. The other man flattened and began to crawl. Thirty or more yards, and he would be even with the rock where Rourke was hiding. The rock was just barely big enough to protect Rourke, and Ethan could see the man now and then shifting his position behind it. The trail behind him was open, so he would not be able to run. He was trapped.

"Rourke!" yelled Ethan. "Give it up. I want you alive. Just come out from behind there and you'll be all right!"

"Go to hell, ya bastard," said Rourke. Ethan stayed alongside the wall of the cliff. There was enough cover there, and he could still see Rourke's rock, and he could see Jesús crawling down the gully by the stream on the other side of the trail.

Slowly Jesús crawled toward a spot opposite Rourke.

"Keep it down, Jesús!" yelled Ethan. "I'll tell you when you're in position! Then find yourself a tree and get behind it."

Jesús kept crawling. When he was at a slight angle from Rourke, Ethan yelled again.

"That's good enough, Jesús! Get behind a cottonwood! You'll be able to see Rourke!"

There were a few yards between the gully where Jesús was crawling and a large cottonwood. Ethan could see Jesús gather himself for the quick dash to the tree. He rose up on his haunches and then launched himself in a dive toward the cottonwood. Just as he was landing there was a shot. Ethan did not see where it came from. He hadn't been watching Rourke for that split second. Jesús yelled as he hit the ground, and he landed behind the tree and lay face down and did not move.

<u>BOOK YOUR PLACE ON OUR WEBSITE</u> AND MAKE THE <u>READING CONNECTION!</u>

We've created a customized website just for our very special readers, where you can get the inside scoop on everything that's going on with Zebra, Pinnacle and Kensington books.

When you come online, you'll have the exciting opportunity to:

- View covers of upcoming books
- Read sample chapters
- Learn about our future publishing schedule (listed by publication month *and author*)
- Find out when your favorite authors will be visiting a city near you
- Search for and order backlist books from our online catalog
- Check out author bios and background information
- Send e-mail to your favorite authors
- Meet the Kensington staff online
- Join us in weekly chats with authors, readers and other guests
- Get writing guidelines
- AND MUCH MORE!

Visit our website at
http://www.kensingtonbooks.com

SHOWDOWN AT
VERITY

T.A. MORT

PINNACLE BOOKS
Kensington Publishing Corp.
http://www.kensingtonbooks.com

For Sondra

One

The half-breed was picking his way carefully. His head was up, his eyes scanning the entrance to the canyon. He sniffed the wind and listened for sounds that didn't belong there. Years of being on the run had made him wary, especially when riding through canyons where there were dozens of places for enemies to lie in wait. His horse was done in, lathered from long hours on the trail. Another reason for caution, for he would not be able to outrun anyone.

Ethan Grey watched from behind a boulder about seventy yards inside the canyon. There were piñon trees on either side of him. He could see his man easily through the branches on his left. Grey's shotgun was leaning against the boulder. Next to it was a shovel, and next to that a pine board that Grey had been writing on. The wind was on Grey's left, so that if he fired, the gun smoke would immediately blow to the side, leaving him a clear view for a second shot. Grey had learned long ago not to fire a shotgun into the wind if he could help it.

Come on, Joe, thought Grey. *Let's finish this.*

Indian Joe rode closer, stopping once to listen and then coming again, slowly. Ethan Grey could see his mahogany face, dark eyes, greasy hair hanging down beneath an old sombrero, a faded serape thrown back over his shoulders. Ethan could see his gun belt with a heavy Navy Colt revolver stuck in it next to a skinning knife. He could see the beadwork on the knife sheath and the brass tacks Joe had used to decorate the stock of the Spencer carbine he was holding in his right hand.

When Joe was thirty yards away, Ethan Grey picked up his shotgun and slowly pulled back both hammers. The gun was a twelve-gauge Purdey, a gift from his commanding officer during the war; it was too good a gun to use on the likes of Indian Joe. It was made for grouse on the moors of Scotland, or ruffed grouse in the autumn woods around his boyhood home in Maine. The English gun maker who had hand-polished the walnut stock and lovingly engraved the scrollwork in the sidelocks never thought that this elegant weapon might be used on a renegade somewhere in the desert of New Mexico Territory. But a shotgun was the right gun for this situation, and Ethan Grey believed in using the right tool for a particular job.

For a second, Ethan thought Joe's horse had heard the soft clicking of the hammers, for the horse seemed to look in Ethan's direction. But no. The horse's ears didn't twitch, and he didn't change his gait. Ethan's own horse was tethered about a mile up the canyon. He wouldn't give any warning.

Soon Indian Joe was just opposite Ethan's blind, almost fifteen yards away. Ethan had waited until this moment because Joe would not be able to swivel easily in his saddle, not be able to bring his carbine to bear. He'd either have to quit or die. Ethan could smell the half-breed's horse. Or maybe it was Joe he smelled. Hard to say.

Ethan stood up and put the shotgun to his shoulder.

"Hold it there, Joe," he said, not particularly loud.

Startled, Joe looked around wildly for a moment, and then saw Grey pointing the shotgun at him. He started to raise his rifle.

"Don't do it," Ethan said, more forcefully this time.

Joe turned in his saddle toward Ethan and pulled the rifle to his shoulder. Most likely it was a simple reflex, something he would not have done had he thought about it. The last thing he saw was the flash of Ethan's shotgun. At fifteen yards the shot pattern was about the size of Joe's head, and he got all of it.

The force of the blast knocked Indian Joe off the side of his horse into a heap on the ground, his face in the dirt. The horse, suddenly riderless, bolted a few paces up the trail and then stopped and looked back, confused.

Ethan watched Joe for signs of movement. He saw none. He shot Joe again, this time hitting him in the side, which rolled him over on his back. Ethan broke the shotgun open and removed the empty shells. He reloaded and fired once more into what was left of Indian Joe. There was no sense in taking chances, he thought. Shells were easy to come by, and half-blooded Utes were hard to kill.

He waited a minute longer and then, picking up the shovel and the board, went down to the body. He had selected this spot from among the many ambush sites in the canyon because there was some soft dirt alongside the hard-packed trail. It was a good place to dig a hole. Ethan had not gone there intending to kill the outlaw. He would have brought him in alive had it been possible. But he also understood the odds and understood his quarry, and so made his plans accordingly.

Ethan looked down at what he had done. Joe was

bleeding from dozens of shot wounds. His lower jaw and left ear were gone.

Well, Joe, he thought, *you aren't as good-looking as you used to be, but you have learned a valuable lesson. Let's get you planted so you can spread the word down below.*

This was not the first time Ethan had killed a man. The other situations had been similar. He felt little, if anything, and he sometimes wondered at this lack of emotion. There was no revulsion, no regret, nothing except maybe a little dark humor that seemed out of place. Now and then it troubled him, this numbness. He knew it was not natural; he had not been born with it. It was something that he had acquired along the way. Perhaps it was a kind of armor. Or perhaps he had seen too many good men killed during the war to worry much about the death of a few bad ones, men who mostly needed killing. Nature's errors. Ethan had even killed some of the good ones during the war. Certainly some of the shells he had ordered fired into Vicksburg had injured and killed people, maybe even some civilians. And he remembered aiming his guns at a squad of Rebel cavalry near the riverbank and ordering the fire that sent shells bursting above the squad, killing men and horses alike. He presumed that many were good men. Indian Joe, by comparison, was simple trash.

Ethan dug a shallow hole, then stripped Joe of his pistol and knife and checked his pockets. Nothing much. Then he rolled Joe into the hole and covered him over. He piled some rocks on top, and then pounded in the board at the head of the grave as a marker. While waiting for Joe to arrive, Ethan had written his epitaph, just to save time:

HERE LIES INDIAN JOE. THIEF AND MURDERER. HE WON'T BE MISSED.

Two weeks later Ethan was having breakfast at his hotel in Santa Fe. He was reading the newspaper, and came across the account of his "capture" of Indian Joe:

DESPERATE ENCOUNTER IN THE DESERT

Pinkerton detective Ethan Grey killed notorious outlaw "Indian Joe" in a duel in Phillips Canyon. Joe was wanted for numerous depredations throughout the Southwest, most recently the holdup of a Wells-Fargo stage during which he killed the driver and two passengers and wounded the shotgun messenger, Albert Bell, who subsequently identified Joe as the assailant.

Grey, a native of Maine and a Civil War veteran, had little choice but to use deadly force against Indian Joe. "I gave him every chance to surrender," said Grey, "but he pulled his gun and I had no other option." The outlaw fired three shots at Grey, narrowly missing him each time. Grey then drew his revolver and fired a single shot, which ended the fracas.

The Pinkerton Agency had been hired by Wells-Fargo to track Indian Joe and if possible bring him back to Santa Fe for trial. Grey's quick actions have saved the county the trouble.

Ethan grimaced as he read the report. He had not talked to the newspaper, so obviously they had gotten their account from the Pinkerton office.

Later that morning Ethan went to see his supervisor, Parker Jones. Jones was a small man, pudgy from too many years of sitting behind a desk. Ethan did not care much for him, but then, he didn't care that much for anyone.

"I saw the newspaper report on Indian Joe, Parker. Seems like somebody's imagination's run off with him."

"Publicity's good for business, Ethan."

"I know that. But that report's a little short on the truth."

"There are different kinds of truth."

"So it would seem." It was not an idea that Ethan agreed with, but there was no sense in discussing it with Jones.

"I read your report," said Jones. "As usual, it was to the point without a lot of detail. So we had to add a little style to it, just so the newspaper boys would be happy. They like a story to be a little colorful. I gather Joe didn't show that much fight."

"He would have. As it was, though, he didn't."

"Well, it was good work, regardless of the details. You may have heard, though, that there was some talk around town about it just after we got the word. Some people wondered why you didn't bring him back to town. The county sheriff, for one. I wouldn't worry about it, though."

"I'm not going to. In the first place, Joe wasn't in any condition to travel. And second, I didn't feel like toting a dead man a week or so through the desert just so some sheriff looking for votes could set him up on the plaza for people to gawk at. Anybody wants him, they can go dig him up. I'll draw them a map."

"No need. Your affidavit is enough to close the case. Plus you did bring in his horse."

"Wasn't much of a horse, but I figured the widow of the real owner might want him back. Decent saddle, anyway."

Jones nodded. He said, "Looks like there'll be some

more work for you coming up soon. We're discussing a project with the Army. It seems there's been some trouble about stolen payrolls around Tucson, but there's nothing set yet. You could take some time off and go fishing or something, if you wanted to. We'll know more in another week or so."

"Might just do that."

The idea of going to the mountains and being around water for a few days was appealing. Ethan Grey had grown up in Oquossoc, Maine, a few miles east of the New Hampshire line, in the Rangeley Lake district. His family owned a sawmill there, but his father's great passion had been the building of the elegant little boats named after the lake, and Ethan had lived most of his early years around these boats and around the water. Fishing and waterfowling had been a way of adding to the larder, but more importantly, had been a way of life for him in those days. He had been a solitary boy, a reader and student, and he spent his free time, the time when he was not needed at the sawmill or boatyard, wandering through the Maine woods with a rod or gun, his sack lunch, and a book. The best times were in the autumn, during that all-too-short season when the maples and birch trees changed colors and turned the mountains into patternless quilts of yellow and red. And he remembered the smell of the forest, the clean moist air, and the call of the loons on the lake outside his front porch; he remembered the smell of birch-bark fires, the sweet smell of split logs burning in the mornings when his mother would be up before first light to fire up the cast-iron stove in the kitchen. He remembered the smell and taste of coffee and flapjacks with maple syrup. When he thought about these things, he wondered what he was doing in the Southwest, so far from things that were familiar, so far from water, so far from the moist and smoky smells that meant home to him. But then he remembered the winters that seemed endless, the iron-gray days and the cold that could never be dispelled no matter how large the fire. Even that, though, was part of home. And he was now a long way from there.

When he turned eighteen, he went off to Bowdoin College to study literature. One of his professors there was the now-celebrated Joshua Chamberlain, the hero of the Little Round Top fight at Gettysburg. The year Ethan finished college the war broke out, and though many of his friends joined the Army, Ethan felt the pull of the water. It seemed more natural for him to join the Navy. He received a commission as a lieutenant, and was assigned first to blockade duty in the Atlantic, and then to a gunboat squadron patrolling the Mississippi. That was how he came to be at Vicksburg, second in command of one of the gunboats that were bombarding the city during Grant's siege. On the day that his former professor was beating back the Confederate attacks on Little Round Top, Ethan Grey received a splinter wound through the calf, the result of a Rebel cannon shot that shattered the railing near where Ethan was standing. He missed the surrender of the city the following day, for he was in the hospital lying soaked in sweat, horrified at the thought that they were going to amputate his leg. But the wound was clean, and no infection set in, so he recovered with no long-term effects except an occasional ache when the nights were cold.

When the war ended, he tried to stay in the Navy, but there was no place for him, so he went home to Maine. The war had left him feeling restless in a way that he could not shake and could not explain. He knew he could not get back into the slow rhythms of village life, and after a month or so he left home again thinking to find work on a merchant ship. His travels took him to Mexico, where he was caught up in a short-lived and abortive action against the Emperor Maximilian. It was entirely accidental, this venture; he had simply been in the wrong place at the wrong time, and he had become involved. In Mexico he met a woman. Maria. Together they escaped from Mexico, staying for a while in Texas before finally going to San Diego, where her parents, also refugees from the war in Mexico, had gone to establish a trading business. Ethan and Maria were married. She was different from anyone he had known before, dark, slim, unfailingly good-natured with a talent for joyfulness, and she charmed him and filled his time with great happiness, and he no longer felt like a restless wanderer, because wherever she was was home to him then. After a while he found a berth as second officer on a clipper ship running to Asia, and he made a number of trips to Japan and China during the first few years of his marriage. The voyages lasted several months, and although being away from Maria was not easy, this was work he liked to do. Homecomings were always sweet. He was content, and gradually began to think that he had actually earned the happiness he felt. He began to believe in it and trust it. But during one of his voyages Maria was swept up in an influenza epidemic, and by the time he learned of it she had been dead three months. And now that was the other ache that he felt, regardless of whether the nights were cold or not.

He left the sea and left his home in San Diego. He did not have the heart for any of it now. After a while he found that he had come to the desert, and after a little more time he came to New Mexico, where he began work as a Pinkerton.

Two

Ten days after his meeting with his supervisor Ethan Grey stepped off the train in Tucson.

More damned desert, he thought, as he looked around the town. The wind was blowing clouds of dust through the streets. The sun was blazing, and there were Mexicans sitting up against the adobe walls waiting out the heat of the afternoon. There was a dead mule lying at the end of one of the streets, but nobody seemed in any hurry to drag him off. A few stray dogs were the only ones interested. At the end of the main street was a café called The Shoo Fly. Aptly named, he thought.

The Santa Cruz River ran alongside the town. It was a poor excuse for a river, just a few feet wide and a few inches deep. The water looked foul, murky and warm. The mountains around the town were rocky and bare except for some scrubby mesquite and the spires of saguaro cactus. The Tucson Mountains to the west were sharply pointed, and reminded Ethan of the mountains he had seen in China. The Catalinas to the north were broader and more massive, and at the lower elevations they were light pink and green from the lichen on the rocks and from the occasional cactus or mesquite. But there was not much soil there, and the pastel colors could not disguise the reality of the rock. At the higher elevations near the summits there was a line of pine trees, and the highest peak was covered by a thin haze of smoke from a forest fire started, most likely, by lightning.

Ethan unloaded his horse from the train. He saddled up and rode a few miles north to Fort Lowell, where he was to meet with his Army contact, a captain named Wilkes.

Like most frontier posts, Fort Lowell was a collection of buildings arranged in a rectangle around a parade ground. There were no walls around the post. The buildings were all made of adobe brick, and the main offices and officers' quarters were trimmed with whitewash around the windows and doors. The fort stood near the Rillito River, a dry wash during most months and a brown torrent during the monsoon rains that hit Tucson in the late summer.

Ethan rode up to the building marked ADJUTANT and went in.

"Captain Wilkes?" said Ethan to the officer behind the desk.

"That's right."

"My name's Jaeger," said Ethan.

Wilkes stood up and shook hands with Ethan. He was not a young man. He had thick white hair worn long, and his face was burnt brown and leathery. His uniform was faded, slightly. He was lean and straight, and he gave the impression of someone who knew what he was doing. Like many career officers, he'd found that the opportunities for promotion were few and far between after the war. Since the war he had been posted to a number of small forts throughout the West, and he'd tried to make the best of it. Unlike many of his colleagues, he had not given in to the boredom and the hardship, had not drunk himself into early senility. Instead, he had made a study of the places he was sent to and of the Indians he was there to watch over and, if necessary, fight.

"Have a seat," said Wilkes. "I've been expecting you. Have a good trip?"

"Tolerable," said Ethan.

"That's about as good as it gets out here. I expect you know that." Wilkes smiled. "Coffee?"

"Yes, thanks." Wilkes poured coffee from a metal pot that was steaming on the cast-iron stove in the corner. Though Ethan was happy enough to get the coffee, he wondered that anyone would keep a stove going in this weather. It was autumn, but it was still hot. As though reading his thoughts, Wilkes said, "You get used to the heat out here. Maybe you heard about the cavalry man who died in Yuma and went to hell and after a day or so down there sent back for his blankets."

"Yes, I have heard that story. Often wondered if it was true." Apparently Wilkes was a professional soldier with a sense of humor, not a common combination in Ethan's experience.

"Every word of it. And no lesser authority than General Sherman himself said that if he owned Hell and Texas, he'd live in hell and rent out Texas. Arizona's worse. But it's pleasant in the winter. Well, this is interesting to me, having you here. I've never met a Pinkerton before. I reckon it's a good idea getting you folks involved in this investigation. To be honest, the Army doesn't have the resources to do this job by ourselves. We're stretched pretty thin, and it's not our specialty anyway. I've been told to give you as much background as I can. That's little enough, I'm afraid. We don't have any idea who attacked our patrol, but whoever did it got away with fifty thousand dollars in Army payroll."

"The reports I read suggest it was Apaches."

"That's one theory, but there are some unusual aspects to this raid that make me think maybe somebody else is involved. If we were sure it was an Indian problem, there'd be no sense in getting private investigators involved. It would be strictly Army business. But there are plenty of other candidates, God knows. Arizona is hell's own training ground. The raids all took place in the Santa Rita Mountains south of here. The wagon and the escort were heading from Tucson to the forts near the border, Huachuca and Bowie."

Wilkes stood and went over to the map on the wall.

"The patrol went south out of Tucson down the Santa Cruz Valley, and then turned east up through Madera Canyon in the Santa Ritas. They were headed up to the grasslands on the other side of the mountains. That's the shortest way to Fort Huachuca. But they never got out of Madera Canyon."

"Are the Apaches active in that area?"

"The Apaches are active anywhere they choose to be and nowhere in particular. But yes, that country and all the way to New Mexico has been the traditional stronghold of the Chiricahuas, for one. I expect you remember Cochise and that gang. Well, about two years ago, the Chircahuas were removed from their reservation in the mountains—this was after Cochise had died—and they were sent up to San Carlos and mixed in with the other Apache tribes. Nobody's very happy with that arrangement. Most people think an Apache is just an Apache, but it isn't so. They have different bands and jealousies and feuds and whatnot just like any other collection of humans, and the fact is the Chiricahuas don't like it up there in San Carlos. Every now and then, a few of them will prove it by running off and raiding into Mexico just like the good old days, and on the way they don't scruple to steal some rancher's stock and kill any white folks who happen to be in the area. It's the way they've made their living for centuries, and a lot of them see no reason to change. Just last April, Geronimo and Juh and a bunch of their people jumped San Carlos. They're probably raising hell down in Mexico even as we speak. There are times when I think I'd do likewise, if I was in their shoes. Beats farming. They are an interesting people, but cruel. Which is the one thing that makes me wonder if they're responsible for this robbery."

"How so?"

"None of the soldiers was mutilated. No sign of torture. Just efficient killing from ambush. Then they grabbed the money and stock, burned the wagon, and left. They took the soldiers' uniforms and boots and weapons, maybe to make it look like an Indian attack, but whoever it was didn't have any interest in, or maybe any stomach for, the sort of things that Apaches generally do to their victims."

"White men, you figure?"

"Perhaps. Or maybe Mexicans. You know, that's right near the border, and there has been a long tradition of Indians and white men and Mexicans all going both ways across that line killing each other and stealing whatever there was to steal. An Army payroll would look pretty tempting to any of them."

"How many men were guarding the shipment?"

"Six troopers plus the corporal in charge. And the paymaster. Eight men in all." Wilkes paused. "You're wondering why we didn't send more men, I suppose."

"It occurred to me. But I'm sure you know your business, Captain."

"I do know my business, Mr. Jaeger. Our commanding officer, however, is one of those who thinks that one trooper is worth ten Indians or twenty Mexicans. He's new out here." Wilkes said this matter-of-factly, with no irony or implied reproach in his voice. "Everybody's new at some point. It passes soon enough."

"I see. You'd think after Custer, people might see things a little differently."

"Some attitudes die kind of slow. But he's a decent officer and he's learned something the hard way, though not as hard as those troopers. And in fairness, we are stretched thin here, and the troopers he sent were experienced men. Whoever pulled this off knows something about setting up an ambush. When we examined the site, we didn't find any spent cartridges. None of ours, I mean. Our men never fired a shot."

"Which brings us back to the Apaches, maybe."

"I don't rule it out. They are adept at ambush, God knows."

"Were there any other signs?"

"Not really. We found where the attackers hid. It seems like they were wearing moccasins, but of course anyone can get hold of them. We never located where they hid their horses, so there was no telling if they were shod or not. We found their empty shells, but there was nothing revealing about them. A mixture of common calibers. They must have hidden their horses back in the mountains and walked to the ambush spot. Had to've been several miles. Then afterwards, we figure they gathered up our troopers' horses and rode out of there. They circled around so as to confuse anyone following them, and then disappeared. Back to where they had their own horses hidden. Anyway, I'm just guessing, because we lost their trail."

"Who did your tracking?"

"Our Apache scouts," Wilkes said. "Naturally, that raises questions in some people's minds. But we have used Apache scouts successfully for a number of years. It was originally General Crook's idea, and most of the scouts are White Mountain Apaches. They've always been loyal and effective, and lots of them don't care much for the Chiricahuas. It goes back to what I said before—it's a mistake to think of Apaches as just one tribe. These various bands may speak the same language and have the same sort of ways, but they are as different in other respects as a parson and a pimp. Meaning no disrespect to the pimp by the comparison." Wilkes smiled. It was obvious to Ethan that Wilkes had had this kind of discussion before.

"Were the wounds all from gunshots?" Ethan asked.

"Yes. No arrow wounds as best as we could tell. The surgeon wasn't with us at the time to examine the bodies, so we can't be sure. But we didn't find any arrows. Of course, they could have removed them from the bodies, but Indians will generally leave some arrows in a body, as a gesture of contempt. I've seen some dead troopers up in the Plains who would pass for porcupines. So I doubt arrows were used. Looks to me like our boys rode into sudden and concentrated rifle fire. Over in seconds. It has the earmarks of a very disciplined attack, which is another thing that makes me doubt the Apache theory. They generally fight as individuals. They're clever fighters, but not much given to military discipline. Most likely one of them would have jumped the gun, which would have given some warning to our men, enough so that they could at least get off a few rounds in return."

"Makes sense." Ethan admired men who knew what they were doing and who went about it without any show. Wilkes's analysis was all the more credible because he wasn't cocksure.

Wilkes paused. He seemed to be studying Ethan. "Just out of curiosity, is your name really Jaeger?"

"It's close enough."

"That's what I figured. You know, during the war, we used the Pinkertons as intelligence agents. McClellan was fond of Alan Pinkerton as I heard it. So I guess you fellows are used to going around under assumed names."

"That's often the way it works. The fact is, only you and the commanding officer know why I'm here. As far as anyone else is concerned, I'm a reporter for a New York paper, the *Herald*. We have some contacts there who will verify that, if need be."

"So the story is you're out here to write about the great American West for all the ribbon clerks and Sunday school teachers back East. Give 'em a taste of adventure," Wilkes said.

"That's the idea. It's a plausible story, and it allows me to move around and ask questions without raising too many suspicions."

"Makes sense, although if it was the Apaches, I doubt the story'll do you much good. Not if they get hold of you. Press credentials don't impress them."

"That has occurred to me," Ethan said. "On the other hand, if it wasn't the Apaches, then maybe a little camouflage will come in handy. Can't hurt, anyway."

"Well, I guess you know your business, too."

"Pretty well."

"What are your plans?"

Ethan said, "I thought I'd start by looking around the area where the attack took place, and then head down toward the border. I noticed there's a little town, up in the foothills east of the Santa Ritas. Verity. I figured I'd make that my base, maybe meet a few of the locals and sniff around some. If it was somebody other than Apaches, that might be a good place to start looking. From what I hear, there are some pretty rough elements down there."

"That's true. Quite a few of those Verity boys haven't made up their minds yet about which side of the law they prefer. They keep experimenting, so to speak. When you get to Verity, you should look up a man named Septimus Harding. He runs a little newspaper there. He's a good man and a bad poker player, which is why I like him. Calling on him would make sense, you being a reporter. He can give you all the local gossip and fill you in on the cast of characters. Verity's not much of a town, but there are some big ranches in the area, and a lot of little ones, too. And generally, the smaller the ranch, the more liberal the rancher's interpretation of property law. Like I said before, the border's close by, and Mexican cattle seem to drift over the line with fair regularity, if you follow me. Can't keep away, seems like. Some of those ranchers have hay and beef contracts with the Army, and by the time we get the beef, the original brands are as distant a memory as a whore's First Communion. The Army thinks Mexican beef tastes about the same as American, so we don't ask a lot of questions. We wouldn't get any answers even if we did. I expect the hay's one-hundred-percent American, though."

"It's a wicked world, Captain."

"So it is, Mr. Jaeger."

Three

Early next morning Ethan went to the livery stable in Tucson to buy a pack mule. There was only one available, a red mule with a squint. He looked sound enough. The livery man was a wiry old coot, bearded up to his cheekbones. Tobacco stains colored his chin whiskers. And he had a wary look in his eyes as he tried to determine whether Ethan was a tenderfoot who could be safely cheated.

"If you're lookin' for a mule, then you need look no longer, friend. This is the animal for you. A regular daisy. Half brother to the mule General Crook used to ride when he was down here chasin' the Apaches. Gentle. Smart. And good company, too. Never says a word. Won't bite or kick, much. And he's broke to the pack, yessir. Nothing he likes better than two hundred and fifty pounds of gear strapped on him. Go all day and ask for more come sunset." He spat for emphasis.

"What's his name?"

"Name? Well, jest Mule, I guess. He never said otherwise. No, you can't go wrong with a mule like this one. Where're you headed?"

"South. Down towards Verity."

"Well, then, all the more reason why this is jest the mule for you. He can smell Indians a mile away. Doesn't care for 'em one little bit. You watch his ears and if they start twitchin', well, then, you look sharp. More'n likely it means there's Indians around. Course I don't say that he can tell the difference between an Apache and a Papago. He ain't *that* smart, but at least he'll give you some warning. Yessir, I've seen it a dozen times, and never known him to make a mistake. Saved my hair more 'n once, and that's the gospel truth."

"I'm surprised you'd let a mule like that go." Ethan didn't believe any of it. His experience with mules was that when their ears started twitching, they were getting ready to run off. And the only mule he'd ever seen that wouldn't bite or kick was the one that had been lying in the street the day before. But he was now getting into his role as a reporter, and figured a little gullible conversation was appropriate.

"Hate to do it, I surely do," said the livery man. "I'd sooner sell my old woman, but she wouldn't be much good to you because she refuses to tote a pack and what's more, she'd most likely founder before you got out of town, so you're better off with this here animal. Besides, times is hard and business is business."

"How much?"

"Well, like I say, time's is hard jest now, so I'll let him go for, say, forty dollars." Ethan said nothing. "And I'll throw in some hobbles. Mexican hobbles, at that."

Ethan considered, then said, "Seems fair enough."

The livery man looked disgusted, feeling that he hadn't asked enough. "Course that don't include the bridle and such," he added.

"Yes, it does, friend."

The livery man looked at Ethan and didn't care for what he saw. He wisely decided forty dollars in hand would do.

"Good decision," Ethan said. "Come on, Priam. Let's get you packed up."

"Priam?"

"Everything's got to have a name, friend. That's how you know what's what and who's who. Without that, we're all just wandering in the wilderness."

"Maybe so. But if you're going down to Verity, that's jest exactly what you *are* going to be doin'."

At sunup the next day, Ethan headed south from Tucson. He followed the river past the Spanish mission of San Xavier del Bac on his way to the little town of Tubac thirty miles or so from Tucson. The Army patrol that had been attacked had followed this same road, although they had turned off into the mountains a few miles north of Tubac. Ethan's plan was to spend the night in the little town. Perhaps he could pick up some scraps of information, and besides, he disliked camping and avoided it whenever possible. The next morning he planned to backtrack north and turn east into Madera Canyon and investigate the attack scene. From there he would follow the pass east through the Santa Ritas to Verity.

Priam seemed fairly tractable carrying Ethan's camping equipment and extra food and ammunition. He plodded along behind Ethan's horse apparently indifferent to the weight of the pack or the heat of the day. But Ethan didn't trust him yet, so he carried his water and some food in his saddlebags, and he kept his rifle in his scabbard and wore his two Schofield pistols and a bowie knife on his belt. His Purdey was packed in a mutton-leg case and strapped behind the saddle. If

Priam decided to run off, he would not be taking anything that meant the difference between survival and death in the desert. Ethan wasn't going to let some fool mule run away and leave him unarmed.

On the ride south, Ethan saw no one. The road followed the river. There were cottonwoods to the east at the base of the Santa Ritas. To the west was another mountain range. The valley between was dotted with mesquite bushes and a few scrubby junipers and cactus here and there. The ground was hard-packed, more rock than soil. Everything looked brown. The heat of the sun pressed on Ethan's head and back; his clothes and hat were soaked with sweat. The light ahead shimmered in waves and distorted the trail. Nothing was moving except some ravens soaring above the mountains.

Ethan reached Tubac around sunset. The town had been there for 130 years or so and looked it, just a couple dozen single-floor adobes arranged around the dusty plaza. During the Civil War, when the Army had pulled out, the Apaches had stepped up their attacks and had made the countryside around the town a no-man's-land. The people drifted away and the mines that were in the mountains around the town failed; there was not much reason for anyone to be there. Since then, though, people had come back slowly, and in the last year or so some Anglos had even opened a small hotel and a general store. But there weren't many Anglos there yet, mostly Mexicans. This suited Ethan. Since his marriage he had found that he preferred the company of Spanish people, who seemed to have something that he lacked—a lightness of heart.

Ethan took his horse and mule to the livery stable, and after unpacking his gear and storing everything except his guns with the livery man, went to the cantina. The sign above the door said JESÚS SANCHEZ, PROP.

The cantina was dark and dingy. The floor was hard-packed dirt. There were a few tables in the corner where a couple of men, teamsters by the look of them, were eating tortillas and frijoles and drinking mescal. A slim girl wearing too much rouge sat with them, but they ignored her. A Mexican man was sitting alone at another table.

Everyone looked up when Ethan walked in, made their assessments, and then went back to minding their business.

"Buenas tardes, señor," said the man behind the bar. Apparently, this was Sanchez. He was smiling at the pleasure of more business and at the novelty of a stranger. He was a short, heavy man with a thick black mustache and a bald head.

"Good day, amigo," said Ethan. "You wouldn't happen to have any cold beer back there somewhere, would you?"

"Nothing is cold in this country, *señor,* except the hearts of the Apaches. But the beer that I have is cool, that I can say. Our cellar is the coolest in the town. And the beer is excellent."

"Fair enough." Ethan dropped a dollar on the bar and received an earthenware mug in return. Sanchez was right about the beer, though anything would have tasted good after a thirty-mile ride.

"What brings you to this place, *señor?*"

"It's a long story."

"Ah, yes. Most of the people who come here have long stories. People with short stories stay where it is civilized."

"Seems you're a philosopher."

"Perhaps. One sees things from behind a bar. Even though it is dark much of the time."

"I'm looking for a room for the night," said Ethan.

"We can do that, *señor.* We have two very fine

rooms. Those men over there are in one, and you can have the other. The bed is clean, and there are no scorpions, except only rarely."

"Hard to pass up a recommendation like that."

"Where do you go, *señor?* Tucson?"

"No, the other way. Over the Santa Ritas to Verity." Ethan had decided to be somewhat forthcoming. It was not his normal way, but he had learned that casual conversations often yielded small nuggets of information.

"Over the mountains? Ah, Chihuahua, *señor.* That is a perilous trip. You would be better to go south from here toward Pete Kitchen's ranch and from there go east to Verity. Go around the mountains. Nothing good lives up there. Besides, you have already come pretty far south. Why go back to the pass, *señor?*"

"Well, I came here because I heard about your beer." Ethan smiled at the barman.

"Well, it is your business, of course. Perhaps you are a miner?"

"No, I like gold as much as the next fellow, but I don't care that much for shovels. Fact is, I'm a newspaperman from back East. I'm doing some articles on this part of the country. The Apaches. The Army. The way people live out here. That sort of thing. And you've got to see it before you can write about it. That includes the mountains." Ethan was aware that the two teamsters and the girl were listening. The Mexican man was staring straight ahead at nothing.

The barman raised his eyebrows. The gesture implied that the information was not worth the risks of acquiring it.

"Perhaps you do not know, *señor,* that not long ago, no more than a month, an Army patrol was killed, all of them, in that pass you want to look at. Apaches. If it were me, I would look at the mountains from down here and just *imagine* the pass. The readers of newspapers would not know the difference."

"Things are often done that way, but it is not my way." It occurred to Ethan that this was the truth.

"Well, *señor,* at least you are well armed." Sanchez gestured toward Ethan's pistols and the rifle he had propped against the bar. "I hope you are adept."

"Adept enough. So far, at least." Ethan drained his beer.

"Bueno. Another, *señor?"*

"Another, yes. And maybe some food."

"Of course. My Rosa makes very fine tortillas. And although we lack many things in this country, beef is not one of them. So perhaps a steak to go along, and some tomatoes from my garden? They are very good this year."

"That'll do fine."

Ethan took his Henry rifle and his second beer and sat down at one of the tables while Sanchez went into the back room to arrange for the food. He rested his rifle on the table and surveyed the other people in the room. The Mexican had fallen asleep, his head resting on the table. The two teamsters were a rough-looking pair, heavily bearded and dirty. Their clothes were dusty from long hours on the road. They each wore a pistol on their belts. They were eating with their hands and talking to each other in low tones, occasionally gesturing in Ethan's direction and smiling. One was a tall, heavy man. He had a brutish look in his eye, truculent from mescal. The other was small and wiry, and although he too was drunk, he looked more or less harmless.

The girl, whom they had been ignoring, looked over at Ethan and smiled. Ethan nodded at her, out of politeness. Encouraged, she got up and came over to Ethan's table.

"You like some company, *señor?*" Ethan figured she was maybe seventeen.

"Hey," said one of the teamsters, the big one. "Come on back here and sit down. You're with us. And we ain't finished with you yet."

"We ain't even started," said the other. He laughed drunkenly.

Here we go, thought Ethan. The first teamster got up, lurched over to Ethan's table, and grabbed the girl by the wrist and pulled her to her feet. "Come on, honey. We got business to discuss. This fella ain't your type. I doubt he likes girls." He looked at Ethan. His eyes were not focusing, and they were red from a combination of dust and too much sunlight and mescal. He smelled like a goat.

Ethan put his hand on his rifle and turned it a few degrees so that it was pointing at the teamster's midsection. He cocked the hammer.

"Friend," he said, "you may not be as dumb as you look. You might even know what a fifty-caliber bullet will do to your innards at this range. Then again, maybe you *are* as dumb as you look, in which case you're about to learn something."

The teamster dropped the girl's wrist, surprised at Ethan's manner. Ethan could see him considering what to do next.

"You ain't got the guts to pull that," he said after a moment.

"Yes, I do, friend, and when I do, you'll be the one without the guts. They'll be splattered over there on that wall." Ethan looked at him steadily.

The teamster considered some more. He was suddenly aware that he had possibly made an error.

"You ain't got a round in that chamber. No one carries a rifle with a round chambered."

"Fact is, I always chamber a round when I come into

a place where I might run into a couple of dumb sons-abitches like you two. So just leave little Chiquita here alone and go on back to your table. You'll be glad you did in the morning."

The teamster hesitated, for form's sake. He was drunk enough to worry about saving face.

"Come on, Clem," said the other one. "He ain't worth it. Come on back."

"You talk big with a Henry in your hands," said Clem. He was backing away. His eyes shifted back and forth from Ethan's face to the rifle.

"A civilized man understands the value of tools," said Ethan.

He looked forward to the day when he could walk into a place and not run into a drunken peckerwood who was out to prove something that wasn't worth proving. He was about to say those things, but thought better of it. There was no sense antagonizing Clem further.

"Let it go, Clem," said the other one.

"All right, this time, mister," said Clem. "But you ain't heard the last of this."

"I'll be around if you want me," said Ethan.

"Come on, Clem," said the other teamster. He had gotten up from the table and was collecting their things. "Let's get out of here. I ain't staying in this place. They've got better rooms at the hotel. There's too many greasers here, anyway."

"All right," Clem said. "Too many greasers here is right." He got his hat from the table, and then the two men backed out the door, the little man pulling the big man by the elbow. Ethan watched the window on the other side of the room. He half-expected Clem to take a shot at him from outside, but he could see no movement through the window. Sanchez, who had watched the scene from the back room, came back in.

"They have gone, *señor.* I don't think you will have more trouble. They are rude men, but not especially bad. They drink, and they talk loud and say things that are not polite. But mainly they are drivers of mule wagons, nothing more. Mescal does not agree with them. It is the same with many Anglos. Still, I will close the shutters. It is prudent, I think. Yes?"

"Yes." Ethan lowered the hammer on his rifle. He did not have a round in the chamber, of course, but he could lever one in fast enough if the need arose. Sanchez closed and bolted the shutters and then brought Ethan his dinner.

"I will sit with you, *señor?*" said the girl. She didn't seem frightened by what she had seen. She had probably seen such things many times.

"Sit wherever you want to, honey. But I'm not in the market."

"Perhaps you will change your mind." She gave her best imitation of a leer and bent over to show her breasts, what there was of them.

"Not likely. Nothing personal. I'm just not in the mood." Actually, he was sort of in the mood, but this girl was too young, too skinny, and too desperate. To do such a thing would be depressing afterward and, most likely, during. "I'll buy you a drink, though, if you like. And dinner."

"Yes. I like that, too." She smiled. Her teeth were very bad.

After dinner, Ethan went to his room and lit the kerosene lamp. He closed the solid wooden shutters and checked the floor and the bed before taking off his boots and gun belt. He stuck a chair under the doorknob, put one of his Schofields on the table next to the bed, and then lay down. The room was small but clean.

The walls were painted white, and the ceiling was dark brown and made of saguaro spines and mesquite beams. There was a rudely carved and painted crucifix on the wall opposite the bed. Ethan studied it a while. The wounds from the thorns and the nails and the spear thrust were very graphic, and the blood looked fresh. Whoever carved it, some mission Indian probably, had understood physical pain and had shown his understanding in the figure's body and in the expression on the face.

"You poor bastard," thought Ethan, "to die like that, for this." Then, as he did each night, he thought about Maria, and afterwards, much later, fell asleep with the lamp still burning.

Four

It was well past sunrise when Ethan woke. The lamp had run out of oil and the shutters kept the sunlight from the room. Ethan checked his watch, and then dressed with no particular hurry. He opened the shutters and looked out on the town. There was no sign of the two teamsters. They had gotten an early start for Tucson. Ethan went to the main room of the cantina to get some breakfast. Sanchez was there, alone.

"*Buenos dias, señor.* I have been waiting for you." Sanchez seemed nervous about something. "Perhaps you would like some coffee?"

"Coffee, yes. And maybe some *huevos* and tomatoes."

"Yes, of course. I will have Rosa make them for you." He went to the back room for a second and then returned. There was obviously something on his mind.

"*Señor,* I have something to ask you. Last night, after you went to your room, some people came. More teamsters. They had just come up from Pete Kitchen's ranch, which is about twenty miles south of here.

Before that they were in the town you are going to, Verity."

"And?"

"They brought some bad news to me, *señor.* My brother, Tomás. He works at the big ranch there, and someone has shot him. Indians, perhaps. No one knows. He was out herding alone, and someone shot him from ambush. He was able to get away from them, but he is very bad, *señor.* Very bad. I have great fears that he will die. I must go to him, *señor.* I cannot let him lie there alone."

"That is bad news." Ethan knew what was coming. "Is there a doctor?"

"Yes, *señor.* And the teamsters say the doctor has hope, but still I cannot rest here not knowing. I must go there."

"I can see that."

"And so, *señor,* I am asking to go along with you. The road is very dangerous, as I have said. It would be better for two men. I would not ask, except that there are no stages or other teamsters heading there. I would have to go alone, for I must leave today. And so I hoped. . . ."

"I understand." Ethan thought about it. He generally disliked traveling with other people. They were distractions. On the other hand, Sanchez seemed like a good man, and there might be some merit in having him along in case they did run into Apaches. It might be good to have some company on the trail for once.

"Do you have a gun?"

Sanchez brightened. "Everyone has a gun, *señor.* The question is, can one use it with efficiency? In my case the answer is yes, up to a point. I can hit what I aim at provided it is willing to stand still. Otherwise. . . ." Sanchez shrugged. "I say this to be honest with you."

"Well, it's good to be honest with yourself about your marksmanship. It's the people who aren't that generally run into trouble."

"Yes, *señor.* That is true about many things, I think."

"You understand that I will be going over the mountains, through the pass where the Army patrol was attacked? That is something I must do, regardless of your brother."

"Yes, *señor.* I assumed that you would. It is more dangerous, but it is shorter. There is that advantage. And since I must hurry, I can make myself believe that the way of the pass is better for me, too."

"Well, I can't see the harm in it, Señor Sanchez. Soon as I eat breakfast, I'll get my things together and we'll go. Can you be ready in about an hour?"

"I am ready now, *señor.* As I said, I have been waiting for you. And *señor—muchas gracias.*" Sanchez took Ethan's hand. "You are a kind man. My Rosa will say her prayers for you as well as for me."

"Can't hurt. While she's at it, have her pray that whatever you have to shoot at doesn't jump around too much. That'd be a real blessing."

"Yes, *señor.* She will wear out her knees praying for stationary Apaches, although such a thing is a rarity. And now I will get your *huevos.*"

After breakfast, Ethan went to the livery stable to get Priam loaded up. At the appointed time, Sanchez came there. He was riding a serviceable-looking horse and leading a burro that carried his packs. Ethan noticed that he had a rifle in his saddle scabbard. He had a cartridge belt that was filled with ammunition wrapped around his waist, and was wearing a wide black sombrero and a leather jacket decorated with silver disks. He looked the part, at any rate. A big yellow dog was tagging along with him. It looked like there had been some Labrador retriever in his lineage at some point, mixed in maybe with some coyote and some other indeterminate breeds. He appeared to be a businesslike dog. Apparently, he'd had his share of fights. There was a long scar on his muzzle and a V-shaped notch in one ear.

"We are here, *señor.* Ready for the mountains, I hope."

"That dog going along?"

"Con su permiso, señor. I think he will be useful unless you have an aversion to dogs."

"I like them well enough. What's his name?"

"His name is Cesar, *señor,* but he goes by Nariz. He seems to prefer it. Nariz is Spanish for . . ."

"Nose. I know."

"Ah, you speak Spanish. That is good."

"A little."

"Yes, he is called that because he has a genius for hunting. He is a serious dog, *señor.* Very loyal in his own way, although he has his own ideas about some things. I think it would be well to have him along, as a precaution against surprises."

"Can't hurt. Well, if you're ready, let's get going."

They headed north. The day was clear and warm, but the wind was howling, blowing dust across the road. At least the wind took some of the heat away, thought Ethan. He could see there were clouds on the tops of the Santa Ritas. It was the time of year when the weather at higher elevations could be unpredictable, and the southwest wind was a sign that there were changes coming.

They rode in silence, side by side, with their pack animals behind. Sanchez was a friendly man who liked to talk, but he also knew when conversation was not welcome, and he had evidently determined that this was such a time. He seemed content to let Ethan dictate the terms of the relationship. The dog ranged ahead, probably hunting for jackrabbits. He would disappear for long periods and then come back, as though to check on the men. Then he would disappear again.

"What's he after, do you suppose?" Ethan asked.

"The dog? Well, anything that he can eat. He has a fine appetite, yet I rarely have to feed him. To a man the desert looks very empty, but not to a dog. There are many things in the desert to interest him. And he is not particular in his tastes. It is a good quality in a dog."

Now that Ethan had opened the conversation, Sanchez felt it would not be impolite to continue. "If you will pardon me, *señor*. I would like to know your name. It seems strange to travel together not knowing such a thing."

"Well, you're right. I apologize for my bad manners, *señor*. Name's Ethan Jaeger."

"It is a good name. And I am Jesús Sanchez, as you may have known from the sign on the cantina."

"Yes, I figured that."

"Since you seem to know something of the Spanish people, *señor*, does it not seem strange to you that so many of us are named Jesús? I never met an Anglo with that name. But many Mexicans have it. Perhaps it is because we pronounce it differently so that it does not seem like the same name to you. But I have always thought that was strange."

"It's occurred to me," said Ethan. "We have a different way of looking at things, I guess."

"Yes. That is true, of course."

"Maybe our way of looking at it comes from the Jews. You know, they never had a name for God. They called him Yahweh, which means the unnamed one, or something like that."

"Truly? That is interesting. I will have to discuss that with my friend Goldberg, who has opened the general store in Tubac. Perhaps he can explain this way of thinking. For myself, I think it is a good thing to know your God personally. Especially when you live in a country like this. A God who does not even want you to know his name must not care much for your troubles. It would be very lonely in this country with such an arrangement."

"You're right about that, Jesús."

After about three hours they turned east, crossed the narrow river, and began to climb. The trail apparently led straight into the mountains. There were two peaks looming above the rest of the range, and unlike the bare mountains to the west, the slopes were thickly wooded. The colors were dark, with just an occasional smattering of gray rock, though toward the summits they both grew more bare and rocky again. With their covering of vegetation, they seemed less inhospitable than the other nearby ranges.

"These mountains, *señor,* the highest peaks, I mean, are called Wrightson and Hopkins after two men who came here to survey just after the war between your states. The Apaches killed them, and so these are their monuments. The road to Verity lies through them, *madre mia.*"

"It looks like pretty good country up there, though. We should be able to find water, and grazing for the animals." In fact, Ethan had a detailed map that Captain Wilkes had given him. He had a good idea of places to camp.

"Yes, there is good water and grass there. With this wind, I am afraid that we may get some rain tonight. I have often sat outside my cantina and watched the storms here. They are things of great violence but beautiful, if you are watching from a distance. The lightning is like nothing in this world, *señor.* There is metal in these mountains. Silver. Copper. And the miners say that the lightning is seeking this metal, like a man seeking a woman when they are both new to each other. And like love, they often come to nothing after the first flashes. But at other times, *madre mia,* there is great disaster. Fires or floods where everything is washed away. The important thing is to stay out of the way."

"You talking about love or lightning?"

"Lightning, *señor.* There is nothing wrong with love. Women are God's gift, although after a time, the quality of their tortillas becomes as important as the quality of their kisses. But this is natural."

Ethan laughed. "Like I said when I met you, Jesús. You're a philosopher."

"Yes. There is always time to think about such things in a cantina."

The climb toward the mountains was very gradual. They were travelling through a broad meadow, where the grass was knee-high, yellow in the autumn light, but there were prickly pear cactus and chollas and the wicked-looking spikes of ocotillo to remind them of where they were. And now and then, there were the barrel cactus with their fish-hook spikes. The higher they climbed, though, the better the country would be, until finally they would leave the desert behind.

The road, such as it was, was an old miner's trail. It lead from the river valley, which lay at about 2500-feet elevation, up over the pass at about six thousand feet, and from there down into the Verity Valley on the other side of the Santa Ritas, which lay at about five thousand feet. It would take two days to get there. They would not go through Madera Canyon to the south at a right angle to the trail. But they would stop there for the night at the base of the canyon entrance, because it was roughly halfway and because there was a good spring there and grass for the animals and plenty of firewood. Also, Ethan wanted to scout Madera Canyon, since it lay at the base of Mount Wrightson, the highest peak in the area. There was a trail to the summit that he wanted to investigate. Ethan knew how eager Sanchez was to get to Verity, but having seen the terrain and the way the mountain ranges lay, he decided that he would have to take the time to climb Mount Wrightson. That would delay them by a day. Sanchez could either wait for him in camp while Ethan explored, or continue on to Verity by himself. That was up to him.

They reached the camping place an hour or so before sunset. The wind had diminished, and the clouds that had been covering the summits were gone. The night would be clear, but the temperature had dropped both from the higher elevation and from the wind, so the night would also be cold.

They unpacked their animals and hobbled them and turned them loose to graze. They set up camp next to the spring. There were a few sycamores grouped around the spring, and Ethan could see in the mouth of the canyon that there were more sycamores and oak trees lining the trail as it ascended into the canyon and led to the base of Mount Wrightson.

"Well, this looks like a pretty good spot," said Ethan. "It's good to get away from the dust."

Sanchez had other things on his mind. "I have heard it said that the Apaches are not happy to fight when it is dark."

"I have heard the same thing," Ethan said.

"Is it true, *señor?*"

"I don't know. I suppose it could be." Ethan imagined that if Apaches ever did attack someone in the dark, no one ever heard about it afterward. But there was no sense in getting Sanchez more worried than he already was.

"Let us hope that is true and that the darkness comes quickly," said Sanchez. "Meanwhile, I will gather some firewood. A fire is always a good thing, and tonight, especially so. I am afraid it will be cold."

Ethan went through one of his packs, and pulled out two collapsible tripods each about four feet long. He found some firm ground under one of the sycamores, pounded the tripods into the earth, and then, a few feet away, pounded in two tent pegs and strung a tent rope from them to secure the tripods. Then he slung a hammock between the tripods.

Sanchez returned with some wood. "Ah, Chihuahua, _señor._ A hammock. It is ingenious."

"No sense sleeping on the ground unless you have to. Besides, an old Navy man gets used to sleeping in hammocks. You get so you prefer it to a bed."

"And you do not risk sleeping with centipedes or scorpions or snakes. This is the thing I have against sleeping on the ground," Sanchez said.

"There's that, too. Say, where's that dog? I haven't seen him in a while."

"Hunting, I am sure, _señor._ His appetite is a prodigy, but even more so is his curiosity. Therefore, he is gone for long periods of time. But he is in the area somewhere, and if someone should try to approach us undetected, he can be trusted to give the alarm. Unless they kill him first, which is always a possibility."

They built their fire and cooked dinner. Sanchez's wife Rosa had done most of the work, so they only had to heat the _chile rellenos_ and beans and to grill the beefsteaks and boil the coffee. They ate in silence. And as they were finishing, the last of the light disappeared, and the crickets and hoppers began to sing. In the distance, a pack of coyotes started yipping and howling.

"It is a lonely sound," said Sanchez. "No one likes coyotes. I meant to ask you before, *señor,* when we were talking about women, whether you have a woman yourself. Someone at home."

"Not anymore."

Just then, beyond the glow of the firelight, Priam started braying. In the stillness of the night it sounded like fiends from hell let loose. Ethan grabbed his rifle and ran toward the sound. The mule was nervously stamping and tossing his head and, Ethan noticed, his ears were twitching wildly. He let out another deafening bray while Ethan peered into the darkness looking for movement. The other animals seemed calm enough. Sanchez's burro was asleep on his feet.

"Hallo the camp!" came a voice from the direction Priam was looking at. "Hallo! Don't shoot. It's only me, Ed Phillips. I'm coming in. Don't shoot. It's just me and Willy."

Gradually, Ethan could make out a man leading a burro. Evidently, he was a prospector. Tagging along with him was Nariz, lolling out his tongue and wagging his tail.

"Good evening, amigos. I am damned sure glad to see your fire. Hello, Sanchez. I figured you must be around somewhere when I ran across Nariz about a half mile from here. Howdy, mister," he said to Ethan. "Name's Ed Phillips, and this here's Willy." He gestured to the burro. "My friend Jesús will vouch for me, won't you, Jesús."

"Of course. I am very glad to see you again. When a miner leaves for the mountains, one is always aware that that sight of him could be the last. We are just finishing dinner, but there is some left."

"Much obliged. I am tired of my own cooking, that's a fact." Phillips was a short, stocky man. He was dressed in canvas pants secured with a wide belt and suspenders. He wore a red flannel shirt and a battered hat. His face was covered with long stubble, but he looked less like a man with a beard than someone who badly needed a shave.

Sanchez got him a plate while the miner secured his packs and burro.

"Where have you been, since I saw you last, Ed?" Sanchez asked.

"Oh, dodging Apaches and Lady Luck, too, seems like. One of 'em's interested in me and the other one isn't. I just come up from Verity. I guess you heard about your brother, Tomás."

"Yes, that is why I am traveling there. Do you have news, Ed? How is he?"

"Why, he's in pretty good shape. Last time I saw him he was sitting up in bed taking nourishment—tequila. Playing cards with the girl who works nights at the saloon, name of Sally Rose. She's been there about six months now, and before that worked in Tucson. Aside from her other talents, she sings some and plays the concertina."

"*Madre mia.* Do you mean Tomás is out of danger?"

"Well, if you don't count Sally Rose, yes, I would say so. Doc said he got over the fever and the loss of blood, and he'll be good as new in a couple of weeks or so. He might limp a little when he does the fandango, but all things considered, it could have been worse."

"You are sure of this?"

"Saw him with my own eyes in the doc's office. I had a bad case of scours, and Doc gave me some of those blue pills which stoppered me up just fine, a little too fine, if you want to know the truth. But I had a nice visit with Tomás. He's a little weak still, but there's not much else wrong with him. Course, he's mad as hell at being shot, but that's normal."

"Gracias a Dios," said Sanchez. There were tears in his eyes suddenly. *"Gracias a Dios."*

Ed turned his attention to Ethan. "Where're you headed, amigo?"

"Verity."

"Señor Jaeger is a writer of news articles," Sanchez said.

"A newspaperman? Well, that's a fine thing. Yessir, when I strike it rich you can make me famous. Only, I haven't struck it yet. It's there, though. I expect you heard about Ed Shiefflin over in the San Pedro Hills. That's out beyond Verity forty miles east or so. Struck the richest vein of silver anyone's heard of since time began. He went out there by himself, just like me, even after the Army boys at Fort Huachuca told him he'd never find anything but his own tombstone, because of the Apaches. Well, he's got the last laugh, 'cause that's what he's calling his little camp over there. Tombstone. People are starting to pour in there now. Few more months and the place will be overrun with miners."

"Seems like you're going the wrong way then," Ethan said.

The old codger shook his head. "I know there's metal in these mountains. I can taste it. Why compete with all those people over there when I can have this whole range to myself? Yessir, boys, one of these days I'm going to be drinking the whiskey instead of just smelling the cork. Speaking of which, I don't suppose you've got a drop of anything around here. At the end of the day, I like to take a little something as a precaution against hives, but my bottle must of sprang a leak on the way up here."

"We have some mescal," said Jesús.

"That'll do."

"Is there any news of the Apaches?"

"Nothing recently. Of course, no one knows who shot at your brother. Could have been Apaches. Most people seem to think that Geronimo and his gang are down in Old Mexico in the Sierra Madres. No way of telling for sure. You know how it is with them—borders don't impress 'em much."

"Just out of curiosity, Ed," said Ethan, "do you have any Indian blood in you?"

Ed thought about it a moment. "Not so's I know about it. Why?"

Ethan looked over to where Priam was grazing. "Just wondered."

"Course, I was married to one for a while. A White Mountain woman. But she took after me with a knife one time too many, and I had to leave her. Good cook, though, I'll say that for her."

Five

The morning was clear. Ethan explained that he wanted to explore the canyon and, perhaps, Mount Wrightson. Sanchez was happy to stay in camp, for although he still wanted to go to his brother, the urgency was gone. Ed agreed to stay for the day and keep Sanchez company.

"Won't hurt to give Willy a breather," he said.

"How's the trail to the summit?" Ethan asked Ed.

"Well, the last time I was up there it was perfect for a mountain goat. But I believe you can make it all right. I doubt your horse would admire the trip, though. If I was you, I'd ride to the base and leave him and walk the rest of the way."

"Can a mule make it?"

"More'n likely, though I wouldn't ride him. There are some places there that are tighter than a virgin's quim, so if you need your packs with you I'd walk and lead him. I'd lend you Willy, but he can be particular. You'd be better off just going by yourself, if all you're after is seeing the sights. It's about four miles from here to the base and another four or so to the top. Good stretch of the legs."

"No, I think I'll ride as far as possible."

Ed shrugged. "It's your party."

After breakfast, Ethan loaded his packs on Priam, caught his horse, and set off.

"Vaya con Dios, señor," said Sanchez. "We will have the fire burning for you."

As soon as Ethan entered the canyon, the land around him changed. The sycamores grew thicker around the dry watercourses. And soon there were oak trees mixed in, not the oak trees of the East, but the live oaks that stayed green throughout the year. Yucca plants and agaves mixed in and grew on the rocky outcroppings, but there was good grass, too, and the dominant colors changed from the browns of the desert to the greens of a higher elevation. On entering the canyon and climbing toward the base of the mountain, it seemed to Ethan that he had come to another country. The higher he climbed, the more he encountered pine trees and the thicker the oaks were clustered. And mixed in were red-limbed laurels called manzanitas. There were so many places for an enemy to hide that Ethan stopped looking for them and settled into his normal mode of relaxed awareness. He rode slowly for about an hour, content to be alone again.

At the base of the mountain he found a small spring shaded by sycamores. He tethered his horse near the spring in a patch of grass and unsaddled him.

"You wait here, Rangeley," he said. "I'll be back for you."

He took Priam's lead and, holding his Henry in his other hand, started up toward the summit. The trail grew rockier as he climbed. According to his map the summit was at 9500 feet, which meant he would have about 3500 feet to ascend. The trail clung to the side of the mountain and wound its way narrowly up in a series of switchbacks. Priam moved easily and did not try to scrape off his packs, even though there were trees close to the trail, and here and there a boulder nearly blocking the way, obstacles that Priam could have easily made use of if he'd wanted to.

"I'm beginning to like you, Priam," said Ethan. "Maybe that old buzzard in Tucson knew what he was talking about."

They climbed for about two hours. Ethan could see the rocky summit looming before him. The sun and dry air wicked away the sweat, and he was beginning to get cold when he arrived at a plateau on the north side of the mountain a few hundred feet from the top. To the north he could see Tucson lying at the base of the Catalina Mountains. To the west was the valley of the Santa Cruz with Tubac baking in the sun. To the east lay the Verity Valley. It stretched for miles. Thick grass, gold in the sunlight, covered rolling foothills dotted with oak trees that from this distance looked like herds of buffalo grazing.

He could just make out the little town of Verity sitting in the middle of the grasslands. Scattered around the valley were the windmills that serviced cattle tanks and ponds, shining like silver dollars. The Whetstone and Huachuca mountain ranges were the eastern borders of the valley, and beyond them, the Dragoons, where the Chiricahuas used to have their stronghold.

"I think this'll do," he said.

He hobbled Priam and unloaded the crate he had been carrying. It was marked U.S. ARMY. He pried open the crate, took out the heliograph, and set up the tripod, and then assembled the mirrors and the signaling devices and pointed it toward Tucson and Fort Lowell.

The heliograph had been Captain Wilkes's idea. The Army had used them occasionally in the Southwest where the reliable sunlight and clear air allowed for long-distance signaling.

"This thing has a range of about forty miles," said Wilkes. "And you cannot beat it for security. No wires to cut. Of course Indians have used signal mirrors for years, but we've got the advantage of Morse Code. If you set this up somewhere in the Santa Ritas, I'll make sure we have a signalman on duty at a particular time each day to watch for your messages."

They had agreed on two o'clock. Ethan had been used to using signal devices in the Navy, and he had not forgotten his Morse Code. He spent the next hour or so practicing with the signal levers, and then a few minutes before two o'clock he arranged the mirrors to catch the afternoon light so that it would flash directly toward Fort Lowell.

At two he sent his first message.

"Jaeger to Wilkes. In place Mount Wrightson."

He waited, using his binoculars to watch the spot in the Catalinas where Wilkes had placed the fort's heliograph. There was a single-wire telegraph between the heliograph station and Wilkes's office, so that incoming information could be relayed to the fort without delay. In a few minutes Ethan saw the reply flashing from the Catalinas: "Message received. Good hunting. Wilkes."

"All right, Priam," said Ethan. "We're in business."

He covered the heliograph with a canvas tarp and secured the tarp with tent pegs. The spot was protected from the westerly winds, and the canvas would keep out the rain. He cut some brush and arranged the branches around the tarp. It wasn't a perfect job of camouflage, but sufficient.

As he was finishing, he noticed that Priam was acting nervous. He was tossing his head and nickering. Suddenly, he kicked out his back legs and started braying. Ethan reached for his rifle and crouched behind the heliograph, expecting an Apache to come bursting out of the undergrowth, but he saw nothing. Priam kept bellowing and bucking. Then Ethan noticed some subtle movement in the manzanita bushes about ten yards away. At first he could not see what caused the movement. But then he saw the mountain lion. It had thrust its head almost to the edge of the manzanitas. Ethan could see its yellow eyes shifting from him to Priam and then back again. The cat uttered a low growl. Ethan raised his rifle, but the cat turned at the movement and disappeared. Ethan did not fire. If there were other enemies in these mountains, there was no sense in alerting them. Sound, like light, carried a long way in this country.

Ethan waited a few minutes for Priam to calm down, and then unhobbled him and gathered up his lead.

Ethan reached camp an hour or so after dark. He had been anxious about his horse on the trip down the trail and he had hurried. The possibility that the lion had discovered Rangeley worried him. But the horse was grazing peacefully when Ethan got to the base of the mountain. From there it was a short ride back to camp.

When he got to camp, Sanchez and Ed were arguing about dinner.

"Come on, Jesús. Dish up them frijolies. My innards are grumbling worse than a bear with a sore head."

"Beans are like other good things in life, *señor*. They require some waiting."

"Mebbe so," said Ed. "But a smart man knows when he's reached 'good enough,' and seems to me that's where we are as far as these beans are concerned. Toss some of those chiles in there and let's eat. Otherwise I'm likely to get grumpy, and that ain't good for my digestion."

Sanchez shrugged and smiled at Ethan, as if to say, there's nothing to be done about Philistines.

"Was your journey a success, *señor?*" Sanchez asked Ethan.

"Pretty good. We ran into a mountain lion near the top. But otherwise it was uneventful. You can see a long way from up there."

"Did you kill him?"

"No. He took off too fast."

"Just as well," said Ed. "I've et lion before and I'd do it again, but only if I was starving. It's real stringy and strong-tasting. Sort of like my second wife." He shook his head at the memory. "Funny thing, she took after me with a knife, too. Must be something about me that sets 'em off like that."

"Can't imagine what it would be," said Ethan.

"Me neither. If the current one acts up like that, I believe I'll give up on matrimony. Too derned dangerous."

They were ready to get under way at first light the next morning. Ed was going west, while Ethan and Sanchez were headed east.

"So long, boys," said Ed. "Keep ahold of your hair. If you run into my third wife in Verity, tell her I didn't really mean it. She'll know what you're talking about. If she starts cussin', just set back and enjoy it. She's real gifted along that line. Come on, Willy."

"*Vaya con dios,* Ed."

"You, too, boys."

The trail east continued to climb. It narrowed as they traveled, and led up the side of a tall cliff. It was just barely wide enough for a small wagon to travel. The cliff was on the left side of the road and was studded with yuccas and agaves. To the right the hillside dropped off into a deep canyon. The road was eroded in places where the runoff from rainfall had washed down the cliff. According to Ethan's map, they were not far from the site of the attack on the Army patrol, and Ethan was anxious to investigate the scene.

Should be just up at this bend, he thought. The road curved around the cliff and then turned sharply to the right before continuing up the hillside. It was at this curve that the attack took place, and Ethan could understand why the attackers had picked this spot. The Army wagon would have had to slow nearly to a stop in order to negotiate the turn. Soldiers would have been bunched up behind, waiting. There were boulders on both sides of the road, places where the attackers could hide and then shoot from two sides directly into the line of riders, enfilading them while giving them no chance to respond, no place to turn around, and no way to go forward. It reminded Ethan of the technique of Naval gunnery called "crossing the T," which meant firing into a line of ships with your broadsides while the target ships could not bring their guns to bear. A perfect spot for an ambush. It would even be possible to get a couple of men with each shot, the bullets passing through one and then hitting the man behind. Even without that, it would not take more than three men firing rapidly to kill eight soldiers who were virtually standing still. The attackers would have been able to watch the soldiers climbing up the trail and could have marked their targets in advance for greatest efficiency. Ethan could understand how Wilkes had been impressed by the disciplined nature of the attack. Whoever did it could shoot with coolness and accuracy. A few seconds and it would have been over. An execution.

Ethan dismounted at the curve.

"I'd like to take a look around here for a minute, Jesús. This is where those Army boys were attacked."

"Madre mia. It is a bad place, *señor.* Why do you want to see such a thing?"

"Readers back East, Jesús. They want to know about such things."

"That is because they are thousands of miles away. If they were here, now, they would want to move away quickly."

Ethan went to the edge of the road and looked into the canyon. The charred remains of the Army wagon lay about a hundred feet below.

"I think I'll go down there a take a look."

"I will stay with the animals, *señor."*

The hillside was steep, but Ethan was able to find a kind of path down to the wagon. He slid a few feet in the rocky soil, but saved himself from falling by grabbing an agave. Near the bottom he flushed a covey of quail. They took off like an exploding shell right under his feet and startled him badly. He reached for his pistol as a reflex, and stood watching as the birds sailed away in every direction.

"Dammit," said Ethan.

"Fool's quail," shouted Sanchez. "Very good to eat."

The wagon was overturned. It was blackened and the wheels were smashed. There was a jug of coal oil lying near by. The raiders had used the oil to fire the wagon, and it was the greasy black smoke that had first alerted people on the outskirts of Verity to the fact of the attack. About ten yards away, stuck on a prickly pear cactus, Ethan found a cotton bandanna. It might have been the kind worn as a headdress by the Apaches, or it could have been a soldier's neckerchief. There was nothing else around the wagon.

Ethan struggled back up the hill.

"Anything down there, *señor?*"

"No. Just the burned-out wagon."

Ethan then looked behind each of the likely boulders, but any tracks had long been washed away or blown away. The Army had collected the spent cartridge cases, so aside from the wagon there was no indication that anything had ever happened in that place.

He was about to leave when he noticed a small patch of red wedged under one of the boulders on the cliff side of the trail. It was an empty shotgun shell. A twelve-gauge. It was a paper cartridge and still in good condition. There was no way to tell how long it had been there. Wedged under the boulder, it would have been sheltered from the rain and the bleaching effects of the sun. It could have been used in the attack, or it could have been left by a bird hunter a year or more ago. There was a name printed on the shell: *Rigby.*

Ethan pocketed the shell and then mounted up.

"Come on, Jesús. I've seen enough."

"And I, too, *señor.*"

"Say, where's that dog?"

"God knows, *señor.* As I said, the dog has his own ideas."

Six

Verity was a crossroads. The east-west road ran between the Santa Cruz Valley to the west and Fort Huachuca to the east. The other road came down from Tucson to the north, and then petered out in the ranchlands near the Mexican border. The trail that Ethan and Sanchez had followed was a shortcut over the mountains that ended in the rolling grasslands northwest of the town. The Army patrol that had been attacked had chosen that route as a way of saving time on the way to Fort Huachuca. From the end of that trail it was a short ride through the pasturelands to town.

The town had a dozen or so adobe buildings arranged on each corner of the crossroads. Many of the buildings had tile roofs. A few had false fronts, but most had broad porches leading directly from the flat roofs and supported by mesquite beams. There was a wooden sidewalk running in front of all the buildings. Many of the buildings had *ristras* of peppers hanging from the porch roofs; others had pots of flowers. On one corner there was a Mexican man selling vegetables and fruit in the open air. Altogether, it was a more settled place than Ethan had expected.

Ethan and Jesús went immediately to the doctor's office. Waiting on the porch outside the office was Nariz.

"That damned dog must be clairvoyant," said Ethan.

"He and Tomás are old friends, *señor*. It is natural that he would come here immediately."

"Well, I expect you'll want to spend some time with Tomás. I'll look after the animals and maybe we can get together later for dinner. I'll arrange for some rooms at the boardinghouse. I suppose Nariz can look after himself."

"*Gracias, señor*. I will find you later."

Ethan stabled the animals and stored their packs. He then went to the boardinghouse and rented a couple of rooms. He debated having a bath and a change of clothes, but it was getting close to five and he decided to put that off in favor of meeting Harding, the editor of the local paper.

The newspaper office was across the street from the boardinghouse. A man was sitting at his desk poring over proof sheets when Ethan walked in. He was about sixty, and he reminded Ethan of a Presbyterian minister that Ethan knew as a boy—thin, white-haired, mild, and benign-looking, gold pince-nez perched on his nose, slightly stooped, clear-eyed and ruddy-complexioned, an air of kindliness written in his features. His jacket was on a peg on the wall, and he was wearing a green eyeshade and black sleeve garters to protect his white shirt and cuffs. He looked up from the copy he was proofreading.

"Who the hell are you and what in hell do you want?"

Ethan laughed. So much for appearances. "Name's

Jaeger. I sent you a telegram from Tucson the other day."

"Oh. Sorry. You don't look much like a New York City reporter. More like a gunman."

"When in Rome," said Ethan.

"That's a fair comment. Well, welcome to Verity. I'm Sep Harding. I'd shake your hand, but you'd end up covered in ink to go along with the dust you're wearing."

"I plan to do something about the dust pretty shortly, but I wanted to stop by and say hello before you closed for the day."

"Well, I'm glad to meet you. It ain't often we have someone from the East coming to visit. Fact is, you're the first, so far as I can remember, which is pretty far."

"Seems like a nice place. Coming over the pass from Tubac, it's kind of surprising to find so much grass and open country. Doesn't seem much like the desert."

"It ain't the desert," Hardy said. "The elevation here's about five thousand feet, so we aren't troubled with cactus and that sort of stuff. We get more rain and rain means grass, and grass means cattle, and cattle is why we're all here, either chasing after them or looking after the people who do. Have a seat."

"The town's bigger than I thought, too."

"Oh, we have a thriving little community here. Most everything you could ask for in the way of services. We have a doctor who doubles as the undertaker—a conflict of interest, I suppose, but convenient. He also dispenses pills, pulls teeth, and cuts hair. Talented fella. Got a general store with a wide selection of ammunition and dry goods, a saloon with professional companionship available at most hours of the day or night, a Chinese laundry run by a genuine Chinaman name of Hop Sing, neither of which he will do, by the way.

Then there's a boardinghouse that calls itself a hotel and a restaurant where nobody's been poisoned lately. There's even some talk of building a church, but majority opinion's against it, since every month or so an itinerant parson comes down from Tucson, and that seems to satisfy most people. He sets up a tent and preaches to the righteous. And we have a schoolhouse with a teacher who can actually read and do sums. So we got just about everything."

"Including a newspaper."

"Yep. The surest sign of civilization after the saloon. Speaking of which, you look like a man who needs to replenish his fluids. Dust on the outside's one thing. Dust on the inside is something else. I was just about to close up and wander over across the street to the Big Steer and gather up some news. Why don't you join me."

"I'd like that. How about if I go brush off some of this dust and then meet you over there."

"Sounds good. I'll be the one behind the large glass of beer reading the Bible and humming hymns to myself."

Ethan went to his room and sponged off with the water in his pitcher. He changed his shirt and put on his black broadcloth suit coat. It seemed more appropriate to his role as reporter. He took off his Schofields and left them on the bed. Harding's comment that he looked like a gunfighter made him decide to leave his pistols behind. To be on the safe side, though, he got a derringer out of his saddlebags, loaded both barrels, and put it in his pocket.

The Big Steer Saloon was a frame building made of board and battens. It was gray and dingy on the outside, and looked like the kind of place where you wouldn't want to drop a match accidentally. Ethan pushed through the swinging doors and saw Harding sitting at a table in the corner. There was a long bar down one end of the room. The bartender was a Mexican woman. Ethan ordered a beer and then went over to Harding's table.

In the corner opposite the bar there was a girl in a cheap satin dress wailing a sentimental song:

> Just before the battle, mother,
> I am thinking most of you.

A cowboy was sitting at the table next to her. He was obviously drunk and had tears streaming down his cheeks.

"That song sounds strange on a concertina, don't it?" said Harding. "I know I should say 'doesn't it,' but like you said, when in Rome."

"Strange is not the word for it," said Ethan.

"That's Tramp Ellis over there with her. He works at the Double S. Got his name by being run over in a stampede one time. Used to be 'Trampled On Ellis,' but it got shortened, like his leg. He was in the Confederate Army and always asks for that song once he's had about a pint of whiskey. Brings back memories, I guess. It may sound bad now, but it's worse when there's nobody to sing it to him, because he sings it himself. Sounds like a cow with the bots. Nobody says anything about it, though. He's a mean drunk, as they say. Fact is, he's pretty mean even when he's sober. So people put up with it."

"I'll say one thing for that girl. She can't sing worth a damn."

"No, nor play the squeeze box, either. But in a small town you make allowances. Her name is Squirrel Tooth Annie, though between you and me I think she gave herself the Annie part. She borrowed that concertina from the other girl who works here. She can't sing either, but she's better-looking."

The girl finished the song and then immediately started up with "Was My Brother in the Battle?" but Tramp Ellis took some offense and grabbed the concertina from her.

"That's a Blue Belly song. Here's a real tune." He started bellowing, "'Oh, I'm a good old Rebel, that's just what I am, and for your old Abe Lincoln, I do not give a damn.'" He was working the concertina erratically, creating a mixture of unrelated notes.

Ethan looked at him and grimaced. Tramp Ellis saw the look, stopped playing, and stared back, dumbfounded. He seemed surprised that his audience would not be listening with rapt appreciation. He staggered over to the table.

"You got something against my singing, boy?"

"Yes. I'm a music lover." Ethan had placed both his hands on the table, palms down.

"I don't know you. You look like a dude. Are you some sort of dude, er what?"

Ethan said nothing, but regarded Ellis steadily.

"Yeah, you're a dude. I can always tell a dude. Maybe you'd like to do a little dancing while I sing," said Ellis. He started fumbling for his pistol.

Ethan turned his right hand over like a gambler turning over an ace. He pointed the derringer at Ellis's throat and cocked the hammer. Ellis froze and turned white.

"Friend, if you move that gun hand one more inch, I'm going to blow a hole in your voice box that'll put a merciful end to your musical career. The artistic community will thank me for it, and you will have learned a valuable lesson, which is, it isn't polite to ask strangers to dance."

Ellis stared at the derringer. "Hold on there, mister. I don't mean nothing by it." Ellis had his hands raised.

"Not now, you don't. That shows good sense. Why don't you take off that gun belt and leave it here. You can pick it up tomorrow morning once you realize you still have a future to think about."

Ellis unbuckled his belt and let it drop.

"Now, go on out of here," said Ethan.

Ellis stood frozen trying to come up with something to say that would salvage the situation, but it was beyond him. He turned and staggered out the door. Ethan picked up Ellis's pistol and removed it from the holster, checked the loads, and placed it on the table. If Ellis came bursting back into the saloon with a rifle, Ethan would use his own pistol on him. A derringer wasn't very accurate beyond a few feet.

"Good God," said Harding. His eyes were wide with amazement. "You're a cool one. It's not the sort of thing you'd expect from a New York newspaperman."

"New York's a tough town," said Ethan.

"Must be. Never been there, myself. Now I'm not so sure I want to."

Squirrel Tooth Annie came over and retrieved her concertina. "You fellows have any special requests?"

"Yes," said Ethan. Do you know 'Silence Is Golden'?"

"No, I don't think so."

"Good."

She looked confused.

"Tell you what," said Ethan handing her a dollar. "Buy yourself a drink. And think of the next half an hour or so as an intermission."

"Sure. You want me to sit with you?"

"Some other time."

After she left, Harding, who had apparently been thinking about something, said, "Your accent. I'm trying to place it. Sounds like something out of New

England or thereabouts. Am I right? It's not New York, is it."

"Maine."

"Maine! Well, you're a long way from home. I'm from Missouri, myself. Near St. Louis." He thought some more. "Maine, eh? Well, it's a big place, so I don't suppose you ever ran into General Howard, the fella who made the peace treaty with Cochise a few years back?"

"I knew him, some. We went to the same college, although he was there before me."

"What did you think of him?" Harding asked.

"A little too pious for my taste. But he is a good man, I suppose. Not much of a general, though, the way I hear it. I know he was involved in getting Cochise to come to terms, though. So he must be well regarded around here."

"Well, there are two things that everyone around here agrees with. First, the price of beef is too low. Second, the best place for the Apaches is under six feet of caliche dirt. Now I don't necessarily subscribe to the second proposition. Far as I am concerned, the best thing to do with the Apaches is get them a rooming house in Washington, D.C., right next door to Congress, and then maybe we'd see some different attitudes. Better yet, next door to the Quakers who run the so-called peace party, Sunday school teachers whose idea of an Indian comes from reading James Fenimore Cooper. But I doubt my policies will be adopted back there."

"But Cochise did keep the peace, didn't he? The deal did work."

"Yep, he did. And if you look at that treaty, you'll understand why. Howard's deal with Cochise gave his band a reservation right where they'd always lived, in the Dragoons and Chiricahua Mountains, which, you might say, is only right. But it meant they could go on using Mexico as a commissary just like always. They'd head on over the border any time they felt like it, and when they'd gathered up enough stock and captives and whatever else they went down there for, they could skedaddle back to the reservation on this side of the line and the Mexican Army would be able to do damn all about it. Now, if you were a Cochise, wouldn't you appreciate that sort of deal? We were protecting them, in effect subsidizing their raiding, buying peace for ourselves with Mexican plunder and blood. You remember Br'er Rabbit, don't you: 'Please, Br'er Fox, don't throw me into that briar patch.' Well Br'er Cochise made the same deal with that psalm-singing Howard. You tell me which one was the fox and which the rabbit. It worked fine for us, of course, but the Mexicans had a different view. Can't say I blame them much. Course, now that Cochise is dead and the Chiricahuas are up in San Carlos, there's hell to pay for everyone every time they decide they've had enough of reservation life and head out on a raid."

"What's to be done?"

"Like I said. Send 'em all to Washington with the rest of the rascals. Care for another beer?"

Just then two men came into the bar.

"Here's the local gentry," said Harding.

The two men ordered a drink and then looked over toward Ethan. One was a cowboy dressed in work clothes. The other wore a suit and tie and a new Stetson. He was about fifty and prosperous-looking. He had a broad handlebar mustache and long gray side whiskers. The cowboy was a small man with ferret eyes and a wary demeanor. They came over to where Ethan and Harding were sitting.

"Hello, Harding," said the man in the suit.

"Hello, Shelby. Ethan, this is Sam Shelby from the

Double S ranch. Shelby, this is Ethan Jaeger from New York." Ethan stood up and shook hands.

"How do you do," said Ethan.

"Glad to know you. This is Rourke, my foreman." The small man nodded. "Mind if we join you?" said Shelby.

"Take a pew," said Harding. The two men sat down.

"I understand you had some trouble with one of my boys, Mr. Jaeger," said Shelby.

"Let's say we were on opposite sides of a musical discussion."

"Well, I'm here to apologize for him. He'd do it himself, and will later, but I sent him back to the ranch to get sober. He's not at his best when he's been drinking. He's not unique in that, of course. But it was unfortunate. At least nobody got shot."

"There wasn't much danger of that," said Ethan. "Not to me, anyway. But I appreciate your coming here to straighten it out."

Shelby studied Ethan for a moment. "New York, eh? You're a long way from home."

"He came out here to write some articles about the Apaches and the Army and the ranchers and so on. Works for the *New York Herald,*" Harding said. He seemed a little guarded, or so Ethan thought. He couldn't quite decide why, however, because Shelby's manner was friendly enough. He had a trace of an accent, not exactly English but something close, as though he had been here many years but still retained traces of some other country in his speech.

"That right?" said Shelby. "Well, that's fine. It's about time people back East understood what we're up against out here. It seems funny to me, though, that one of my boys could have been faced down by a reporter from the East. No offense, you understand."

"No, I can understand why you'd see it that way."

"You don't exactly sound like the people I've met back in New York, though."

"I was raised in Maine. That probably accounts for it."

"Maine? Beautiful state. I ran into some of you boys from Maine back at Gettysburg. I was damned lucky to get out of there in one piece. Were you with them by any chance?" There was a slight edge in Shelby's voice that Ethan could not identify. Was he still holding a grudge after fifteen years? Some did, he knew.

"No. I was in the Navy, the brown-water Navy in the Mississippi." Ethan thought it best to stay as close to the truth as possible. The likelihood of anyone knowing about his activities as a Pinkerton in New Mexico was small, he figured, far smaller than the chances of slipping up and contradicting some aspect of an elaborate fictional history. And it seemed to Ethan that Shelby relaxed a bit.

"Well, you missed a hell of a scrap. I was with the 15th Texas Regiment. We tried to take Little Round Top from your boys of the 20th Maine under Chamberlain. I expect you know him." Again, it seemed like a probing question rather than casual reminiscence.

"Can't say I do. I was born on the other side of the state. Course, he's been governor a few times since then, but that was after I moved away."

"I see. Well, that was a long time ago. So, what are your plans? For writing your articles, I mean."

"Nothing in particular. I want to look around a little. Talk to the local folks. Just get some background on how people live here, especially now that Geronimo is on the loose."

"He's a black-hearted bastard, that one. You can put that in your paper. I guess you heard about the Army patrol he wiped out."

"Yes, in fact, I came through the pass on the way out here. I saw the burned-out wagon."

"A terrible thing. That's a beautiful pass, though, isn't it? We used to go quail shooting in there quite a bit before this trouble with the Apaches."

"I can believe it. I flushed a covey myself. Nearly gave me heart failure."

The other man laughed. "They'll do that. Are you a shooting man, yourself?"

"When I can. Yes."

"Well, then, how about coming out to the ranch tomorrow? I'll take you out. I've got the best bird dogs in the county, if I do say so. There are lots of places to hunt around here. There's no sense going back into that canyon until the Army nails Geronimo's hide to the barn door. And then stay for dinner. Danielle—that's my wife—will be glad to have someone other than me and the other reprobates in town to talk to."

"That sounds fine to me. I appreciate the invitation."

"Good. The ranch house isn't far from here. A couple of miles. Anyone can tell you the way. Let's say around eight in the morning."

"I'll be there."

Shelby and Rourke stood up. "Well, it's been good to meet you," said Shelby. "I'll see you tomorrow, then. And once again, I apologize for Ellis." And they left.

"So now you've met the big man around here," said Harding.

"You don't sound like you like him much."

"It's not that. He's a nice enough fella. But you know how it is, the richest man in town can be a little overbearing now and then. Nothing too bad, but noticeable. The rest of the town depends on him a fair amount in one way or the other. And he's aware of it."

"Where's he from? He mentioned Texas, but he doesn't sound like a Texan."

"He came here from Texas after the war, trailing a big herd of longhorn cattle. But he's originally an Irishman. He came to this country as a young man before the war, and settled in Texas, the way I hear it. His father was a big landowner in the west of Ireland, but he had an older brother who inherited the estate, so Shelby went into the British Army for a time and then decided to try his hand over here. Bought a place in Texas, but went bust during the tough times after the war, so he rounded up his own cattle and maybe some others and came out here. That was about twelve years ago. He's done well since then, what with the Army beef contracts. Plus he sends a lot of cattle to the Northern markets. Lives like a lord, which in a sense he is, I guess, almost. Couple of years ago he went back to Europe and came back with a new wife. His first one died just after he got here. This new one is a lady, I'll say that for her. Beautiful woman. You'll enjoy meeting her, I expect. Well, what do you say? Have time for another one?"

"No, I better not. I promised to meet a friend of mine for dinner, Jesús Sanchez. He came over with me from Tubac."

"Oh, right. I know him. Nice fella. His brother was shot a couple of days ago. I hear he's doing okay, though."

"Any idea who did it?"

"Not really. There are plenty of candidates, though. This can be a hard place to stay alive in."

"I can believe it."

Seven

Ethan met Sanchez for dinner at the boardinghouse.

"How is Tomás?" asked Ethan.

"Well, *señor,* he is doing fine, it seems, although he feels much pain. The wound is in the upper part of the leg, and though no bones were broken, the muscles there are torn badly. But he is out of danger, thank God. If the bullet had hit the artery, *madre mia,* he would have bled to death in minutes. So, all things considered, he was very fortunate."

"Does he have any ideas about who did the shooting?"

"Oh, yes, *señor.* It was not Apaches. That he is sure of. You see, he was riding alone on the range south of here, just above the Mexican border. There is a beautiful valley there called the San Rafael, very good grass there. Anyway, he was looking for some steers that might have wandered off the Double S range. You understand that he was probably fifteen miles away from here. There is a small ranch down there, run by a family of very poor character called the Curtains. Old Man Curtain and his three sons, each one worse than the next. They are thieves, *señor,* and worse. So it is said, anyway. They steal cattle from Mexico, and they are also artists with the running iron."

"Meaning they will change the brand on cattle from around here, change it to their own brand."

"That is correct. So, since Tomás was in the vicinity of the Curtain ranch, he thought he should go over there to make sure none of the stock of the Double S was mixed in. And he was about four miles from the house when he saw some horses, about eight or ten, he thinks. They were in a small corral in a canyon just off the trail. They were not exactly hidden, but the corral was in an out-of-the-way place. It just happened that Tomás had come that way. He stopped to look, and it was then he was shot. They shot several times, but only one bullet hit Tomás, thank God. Tomás saw them, *señor.* Although he could not identify them, he can say that they were white men. *Muy malos gringos.* Oh, pardon, *señor."*

"No pardon required, Jesús."

"Thank you, *señor.* But to return to the story, here is the interesting point—Tomás is sure that the horses had Army brands."

"That is interesting news. Has he told anyone else?"

"No, *señor.* He is afraid. You see, this town is not always what it seems to be. There are some strange and, you might say, unholy alliances among some of the people around here. The town marshal, for example, is known to be a dishonest man from New Mexico who came here originally to escape the authorities there. And yet he is the closest thing to the law that they have here. And since he runs the telegraph office, all communication in and out of town comes through him. The county sheriff is in Tucson fifty miles away, and the county itself is very large. He cannot police so much territory, and his deputies only come here now and again. Also, the Curtains are not the only such group in the area. There are several gangs of bad men who pose as ranchers but who are really just thieves, and they have a kind of freemasonry among themselves."

"So Tomás, having been shot once, is wary of telling his story, because he may be telling it to someone allied with the Curtains, or whoever did the shooting."

"That is correct, *señor*. And I must tell you, I cannot blame him. One feels differently about things with a bullet hole in the leg."

"I agree."

"When he recovers and is able to travel, I want to take him back to Tubac. He can help me in the cantina where the customers are sometimes rough, but rarely try to shoot you when you are not looking."

"That is a good plan. But I would like to see this place where the corral was, Jesús. Could you ask Tomás to draw a map for me?"

"Madre mia, señor. What can be the point of that? The Curtains will have moved the horses by this time. And surely that is not the kind of news the readers in the East want to receive."

"You'd be amazed at what they want to read, Jesús. And I would like to satisfy my own curiosity."

Sanchez shrugged. "Well, *señor,* if you must. I am sure Tomás can draw a very fine map for you. But if you take my advice, I would imagine the corral and the horses and the horse thieves, and then put your imaginings on paper. The readers in the East will never know the difference."

Ethan laughed. "We have had this conversation before, Jesús. And as I said to you then, things are frequently done that way, but it is not my way."

"I understand, *señor.* But your way is not the way of a prudent man. But that is your choice, of course, and after dinner I will go back to Tomás to get a map for you. I think it would be better if I ask him on your behalf, for he is still somewhat shy of strangers. In this town, one cannot be sure, or so he tells me."

That night Ethan considered going out to the Curtain place in the morning. Tomás had drawn a useful map, and Ethan's curiosity was aroused. If they were Army horses, were they the ones taken in the raid, or had other Army stock been stolen recently? If they were the horses from the raid, did that eliminate the Apaches from consideration? Would they have taken the horses only to sell them to the Curtains? Such things were possible. In other parts of the West there were these kinds of arrangements between Indian renegades and white renegades. And Wilkes had said that the Apaches were not one monolithic group, but rather a collection of bands. One band might have acquired the horses from the group that attacked the Army and then sold them to the Curtains. It was possible, although unlikely. The most likely theory was that the Curtains themselves had attacked the Army and stolen the payroll. But would they be stupid enough to corral the horses on their own land, even if the corral were off the beaten track? That was the reason Ethan wanted to see the place. If it were well hidden and if Tomás had merely stumbled across it, the Curtain explanation would make sense. If not, then there might be other explanations.

On the other hand, Jesús was undoubtedly right, the Curtains would have moved the horses as soon as they had been spotted. There was no urgency about seeing an empty corral. And so he decided to visit the Double S ranch the next day, as planned. A little quail hunting followed by a decent dinner would be a welcome break. The Curtains could wait.

* * *

In the morning Ethan stopped at the newspaper office. He had written a story about the attack. The gist of the story was that people in Verity believed that the Apaches had been responsible. Ethan had his doubts about that theory, but the story was in essence true. People did believe that, and Ethan wanted Harding to send the story through the telegraph office. It would help to establish Ethan's bona fides as a reporter, for he assumed the marshal/telegraph operator would spread the details around town. The story was to be sent to an assistant editor at the *Herald,* a man who had cooperated with the Pinkertons in the past and who would merely file it away unless and until he received another coded message to the effect that the story should run. This was in case Ethan's cover needed to be strengthened.

Harding was at his desk, apparently lost in thought.

"Morning, Sep. You're up early."

"The search for news is never-ending," said Harding. "Besides, I have a sour stomach. Must have been those tamales. Of course, I did have seven or eight glasses of beer, but that generally has a soothing effect on me. Must've had a bad pepper."

"I understand. I've had a bad pepper a time or two myself."

"Did you have dinner with Sanchez? How's his brother doing?"

"Pretty well, I guess. We ate at the boardinghouse. Had something called chicken fried steak with fried okra."

"And lived to tell the tale. Your insides must be copperplated."

"I wonder if you'd do me a favor," said Ethan. "I have a story I'd like sent back to New York, and the telegraph office isn't open yet."

"No, his honor the marshal generally likes to sleep late after a night of drinking and playing cards, which means he sleeps late every day except February 30th. I can drop it off for you, if you like. It's best to wait till later in the day, anyway, to send telegrams, because his touch is a little shaky until about three. Before then, he has a hard time distinguishing between the dashes and the dots."

"That's what I was going to ask."

"Sure. I'll take care of it for you. You going quail hunting with Shelby?"

"Thought I might."

"I'd go with you, if I was invited. His ranch is just down the road to the south about a mile. Take the first turning off the main road, and you'll see his gate. Good luck. Say hello to Mrs. Shelby for me. I expect you'll enjoy meeting her."

"Thanks."

The road to the Double S followed a spring creek. The water was only a foot or so deep and maybe four feet across, but it was as pure and clear as any mountain stream, and Ethan could see the watercress growing under the surface and along the edges. Someone could dam up that stream and stock it with trout, Ethan thought. They would thrive in that cold spring creek. There were cottonwoods lining the banks on both sides, and here and there a sycamore. The cottonwoods were turning yellow in the late autumn sunlight. And beyond for as far as he could see, there was yellow grass rolling in waves up to the base of the mountains. The morning was bright and warm, and there were no clouds in the sky. To the west the Santa Ritas rose up in profile, and to Ethan they looked like a titanic god stretched out for a nap, nose in the air and hands folded across the chest. Here and there a meadowlark flushed out of the grass and flew away, white tail feathers flashing.

"Beautiful country, Rangeley," he said. "It's hard to believe the desert is so close by."

Ethan found the turn for the Double S, and crossed over a little bridge that led to the gate. He rode on through pastureland dotted with live oaks and intersected with dry washes and arroyos, products of summer storms and sudden floods. Scrub jays, brightly blue but raucous, flew among the oaks, complaining about something, and in the distance Ethan could hear the trilling of flycatchers. Mourning doves flushed out of the long grass, sometimes in pairs, sometimes in groups of six or more.

In a mile or so he came to the main house.

It was a single-story adobe house roofed with red tiles and surrounded on all sides by broad verandas. There was a wall around the house about five feet high, with a heavy wooden gate that led into a main courtyard. Behind the main house was a long bunkhouse, a barn and a corral and some smaller outbuildings, along with a kennel that had eight or ten separate cages. In the cages were English setters barking and jumping at their fences. Maybe they knew there was to be a hunt today. All the buildings were carefully painted, and there were *ristras* of red chiles and baskets of flowers hanging from the veranda roof in front of the main door. Several sleek horses were tied to the hitching post outside the front door. One wore a sidesaddle. The whole scene spoke of prosperity.

Shelby was standing in the courtyard when Ethan rode through the gate. It was exactly eight o'clock.

"Good morning, Mr. Jaeger. You're right on time. I like that. Step down, please."

"Morning, Mr. Shelby. Punctuality is one of my few virtues. It's a habit left over from my Navy days."

Ethan dismounted and the two men shook hands.

"My name's Sam, by the way. No sense being formal out here, is there?"

"None whatever. Mine's Ethan."

Shelby was dressed for the field. He was wearing highly polished leather boots that reached to his knees, tight knee-length breeches, and a yellow tattersall vest over a white shirt and silk tie. He looked like a British country squire except for his broad Stetson hat. Ethan, by contrast, wore his traveling clothes—blue jeans and a checked shirt. But they were clean, at least, for he had turned his things over to Hop Sing the day before. Shelby noticed the difference in their outfits.

"I apologize for looking like this," Shelby said. "Habits die hard, and I can sometimes make myself think I'm actually back in the old country by putting on this fancy dress." He cast a quick eye over the rest of Ethan's outfit. He noticed the Henry rifle in the saddle scabbard and the quality of the tack and saddlebags. He made a quick evaluation of his horse and nodded approvingly. It was a quick summing up that Ethan had often observed among wealthy people whose first order of business was always to determine whether you were someone to be reckoned with or ignored. Apparently, Ethan passed the initial tests despite his clothes. Then Shelby noticed Ethan's muttonleg shotgun case, which was tied to his saddle. "That's a fine-looking case you have there. What sort of gun is in it?"

"Here, take a look." Ethan opened the case and took out the shotgun, which was broken into two pieces to fit in the case. He assembled the gun and then handed it to Shelby.

"My God. It's a Purdey," said Shelby. "What a beautiful weapon." Shelby mounted the gun to his shoulder a few times to test the fit. "Good Lord, it's as sweet as Irish butter." He ran his hand lovingly over the walnut stock and admired the engravings on the sidelocks. "Beautiful."

"Yes, I agree. It was a present from a friend."

"That's the kind of friend to have, by God. The quail will be lining up just for the honor of being shot by such a gun." The Purdey placed Ethan immediately in a new category. A man might dress any which way he chose, but if that same man owned a Purdey, he must be someone of substance.

Just then a woman came out on to the veranda, and for the first time in a great many years, Ethan felt a stirring in his heart. She was absurdly beautiful.

"Here's the lady of the house," said Shelby. "Darling, this is Ethan Jaeger. Ethan, this is my wife, Danielle."

Ethan removed his hat. "How do you do, Mrs. Shelby."

She stepped off the porch and extended her hand and smiled. "Hello. Please call me Danielle. And welcome to the Double S."

"Thank you. It's kind of you both to invite me."

She was French, although her English was perfect, with just the trace of an accent. She was about thirty, he figured, with very dark hair that was parted on the side and hung in loose waves around her face. Her eyes were so blue that the color seemed to radiate. Her skin was smooth and dark, the color of robust health. She wore no cosmetics, but her lips were red as autumn apples and her teeth were straight and white. She was about five and a half feet tall, and her figure, even in the elaborate riding costume, seemed to Ethan to be an ideal combination of strength and softness and symmetry.

Ethan felt immediately and profoundly depressed. Her beauty was so perfect that his own isolation suddenly seemed that much more acute and unbearable.

She was like a work of art that you could never own, but only look at in a museum and then long for afterwards. It was, for Ethan, not love, but sadness at first sight.

He stood there, at a loss for words.

Fortunately, just then a wagon drawn by two fine-looking mules pulled into the courtyard.

"Here's Octavius," said Shelby. "Looks like we're ready to go." Octavius was apparently the old black man driving the mule wagon. On the back of the wagon were four dog boxes. Each box contained an English setter. The dogs were all jumping and whirling and yipping in the cages, ready for the hunt. The dogs that had been left behind in the kennel were keening piteously, bereft at missing the day's hunting.

"Those are handsome mules, Sam." Ethan was glad for the diversion.

"You a mule fancier?"

"Recent convert, I guess you might say."

"Well, these are a matched pair. Called Victoria and Albert. One-hundred-percent-pure Missouri mules. None finer." Shelby pronounced the word as "Missourah."

"I can believe it."

"I thought we would ride back a few miles into the oak canyons. There are birds all around here, but there's no sense shooting the home coveys. Octavius can follow with the wagon and the dogs."

"You're the boss. Are you going along, Mrs. Shelby?"

"It's Danielle, please," she said. "No, I'm going for a ride. I will leave you gentlemen to your sport today."

"She's a hell of a shot, Ethan. And she's also a hell of a horsewoman. She'll take some jumps that I think twice about, I can tell you."

"I guess there's no worry about the Apaches around here, then."

"Well, one of the boys will go with her, but I don't think Geronimo and that gang are anywhere around these parts. She won't go too far anyway, will you, darling?"

"I will be careful. You will stay for dinner, Ethan, yes?"

"I'd be happy to, ma'am."

"Good. I will see you then. Good luck." She mounted her horse in one easy motion and then trotted out through the gate. The two men watched her leave.

"She's beautiful, isn't she," said Shelby.

"Yes. Truly."

"I met her in Paris the last time I was there. Her father owns a vineyard in Bordeaux. He sends us wines that he thinks will travel well. Rather a nice arrangement, don't you think?"

"The only way it could be better is if her mother owned a cheese shop."

"Ha, ha. You're right. I'll have to suggest it next time I write to her. Well, I think we're all set. How are you fixed for cartridges, by the way?"

"All I have are fours, I'm afraid. They'll be a little heavy, but the last time I used this gun I wasn't after quail."

"Ducks?"

"Yes, ducks."

"Well, that's no problem. Let me get you a box of cartridges. A gun like that and birds like we'll be seeing require the proper size of shot. No sense in tearing them up with size-fours." He went into the house, and came back a moment later with a box of shells and his own shotgun under his arm. He gave the shells to Ethan. "Here, these will be just the thing. I special-order them."

Ethan looked at the label on the box. It said HOL-

LAND AND HOLLAND, LONDON. "Thanks very much. These will be just fine, although I don't know how a Purdey will feel about shooting Holland-and-Hollands."

Shelby laughed. "Well, you'll just have to muddle through. I'm in the same boat with my gun. Here. Have a look." He handed his shotgun to Ethan. It was a Rigby.

"Nice gun," said Ethan.

"Not quite the same category as yours, but I like it. Well, shall we go?"

They rode several miles west. Octavius followed with the wagon. The trail led through an oak forest and paralleled a dry wash that was filled with stones the size of cannonballs. During the season of the heavy rains these washes had been filled with rushing water, and the stones had been carried there from the higher elevations. The floor of the forest was covered with dried oak leaves, for although these live oaks stayed green throughout the year, they did drop their leaves to make way for new growth. The crunching of the leaves underfoot made Ethan suddenly homesick. The day was a brilliant blue, warm and dry, nothing like most of the days in Maine, but the fallen leaves underfoot were a whisper from the past.

"Have you ever shot these fool's quail before, Ethan?" asked Shelby. The two men were riding side by side.

"No. In fact, I've only ever seen one covey, and that was by accident."

"Well, they are sporty birds. They hold very tight, so you have to have good dogs. Otherwise, you can walk right past them and never know they are there, unless you happen to step on them. That's why they call them fool's quail, I suppose. When they get up, they'll go up in all directions and they fly like the very devil was after them. But these are good dogs. They'll put us into birds."

They rode until they came to the mouth of a canyon. The canyon walls were gently sloped and covered with oaks and tall grass. A dry wash ran through the middle and joined the larger wash that they had been following. Up the canyon Ethan could see some huge sycamores that had multiple trunks, each one slanting in a different direction so that the tree seemed to be a clump of hardwoods instead of a single entity. Their trunks were dappled from the mottled pattern of the bark and from the sunlight coming through their browning leaves.

"We'll put the dogs out here," said Shelby. "This is a good canyon. Octavius! Put out Mollie and Maggie."

Octavius stopped the wagon, and slowly went around the back and opened two of the dog boxes. Two English setters burst out and jumped to the ground and immediately started to hunt, running in different directions, noses to the ground. They both wore small bells on the collars. When the bells fell silent, it meant that the dogs were on point, that they had found some birds.

"I prefer to hunt bitches," said Shelby. "Male dogs always seem more interested in smelling each other's privates and figuring out who's boss dog. Females just go about their business without worrying about pecking orders. Males by themselves are fine, but in this country it's better to have a couple of dogs working. We'll just ride along and let these dogs work."

"Is this land part of the Double S?"

"Yes, as far as you can see. Which in this canyon isn't very far at all, I suppose. But out here the issue isn't whether you own the land, but whether you control it and can graze it. There are no fences, so whoever has his cattle on the land essentially owns it. I like that. No boundaries. Just whatever you can take and hold."

"I can understand that."

Shelby looked at Ethan, scrutinizing him for a moment. "Yes, I believe you can," Shelby said. "You'd understand it even more if you came from Ireland as a second son, as I did. Do you understand the law of primogeniture? It means that the firstborn son inherits everything while the ones who come after get at most the honor of a title and nothing more. It's designed to keep the great estates intact, and it does that at the cost of turning second sons into gentlemanly beggars or parsons or Army officers. Those are the choices, generally."

"Yes, I have heard of that practice."

"Most people around here think the Double S stands for 'Samuel Shelby.' But in fact it means the 'second son.' It's a small joke to myself. When my older brother, God rot him, came into the title, he cordially suggested that I join the Army and see a bit of the world because he had no intention of feeding me any longer than it took to get me packed. What small legacy my father left me in cash went to paying for my commission, and so at the tender age of twenty-five or so I found myself an officer in His Majesty's Heavy Brigade of cavalry. Very elegant. And it would have been tolerable enough, except that that same year the war in the Crimea began, and so, rather than prancing around Hyde Park on a dashing charger and making eyes at all the ladies in their carriages and twirling my cavalry whiskers and looking like God's own dandy, I was sent to the Crimea, where the only women were nurses and damned few of them, ugly old hens, though useful. I don't suppose you covered that war. You don't seem old enough."

"No. I wasn't there. In fact, I don't know much about it, really. Except the Charge of the Light Brigade, of course."

"Oh, yes. Tennyson did them proud, albeit it was a

mad venture and a great error. But did you know that Tennyson also wrote about the charge of the heavy brigade? It's true. We never got the same credit because we weren't slaughtered so thoroughly. Still, it was a nasty show, very."

"Where was your father's estate?"

"Rosscommon. Have you been to Ireland, ever?"

"No, although I understand it is a beautiful country."

"It is that, if you have money. If you don't, then it's a very wet place. Green and wet. When you have money, you can look out from your drawing room window and watch the mist or rain and think how beautiful it all is and how it will make your gardens grow. When you don't have money, you are out in that same rain digging praties and wondering which will kill you first, starvation or pneumonia, and whether if you can't pay your rent on time, the landlord will come along and tear down the roof over your head and toss you and yours into the road."

"Praties?"

"That's what the peasants call potatoes. Digging praties in the rain is a peasant's lot, of course. When there's praties to dig. But a second son is out in the rain, too, even though he gets to wear an officer's uniform and sit on a horse as a consolation and a proof that he's a gentleman. Do I sound bitter at all?"

"Not overly."

"I'm not, now. But there were times when I was. Look. There's Maggie on point."

The dog was standing on the side of the sloping canyon, her nose pointing into the tall grass under an oak tree. Her tail was raised and her left paw was cocked. She was quivering, but she held her point perfectly. The two men dismounted, took their shotguns out of their saddle scabbards, and walked toward the dog.

"Usually these birds will be coveyed up this time of day, so you can expect a half dozen or so to go up. They'll most likely fly up the side of the canyon, but there's no way of telling for sure. There's not much wind, so they could go anywhere. I'll take the ones on the right, and you take the left."

Ethan nodded, and they walked slowly to where Maggie was pointing. The other dog, having noticed the point, had circled around and crept up behind. She was honoring the point, not wanting to flush the birds prematurely.

"That's a beautiful sight, I swear," said Shelby.

Ethan circled around to the left while Shelby went to the right. Then they walked past the dogs to where the birds were most likely hiding.

"I can't see any," said Ethan.

"You won't. These birds are so well camouflaged that you rarely see them before they fly."

Ethan cocked the hammers on his Purdey and walked forward. Suddenly, there was a whirring of wings and a dozen or so quail leapt into the air and shot off in all directions going in front and behind the two men. Ethan picked out a bird that was peeling away to the left and fired, and there was a puff of feathers and the bird dropped. He then turned to fire a second time at a bird that was quartering away trying to go up the canyon side. He dropped that bird, too. It fell in the grass about halfway up the canyon. Shelby also fired twice. The sound of his gun going off was loud in Ethan's ear, as if the gun had gone off a few feet from his head. At the sound of the guns the dogs broke and dashed after the fallen birds.

"Damn!" said Shelby. "Missed with both barrels. Did you get any at all?"

"Two, I think. Yes, there's Mollie with one and Maggie with the other."

"That's bloody good shooting. A right and a left the first time out. Damn. I hate to miss." Ethan noticed that Shelby was actually angry. "Reload. There may be others in here. Sometimes they don't all go up at once." In fact, Ethan had already reloaded. It was a reflex action whenever he fired. And then a single bird did flush from the same spot going straightaway down the canyon. Shelby fired both barrels, but the bird kept on. Ethan snapped his gun to his shoulder and shot, and the bird dropped, leaving a small cloud of feathers in the air that reflected the sunlight for a moment and then drifted away in the light breeze.

"Bloody hell," said Shelby. Molly dropped the bird she was carrying at Ethan's feet, and then dashed after the third one and retrieved it.

"Good girl, Molly. Good girl, Maggie," said Ethan. "These are fine dogs, Sam. Damn fine dogs."

"Yeah. Yeah, they are. Did you mark where the singles landed?"

"No, I'm afraid not."

"Well, let's hunt them up. Come on Mollie, Maggie. Birds in here. Hunt 'em up. Let's go." He went walking quickly after the dogs, who were running down the canyon after the quail that had escaped. "Octavius, you grab that horse," he shouted.

Ethan took his three birds over to the wagon and gave them to Octavius.

"That's good shootin', mister." The black man was smiling. "The boss, he don't like missing. Not very much. No, sir. This keeps up, could be a long day."

"Beginner's luck," said Ethan.

"Mebbe so. But I've noticed that the ones who can shoot usually have most of the luck."

Just then there were two more shots in quick succession. Shelby was about fifty yards away, and had killed a single bird that Mollie had located.

"That's better," he shouted. "Fetch 'em up, Mollie. Dead bird in here. Dead bird."

"That's good," said Octavius. He raised his eyebrows and smiled at Ethan. "Funny how a little dead bird can make a man happy. Life will be better now."

Shelby was walking back toward the wagon. He was holding a quail in his hand and smiling. "Well, that's one at least. One for six. You're three for three, Ethan."

"I was just telling Octavius that it was beginner's luck."

"Yes, and I'm the King's first cousin. Well, let's see if we can find another covey."

They found three more coveys before stopping for lunch. Ethan killed four more quail and missed two others. He did not miss on purpose, but he was not unhappy that it happened. He was a guest, after all, he figured. Shelby knocked down two more birds, just enough to brighten his mood somewhat after a difficult beginning. Ethan was relieved, too. He had known aggressive hunters before, men who took dangerous shots when they were having a run of misses and the quail flew in too many unpredictable directions. Standing next to someone who was frustrated was a recipe for an accident.

They stopped for lunch at a grove of sycamores. Octavius set up a portable table and two camp chairs, and then brought out a wicker picnic basket that was filled with fried chicken and salad, bread, and two bottles of wine, and laid the table with porcelain plates and silver tableware and crystal glasses for the wine. He served the food and then watered the dogs, before going over to the wagon to eat his own lunch.

"I hope you don't mind a red wine with chicken, Ethan," said Shelby. He was more relaxed now and had resumed his role as host.

"I don't mind red wine with anything."

"This comes from Danielle's father. Very fine stuff, I think." He poured the wine and tasted it. "Yes, quite good."

"I agree, although I'm no judge of fine wines, I'm afraid."

"So, how do you enjoy the newspaper business? Must be an exciting sort of work, I would think. The war correspondents I met during the War Between the States seemed to be a rakish bunch."

"It suits me. Gives me the chance to travel around and get paid for it."

"You work for the *New York Herald,* I think."

"That's right."

"Do you know a man there by the name of Parker, Alfred Parker?"

Ethan had the sudden sense that this was more than casual conversation. He did know the names of most of the people at the *Herald.* Memorizing the list had been part of his preparation.

"Alfred Parker? I don't think so. No, I'm sure I don't know him. Never heard his name, in fact."

"Ah. I thought he worked for the *Herald,* but maybe I was mistaken. I met him during the war, you see. Perhaps he's moved on to another paper since then."

"Could be. It's a footloose sort of business."

"Since we're on the subject, I wonder if I could ask a favor of you."

"Sure."

"Well, it's just this, you see. I'd rather not have a story about me and the Double S appearing in the papers back East. Oh, it's not that I am a shy young violet, you understand. It's just that the ways out here are different from the ways back East, and some people might not understand how we do things."

"What do you mean?"

"Well, being so close to Mexico, we sometimes have

problems with Mexican cattle wandering over the line and getting mixed in with our herds, and sometimes we don't notice it until the cattle are loaded on the trains for market, and by then it's generally too late to locate the real owners and return the beasts. And after all, by that time they have been eating our feed and grazing our land for so long that half their weight comes from our pastures, if you follow me."

"I think I understand."

"And I don't deny that now and then some of our boys encourage these Mexican cattle in their wandering ways. Sometimes at night, just for a little fun, the boys ride over the border, and if they happen to stumble across a herd that is pining to come home, they just show them the way, as an act of charity. Otherwise, they might get lost and perish in the desert, do you see? Well, it's technically wrong, I suppose, but most of those cows have been stolen from up here anyway, so we're just helping them return to their native land. Looked at in that light, it's a patriotic service of sorts."

Ethan laughed. "I understand what you're saying, Sam. And I can guarantee you that no word of your patriotism will appear in the *Herald,* although it's a shame that such service should go unrecognized."

Shelby chuckled. He seemed relieved. "Well, we're modest people here. Who was it who said: 'that best portion of a good man's life, his little nameless unremembered acts of kindness and of love'?"

"Wordsworth, I believe."

"The very man. Well, that's us. We prefer to do our acts of kindness in obscurity and let the light of the press shine on more worthy subjects."

"You have my word on it, Sam."

"Well, then, that's fine. Have some chicken."

* * *

In the afternoon they found five more coveys of quail. Ethan killed eight more birds, but Shelby had taken too much wine at lunch. He was not drunk, but his shooting eye was off, and he managed to kill just two more birds. But his spirits were better than in the morning, since he had an excuse.

"I should know better than to drink wine at lunch. Couldn't hit a flying cow afterwards. It's a cruel waste of cartridges."

Ethan was pleased and relieved about Shelby's change of attitude, for the other man had not taken any dangerous shots, and indeed seemed quite content with the results at the end of the day.

"That makes fifteen for you and five for me," said Shelby. "Ah, it was a shocking performance. My shooting was diabolical. But on my side of the ledger, I had a far better lunch than you, so I consider ourselves even for the day. What do you say?"

"I agree entirely. And I thank you for a wonderful day."

"Ah, well. It's not over yet. There's still dinner to look forward to, and I am sure Danielle has ordered something especially fine. It's not often we have guests from the East. She'll want to know all the news."

"I look forward to it, Sam. But I'd like to go back to town and get cleaned up some and change my clothes."

"Of course. We generally eat around eight, so there's plenty of time for a wash and a brush-up, what we call in Ireland a tidivation."

They rode back to the ranch. The sun was just setting over the canyons, and the light filtered through the oaks and sycamores, throwing long shadows over the canyon floor. The dogs were back in their boxes in the wagon, exhausted after a day of hunting. After a few minutes Shelby was dozing in his saddle. The only sounds then were the clopping of the horses and mules and the creaking of the wagon as it rolled over the rocky washes and through the dry leaves, and then Octavius started quietly singing a hymn of some sort that Ethan did not recognize. Something about "going home." And Ethan felt suddenly very content. The sounds, the light, the smell of the cool air at dusk—all in all, it was the most beautiful place he had been in in many long years.

When they got back to the ranch house, Danielle Shelby was waiting for them on the veranda. She was still wearing her riding clothes, for she had been out most of the day, too. And looking at her, Ethan felt his mood of contentment drain away. Her smile was so welcoming, her presence so intensely and beautifully female, so artless, so womanly, that he felt an ache in his chest, and he wondered how on earth he was going to make it through dinner that evening.

"Well, gentlemen," she said. "I hope you had a fine day."

"A wonderful day, Danielle," said Ethan, trying her name to see how it sounded coming from his own mouth.

"Yes, very jolly," said Shelby. "Good shooting. Ethan will be here for dinner, but he wants to go back to his rooms and change, so I told him we would dine at eight."

"Yes, of course," she said. "Will you have a drink before you go back to town, Ethan?"

"No, thank you. I'll need every minute to get myself into civilized condition again."

"Well, then, we will see you in a few hours." She went into the house, and Shelby followed her. Ethan was turning his horse to leave, but the window was open and he could hear Danielle talking to Shelby.

"How did you shoot, Sam?"

"Pretty well. Got about fifteen, I should say. That

fella managed to scratch down a couple, too, but he's a shocking shot. I wouldn't mention anything about it tonight. I expect he'd rather forget about it."

Ah, thought Ethan. That's interesting.

As he rode out of the main gate, he noticed Tramp Ellis skulking around the corral, and he remembered that Ellis had made no attempt to apologize for the other night, even though Shelby had said he would. It was a small thing, of course, like lying to your wife about your shooting. But it was a small thing that Ethan did not care for.

Back in his room, Ethan looked at himself in the mirror. It was the first time in a while that he paid much attention to the way he looked, and the man staring back at him was almost a stranger. He was a little above average in height, lean and a little hungry-looking. His thick dark hair was flecked with gray, as was his mustache. He had light blue eyes and a fair complexion. There were some fine lines around his eyes, and a small scar on his cheek and another on his forehead. Some women he had known thought he was handsome. Others didn't.

He decided he needed a bath, and went to Hop Sing's bathhouse, where he paid an extra dollar for clean hot water. He soaked in the water for a long time and then, having brought clean clothes with him, dressed for dinner. He wore his best black broadcloth suit with a white shirt and a black tie, and he left his hunting clothes with Hop Sing for washing. "I guess that'll have to do," he said to himself, and he mounted Rangley and rode back to the Double S.

It was dark by the time he turned off the main road and headed for the ranch house. He could see the glow of the house above the trees. The stars were fully out, strewn over the night sky like seeds sown carelessly, extravagantly. The Milky Way arched over the entire sky like some vaporous rainbow, and the Big Dipper lay low on the horizon. There were few places on earth where you could see stars in such profusion, and it was one of the things about the Southwest that Ethan liked. It reminded him of his days at sea. His Navy years had mostly been spent in patrolling rivers, so that he never got very good at celestial navigation; it wasn't necessary. But after the war, when he joined the merchant ship as a junior officer, he'd had to learn how to navigate by the stars, and he'd spent many an evening with his sextant shooting the angles of the stars. And he remembered how he'd felt, far out in the Pacific, the first time his fix came together perfectly, three lines on the chart that intersected exactly, so that he knew precisely where he was at that moment. It seemed to him to be a very good thing to locate yourself by your relationship to the stars. And at that time, just knowing where he was was enough.

He rode through the gate. The house was ablaze with lights. Shafts of light projected from each window out into the darkness of the November night, as though to welcome him. He rode to the hitching post by the front door, and was about to announce himself when Danielle came out on to the veranda to greet him. She was wearing a white silk dress that was elegant but unadorned. It was cut low over her shoulders, and she wore a string of diamonds around her throat. Her dark hair was loose around her shoulders, as it had been earlier in the day. Apparently, she preferred it that way regardless of the occasion. Ethan felt his throat tighten, and he knew if he spoke just then, it would not be with his normal voice.

"Good evening, Ethan," she said. "Please step down. Sam is still getting dressed. I am afraid he overtired himself today. You had a successful hunt, I think."

"Yes, it was a fine day."

"Come in, please."

The main room of the ranch house was large and well furnished. Persian carpets covered the floor, which was made of smooth, wide planks that were highly polished. The ceiling was made of heavy beams that supported finished planking, and in the center hung a cut-glass chandelier. At one end of the room there was a huge stone fireplace, constructed of the same stones Ethan had seen in the washes that afternoon. A fire was burning, and the wood smoke gave just a touch of sweetness to the air in the room. There were leather couches and wing chairs and mahogany tables and paintings on the walls, portraits of people from another time and pastoral scenes and still-life pictures of flowers. Along one wall were bookshelves filled with well-bound editions of the classics in both English and French. And in every corner and on every other available place on the walls were stuffed animals and birds, trophies of Shelby's hunts, Ethan assumed. A mountain lion crouched atop the bookcase, and a black bear, maybe five feet tall, stood on his hind legs in the corner. Pronghorn antelope and deer heads looked down from the stonework above the fireplace. A variety of ducks were arranged along the walls, teal and mallards and pintails, posed by the taxidermist in positions of flight or with their wings cupped as though they were landing on some pond in the forest. On several of the tables were quail under glass, the kind of quail Ethan had been hunting that day. Standing next to the bear was a gun case that contained six shotguns and rifles, each one well cared for and expensive.

"I see Sam takes his hunting seriously," said Ethan.

"I am sure you discovered that today," she said. It seemed as though there was a hint of disapproval in her voice, but Ethan could not be sure. "He enjoys taking trophies."

"I understand that you go shooting sometimes, too."

"Oh, yes," she said. "I like it very much, although I am not very interested in big game animals. I prefer quail hunting."

"Sam says you are a very good shot."

"Oh, well, I suppose that is true. To tell you a secret, I am much better than he is with a shotgun. But he is an excellent shot with a rifle. That is his forte. As you can see." She gestured toward the stuffed heads above the fire. "Would you care for a glass of wine, or something else, perhaps? I expect Sam will be here soon, but there is time before dinner for a drink, if you like."

"A glass of wine would be fine. Thank you." She poured two glasses from a bottle standing on a side table.

"I will join you. This is another of my father's vintages. Quite nice, I think. Shall we stand over by the fire? The nights are getting cold more quickly now." She raised her glass to him and looked at him and said, *"À votre santé."*

"Et aussi à vous, Danielle. Is that correct?"

She laughed gently. "It is close enough for me to understand. But your accent is execrable." She pronounced it in the French way. "Do you have this word in English? I think so."

"Yes, we have it. It is a word that is often appropriate but seldom used."

"I should ask you what the women are wearing in New York, Ethan. I am French, after all, and supposed to be concerned about such things."

"Well, ma'am, I'm probably not the best person to ask about that. The last time I looked, the men were wearing pants and the women were wearing dresses, and that's about as much as I can tell you. It's not my department, I'm afraid."

She laughed with genuine merriment, not just out of politeness at his tepid joke. She touched his arm above the wrist as she laughed, and Ethan noticed how her eyes reflected the lights of the living room, the candles and the firelight, and how the diamonds around her throat sparkled in the same light. There are more stars than just those in the heavens, he thought. And although he knew that was banal, he also knew that it was true. And then he thought, *I know exactly where I am again. Here. Lost.*

"Well, I will tell you a secret, Ethan. I don't really care. It is treasonous for me to say such a thing, I know. But it is true. Please keep my secret, though. If word should get out that a Frenchwoman cares nothing about fashion, well, it would be a scandal, do you not think so?"

"You may rely on me, Danielle."

"Yes. I believe you. Ah, here is Sam."

"Sorry to keep you waiting, Ethan." Shelby was smiling and apparently in a good mood. He was dressed in a stiff white collar and white tie and a long-tailed dinner jacket and dark trousers. His face was a little flushed, as though he had been drinking, but he did not show it. He looked very elegant, and Ethan again was forced to realize that by comparison he looked a trifle shabby. He wondered if this had been Shelby's intention.

"I think I will check on Juno to see how the dinner is coming," said Danielle. "It should be ready soon. So if you gentlemen will excuse me."

"Reluctantly," said Shelby. Danielle left, and Shelby went to the sideboard and poured himself a drink.

"Well, how do you like our humble castle, Ethan?"

"Very beautiful, Sam. Everything seems perfect."

"It's taken the devil's own time to get it this way, I assure you. But the result was worth it, I think. Now if we can just keep the damned Apaches from burning it down in the night, I'll be well satisfied."

"You seem well fortified here. Do you think they would actually try?"

"They haven't yet, but you never know with them, the creatures. Still, there are enough men around here, and the walls are good and thick, so I believe we could withstand most raiding parties without too much trouble. Also, we're not that far from town, so I doubt they'd risk it. They are pretty sensible when it comes to assessing the dangers of an action. They don't take any unnecessary chances, as a rule. If it were otherwise, I wouldn't feel content leaving Danielle here when I'm gone. Running a ranch this size means traveling a fair amount. The nearest railhead is in Willcox, which is a good fifty miles away, and even there they don't have facilities for shipping large herds. Sometimes we have to take the beeves all the way to Denver. But as I say, there are always men left here to look after the place, so I think we're pretty secure."

"Since we're on the subject. I wonder what you think about the attack in Box Canyon. I assume it was Apaches. At least, that's how I wrote the story."

"Oh, yes. There's no doubt about that. I don't know if you heard, but I and a few of the boys were the first to discover the bodies. We were in the north range, not more than a couple of miles from the scene, and we saw the black smoke from the burning wagon. Of course, by the time we got there, there was nothing to be done, poor devils, and the Indians were gone. I sent a man back to town to telegraph to Fort Lowell."

"I understand the bodies weren't mutilated. That's unusual, isn't it?"

"Yes, it is. My theory is they heard us coming or maybe one of their lookouts saw us, and they scampered off. At least we prevented that. They're dreadful bastards, the Apaches. What do the people back East think of all this? Do you understand the truth of it, do you think?"

"Some do, I guess. It's about like it's always been. There's one group that thinks the Apaches and all the western Indians are just misunderstood natural citizens who are the victims of rapacious white men and criminal Army policy, that if they just got a few more hymnbooks in their hands, they'd show the rest of us how to live in harmony with the universe. Then there's a group who thinks they're nothing more than murdering animals that ought to be poisoned like a pack of coyotes, and the sooner the better."

"What's your opinion?"

"Well, I don't know any Apaches, so I don't have strong opinions one way or the other. I generally make my judgments on the basis of individuals."

"But surely you have some view of these outrages."

"Well, my view is that Apaches are humans, and that means they are capable of evil."

"Ah, you're a bloody Calvinist." Shelby's reaction seemed to be a mixture of amusement and impatience.

"That's one word for it, I suppose. Course, I understand that some groups of people can be worse than others. After all, there are such things as politicians and temperance workers. Apaches may be in that category."

"Ah, you're right about that. Well, you can put in your paper that if any psalm-singing Easterners want to come out here and distribute hymnals, I'll pay their way just for the chance of watching the Apaches use those hymnbooks as kindling to roast them with. It'd be a fine sight. From a distance. Ha, ha."

"Can't do it, Sam. I already promised I wouldn't write about you."

"By God, so you did." Shelby patted Ethan on the shoulder. "And I like a man who means what he says. How about another drink? There are no temperance workers around here, by God. We'd hang 'em, sure."

Just then Danielle returned. "Dinner is served, gentlemen."

They went into the dining room. There was a long table covered with fine china and silver. Two candleabra with six candles in each stood on either side of a bowl of wildflowers, flowers that Danielle had picked that day during her ride. Shelby took the head of the table, and Ethan sat on the side, across from Danielle.

"Sam thinks I should sit at the other end of the table," she said. "But it is too formal, I think. This is more agreeable."

A black woman came in carrying a large tray on which were nearly two dozen quail that had been roasted brown. A bacon strip was wrapped around each, and surrounding the birds were slices of *pain de laitue,* a kind of quiche made from lettuce and cheese. The black woman, Juno, placed the tray before Shelby and then went out to get more platters.

"This looks delicious," said Ethan. "It's been a while since I have been in such surroundings. Delmonico's is nothing by comparison."

"Juno is an excellent cook," said Danielle. "She is Octavius's wife, and I don't think we could manage without them."

"Did they come with you from Texas, Sam?" Immediately Ethan felt that he had made a mistake, for Shelby looked at him with some sense of recognition. For a second he appeared wary and suspicious. He had never mentioned coming here from Texas, and both men knew that he hadn't. He had mentioned fighting with the 15th Texas Regiment, but that was not the same thing, not quite. He considered the situation for a moment and then, having reached some conclusion, resumed his cordial manner.

"I guess you've been talking to Harding. He knows everyone's story around here."

"That's right. A newspaperman's natural failing, I guess, curiosity."

"Yes, and with Harding sometimes you get the story even if you don't want it. But to answer your question, no, they didn't come with me from Texas. I never had any servants in Texas. Things were too tight for that sort of business. And I never owned a slave. I detest slavery. Saw too much of it in Ireland. The peasant there is a slave in every way except legally. Worse off than the slaves here, in many ways. At least our blacks got enough to eat."

"And yet you fought for the Confederacy."

"The war wasn't about slavery. The war was about meddling. Besides, I have a weakness for lost causes. It's the Irish in me. The day the Irish ever win their struggle and throw the English out, they'll suffer national collapse. You can sing till your heart's content about dead heroes, but no one writes songs about bankers and lawyers. Defeat is the poet's favorite muse, and poetry is Ireland's favorite drug, after whiskey."

There was genuine bitterness in Shelby's tone. Ethan noticed that Danielle was uneasy. Apparently, she felt that Shelby was on a subject that could lead to unpleasantness.

"Well, I don't know much about the Irish, but I know that our own war was a long time ago," said Ethan. "These are better times, despite the Apaches." It was not something that Ethan necessarily believed, but he wanted to defuse Shelby's mood.

"Ah, you're right about that. Although we still have the meddlers to deal with. Those folks with the hymnals and the rule books." Shelby noticed that Danielle was frowning, and decided to drop the subject. "Well, that's enough of that, I think. Here, have some of this quail. Juno is an artist, I assure you. And some wine, too." He poured three glasses. "This is Danielle's selection, and she knows more about wine than I ever will. But I think it's a very fine *Graves,* wouldn't you say so, darling?"

Danielle glanced quickly at Ethan and smiled at him, as though to thank him for recognizing the situation and helping to avoid it.

"Yes," she said. "It is a very fine *Graves. À votre santé,* Ethan."

And Ethan lifted his glass to her and thought, *The grave's a fine and private place.* It was he felt, ruefully, a good pun, given the circumstances.

It was about midnight when Ethan came back to town. He was not in the mood to go to bed, so he went to the Big Steer for a drink, even though he had had enough already. The place was empty except for a girl at the table nearest the bar. She was playing solitaire and looked very bored. Ethan ordered a drink and went to a table in the corner. Predictably, the girl smiled at him and came over. She was tall and a little overweight. She was wearing a garish silk dress cut low and a black ribbon around her neck. Her brown hair was piled high and fastened with a silver comb in back.

"You look lonely, honey," she said. "How's about buying me a drink?"

Why not, thought Ethan. He gestured to the empty chair.

"My name's Sally Rose." She had a pleasant smile. She was probably in her early twenties, although she looked older. "What's your name, honey?"

"Robert E. Lee."

"That's a nice name. You're new around here, aren't you? I haven't seen you before, and I know most everyone."

"I'll bet."

She laughed. It was a pleasant sort of laugh, neither silly nor jaded. "Well, you know how it is in the bar business. Sooner or later every cowboy or drummer comes through here, and I'm just the sociable type, I guess. I like people. Nice ones, anyway. Some aren't nice, of course. But you look nice."

"Everyone says that."

She laughed again. "You're that newspaper fella from back East, aren't you? I heard about you running Tramp Ellis out of here the other night." She grimaced. "He's not very nice. Served him right."

"People shouldn't drink. It's not healthy."

"You're drinking."

"Yes, but I make an exception for myself."

"You're making fun of me." She dropped her chin and then looked at him from under her eyelashes. She was getting coquettish. Ethan recognized it as the second phase of the sales process. He decided to cut it short.

"How much for the night?"

She stared at him for a second, understood, and dropped the flirtatious manner. "How's ten dollars sound?"

"Sounds like money well spent. Let's get out of here."

The next morning Sally Rose got out of bed and went to the nightstand to get some water. Then she sat on the stool, lit a small cigar, and looked back at Ethan stretched out on the bed.

"Honey, I'm wore out, and that's the truth. I'll be spending most of today sitting in a bucket of cold water. You must've been on the trail a long time."

"It's been a while." Ethan smiled at her. It had been a little better than he'd expected. She had been soft and responsive and she'd smelled clean enough. When she found that he was not going to be rough with her, she reacted with something almost like affection, though Ethan did not place any significance in that. But at least now he felt calmer than he had for a while, calmer than he had been after dinner, certainly.

"Are you going to be staying in town for a while?" she asked.

"I might."

"You were awfully nice to me last night. Did that mean you'd like me to be your girl?"

"What that meant, honey, was absolutely nothing."

She shrugged. Ethan got out of bed, found a ten-dollar bill in his pants, and gave it to her. She took the money and put it in her small silk purse. Ethan noticed that she had a brand-new twenty tucked away in a side pocket.

"Where'd you get that twenty?"

She laughed. "Who knows? I've had it for a few days. It was after one of those busy nights in the bar. Quite a few cowboys were in, and my memory of that night isn't all that clear."

"Mind if I take a look at it?" He examined the bill. "Would you trade a twenty-dollar gold piece for this bill?"

"Sure. But why would you want to do that?"

"Paper's easier to carry."

She shrugged again, bit the gold coin to verify its content, and stashed it in her purse. Then she got dressed. "Well, so long, honey. You know where to find me."

"Sure. Tell your Sunday school class I said hello."

She laughed gaily, and then looked at him with something almost like tenderness and left.

Ethan lay in bed for a while, thinking about the day before and about Danielle Shelby. After a while he decided that that sort of thinking would get him nowhere, and he got up and got dressed. Longing for another man's woman was a fool's game, he knew, and he was no fool. But still, getting her out of his mind was not something he was able to do just yet. And when he thought about it, he realized he didn't even want to. Not yet, anyway.

Sanchez was in the dining room finishing breakfast when Ethan walked in.

"Morning, Jesús. How's Tomás doing?"

"Good morning, *señor*. Tomás is better, thank you. Every day brings improvement."

"I'm glad to hear it." Ethan poured himself some coffee and sat down with Sanchez.

"I hope you had a good day hunting yesterday."

"Yes, it was very good. Shelby has some fine dogs. Very stylish setters. And there were plenty of birds. Speaking of dogs, what's Nariz been up to? I haven't seen him around lately."

"Ah, *señor*, he has disgraced himself by catching a skunk. He came into town yesterday and was of course shunned. I had to rope him and drag him downwind two miles and tie him to a tree. It was very disagreeable for both of us, I assure you."

"I'll bet. How long do you think it'll take him to chew through that rope?"

"Not long, of course, *señor*, but he has great pride and will resent the indignity of the roping and perhaps return to Tubac or take some other ideas into his head. That is my hope. And then perhaps when he reappears, he will be more *simpático.*"

Ethan smiled. He was planning to go down to the San Rafael Valley today to investigate that horse corral where Tomás had been shot. He was hunting skunks, too, he thought.

Eight

Ethan had brought his horse around to the front of the rooming house, and was loading up his equipment when Squirrel Tooth Annie came up to him. It was mid-morning and she was not looking fresh. Her hair looked like an animal's nest, and her makeup was smeared. She smelled like a chamber pot, and she was still half drunk, or maybe just getting an early start.

"Hello, mister. I've been looking for you."

"Must be my lucky day." Ethan went on with his packing.

"Is your name really Robert E. Lee?" she said.

"Is your first name really Squirrel?"

"No. People call me that on account of my teeth." She bared her teeth to prove her point.

"Is that a fact? I couldn't have guessed. Well, I've enjoyed talking to you, but I have things to do."

"Sally Rose told me you were real nice to her last night."

"She shouldn't take it personally. I'm just a nice person in general. Except when I've got things to do."

But Annie was not easily offended or put off. "She

also told me you bought her twenty-dollar bill for gold. I have one, too, if you're interested."

"I might be. Let's see it."

Annie dug around in the front of her dress and pulled out a folded bill. Ethan examined it.

"I don't suppose you remember where you got this," he said.

"The same place Sally Rose got hers, only she don't remember because she was too drunk that night. She can't hold it like I can."

"It's good to have a talent. So, where'd you get it?"

"From a Mexican vaquero who came through here last week. Name of Julio Vasquez. He was real nice, too. I don't usually go with Mexicans, but like I say, he was nice."

"Your taste does you credit. Where'd he get it, I wonder."

"Oh, I know that too. I'd be glad to tell you, if you're interested. And if you're interested, maybe it would be worth a little extra to you."

"Maybe."

"Maybe an extra five dollars?"

"Sounds reasonable."

"Well, he was working for old Juan Lopez down in Sonora, you know, south of Nogales. Lopez is a big rancher down there, and most people say he's a rustler, too. But anyway, Lopez just finished a big roundup and then paid off all his vaqueros with U.S. twenties, just like this one. Seems kind of funny, don't it?"

"Yeah, I guess it does. What happened to your friend Vasquez? I don't suppose he's still around."

"Oh, no. He left the next day. He said he was going up to Santa Fe. You know how cowboys are, always on the move. Love 'em and leave 'em. It's hard on a girl, sometimes." She affected a melancholy look.

"I'll bet. Well, here's a twenty-dollar gold piece and an extra five. Maybe that'll help to dry your tears."

"Thanks, Robert. But you know, I'll bet that's not your real name."

"You're pretty quick, Squirrel. Actually, it's Stonewall Jackson."

"I knew it. I always know when a man's not telling the truth. Sally Rose, though, she can't always tell. She gets fooled a lot. Stonewall, though. That's a funny name."

"My parents had a sense of humor, same as yours, Squirrel."

She laughed and stuck her tongue out at him. "You might be surprised, Mr. Stonewall Jackson. You might be surprised about what I can do with these."

"That day ever comes, I will be surprised." Ethan mounted his horse. "Give my regards to Hop Sing."

"Hop Sing? Why would I be seeing him? He's a Chinaman, and I don't go with Chinamen. They smell funny."

"It's the soap and water."

"You want me to tell Sally Rose anything for you? Like maybe she should wait up? Or maybe you want me to wait for you. I play the concertina real good." She leered at him and rolled her eyes.

"Well, that's a neighborly offer, Squirrel, but I'm afraid I'll be a little late, and young girls need their beauty rest. Some more than others."

She laughed again. "There ain't no rest around here, Stonewall. No rest for the righteous."

"You're right about that, honey." Ethan tipped his hat to her, wheeled his horse, and rode south out of town.

* * *

It had rained during the night, and as soon as Ethan was a little south of town, he could smell the sweetness of the wet grass. It was a thick perfume, unlike any other scent he had experienced. Rich and clean. The rain clouds had cleared away, and there was just a faint breeze. Ethan headed toward the San Rafael Valley. The map that Tomás had drawn showed the Army horses were corralled in a place called Black Tail Canyon. That was about four miles from the Curtains' ranch house, which lay just astride the Mexican border at the base of the Huachuca Mountains. It would be nearly a twenty-mile ride, but the day was fresh and pleasant and Ethan was looking forward to the trip. He didn't expect to find much when he got there, but it was necessary to investigate the place, just in case.

The trail climbed out of the grassy plains into the foothills. The forest thickened as he climbed. Oak trees and junipers were mixed in with some large mesquite trees. But there was good grass amidst the trees, and here and there a small spring. The trail climbed about a thousand feet and, looking back, Ethan could see Verity sitting in the grasslands. It seemed to have a tenuous hold on the country.

After riding seven miles or so, Ethan reached the top of the pass. Spread out below him to the south was the entire San Rafael Valley. Yellow grass stretched for miles all the way to the mountains on the other side of the border. The grass glistened in the sunlight. Lines of cottonwoods followed the narrow riverbed of the Santa Cruz. To the east were the Huachuca Mountains, and to the west the red mountains called the Patagonias. And beyond in the blue distance, the mountains of Mexico. Here and there Ethan could see some small ponds formed from springs. And crisscrossing the entire valley were canyons, dozens of them, their sides and floors covered with plentiful grass and green live oaks.

Any of these canyons could hold large herds of stock, and no one would discover them except by accident.

Good place to be a rancher, thought Ethan. Or a rustler.

Ethan got out his compass and took a sighting in order to locate Black Tail Canyon, and then eased his horse down the side of the mountain toward the Huachucas. If his map was accurate, Ethan could see why whoever had stolen the Army horses had hidden them in that canyon, for it lay several miles off the trail. And not many people used the trail.

It was nearing nightfall when Ethan arrived at the mouth of Black Tail Canyon. He sat listening for a few minutes, but there were no sounds other than the screeching of a hawk. He rode a few hundred yards into the canyon. Still, there were no sounds, no signs of life.

Then he saw a grove of sycamores about a hundred yards up the canyon. And at the base of the trees was a spring. Rangeley picked up his ears as he smelled the water and nickered. Faintly, there came an answering nicker, and then another. Ethan quickly dismounted and pulled his rifle from its scabbard. He tied Rangeley to an oak tree, and then started up the canyon taking care to move from tree to tree so that he would not offer a clear target. In another hundred yards he came to a barbed-wire fence. The fence stretched from one side of the canyon wall, down across the floor, and then up the other side. On the other side of the fence, near the spring, Ethan saw the horses. There were eight of them. And farther off were two mules.

Ethan waited several more minutes, trying to sense whether there were any people around. But the evening was very still. No sounds, no smells of a campfire nearby.

Cautiously, Ethan crawled under the fence and went

toward the horses. They seemed perfectly accustomed to the sight and smell of a man. Two started walking toward him. As he got closer, he could see that all the animals wore U.S. Army brands. They seemed to be in very good condition, for there was plenty of grass and water in that place. But then Ethan noticed that one of the horses had a wound on its left shoulder. The wound was healing and did not appear to be dangerous. It was not a bullet wound, but rather the kind of jagged cut that might come from a piece of shrapnel or a splinter of rock caused by an errant bullet.

I'll be damned, thought Ethan. *What in hell are they still doing here?*

He walked another few hundred yards up the canyon, but there were no other signs of life, so he returned to where Rangeley was tied and started back while there was still a little light. He found a side canyon that led off from Black Tail. It was well hidden and yet offered a view of anyone approaching from either direction. He would spend the night. In the morning he would call on the Curtains.

Ethan was awake at sunrise. He stayed in the side canyon for an hour or so wishing he had a cup of coffee but not wanting to start a fire. He wanted to see if anyone would come to check on the horses. But no one came. He saddled up and headed west. His plan was to ride several miles before turning south, so that he could come up on the Curtain ranch from the direction of the border. It took him about two hours to work himself into a position above the Curtain ranch. He was in the foothills south of the ranch, and he could see the smoke coming from the grove of trees where the ranch house was located. He moved closer and found a place from which he could watch the ranch house through his binoculars. The house was a motley shack made of cottonwood logs chinked with mud. The roof was shingled and sagged badly. There was smoke coming from the chimney. The space in front of the house was littered with trash, animal droppings, and discarded tools. A pile of wood and a splitting block sat near the front door. There was an outhouse placed too close to the main house off to the left, and a weathered barn beyond that. Behind the house was a corral made of fence rails and barbed wire, and in the corral were a dozen or so horses. A pig was rooting around near the outhouse, and some chickens were scratching in the front yard. A few cows and a tired-looking bull grazed the thin grass not far away. Ethan could see someone he took to be Old Man Curtain doing routine chores around the outbuildings, but he could not see anyone else.

The blessings of civilization, thought Ethan. He watched a few more minutes, and then mounted Rangeley and went down to the ranch house. When he rode up, Old Man Curtain ran into the house and then emerged again with a shotgun.

"What do you want there?" he shouted. He was dressed in work boots, overalls, and a long-sleeved undershirt that was very dirty. His eyes were close to each other so that they appeared to be crossed, and his nose was large and pockmarked. His wiry hair and beard stood out in all directions. He looked to Ethan to be a perfect combination of cussedness and ignorance.

"Buenas tardes, señor," said Ethan. "I am Captain Francisco de Assisi, scout for the Fourth Brigade of the Mexican Federal Army, and I am looking to buy some horses."

"You don't look like no Mexican sojer to me," said Old Man Curtain. He spat some blackish fluid into the dust.

"And you, *señor,* bear little resemblance to an honest rancher, and I say that with all possible respect, which only proves how appearances can be deceiving."

"Whut?"

"Nothing, nothing. The point is, I am not here to exchange philosophical observations, delightful as that may be under different circumstances, but rather to buy horses. We are on the trail of Geronimo, and our men need fresh mounts."

"Geronimo, eh? That bastard around here?"

"South of here, on the soil of my own poor country, *señor*. My men are camped ten miles from here, but yours is the closest ranch, and we hope that you will supply us. We need twenty fresh mounts. And we are prepared to pay well for them." Ethan reached into his jacket pocket and took out a coin pouch. "Yankee dollars, as you say. In gold."

"Gold, huh?" Old Man Curtain put up his shotgun and rested the butt on the ground. Ethan could see his mood brightening.

"Yes, and since our need is extreme, we are willing to pay a very good premium. It is bad business on my part to say so, but I am in a great hurry. Further, since the horses will be going into Mexico, we will not be too concerned with their origin, if you follow me. The technicalities of branding and the accuracy of bills of sale are luxuries we cannot afford at this critical time."

"Whut's that supposed to mean, mister?"

"It means we will not care if these horses were raised here on this ranch or acquired in some other way. My men are not particular. And we have a sense of great urgency." Ethan hefted the pouch of gold a few times and smiled in a conspiratorial way.

Old Man Curtain scratched his head and then his stomach, spat once again, and pondered. "How soon do you need 'em?"

"Immediately, *señor.* Or as soon as you can gather them up from your pastures."

Curtain considered some more. "Well, I don't have twenty horses, that's for sure. And I'll need to keep some for our own work around here. But I guess I can let you have half a dozen or so. Would that suit you?"

"Anything would be helpful, *señor.*"

"Whut I've got is around back here in the corral. They're fine animals, mostly. Whut say we go around and take a look-see."

Ethan stepped down from his horse and followed Curtain around behind his house to the corral. In the corral were a dozen horses, none of them carrying the Army brand and all of them well past their prime. They were all skinny, shaggy, and swaybacked. Their eyes were lifeless and they stood looking at the two men with no curiosity. Only their tails were moving, swishing flies.

"No finer horses north of the border," said Curtain hopefully.

"Which border, *señor?* These horses are mere four-legged bars of soap, although they do not realize it as yet."

"Whut?"

"What I mean, *señor,* is that when I said I needed fresh horses, I meant that I wanted animals that could reasonably expect to live past sunset tonight. I am not interested in starting a museum, but rather in chasing the Apaches. These horses are not suitable. Surely you have others in better condition than these poor brutes."

Curtain squinted at Ethan and looked sharp. "You're just trying to jew me down."

"Far from it, amigo. There is not a trace of Hebrew blood in my illustrious line. I am simply saying that I would not take these horses if you paid me. Again I say, surely you have others. It is not a matter of money, I assure you. I am willing to pay very well for reasonable animals."

Curtain looked sorrowful. "Well, I wish I did, mister. I surely do. But these here is all I've got. Things ain't been that good this year in the cattle business, and maybe these critters ain't had the kind of feed they need. But I believe they'll perk up right smart once you get 'em on the trail. A little forage and exercise, and they'll be good as new. Better even."

"Your faith does you credit, *señor.* But I could not take these horses back to my commander. He would insist on having me shot, and even I would not blame him. Are there no others, truly?"

Curtain shook his head and looked glum. " 'Fraid not."

"Very well, *señor.* I will try some other place. Perhaps if I go up to Verity, I will be able to find more suitable mounts. Tell me, which is the best trail there?"

"Just head north and you'll find it, I reckon. If you don't, I guess you'll be lost. But that ain't none of my concern. I don't like Mexicans, anyway." So saying, he left Ethan by the corral and went back into the house.

Ethan walked around to his horse and mounted. As he turned away from the house, he noticed a face looking out through the window. It was not Old Man Curtain.

Ethan rode north. He intended to go back in the direction of Black Tail Canyon. Since he was in the area, it would not hurt to stop there again to see if anyone had come by. Also, he wanted to see how many possible trails led to Black Tail. Whoever stole the Army stock had driven them from the Santa Rita mountains south to the San Rafael Valley and into Black Tail

Canyon. Obviously, they did not come through Verity on the way. The question then became, how did they get there without being seen?

Tomás's map showed some other possible trails there, trails that made wide loops around Verity and entered the San Rafael from the east and from the west. Ethan decided he would backtrack the eastern trail first. He also decided to leave the Army stock in the canyon rather than driving them back to Verity. Whoever put them there would have to return for them sometime, and when they did they might leave some trace or trail that would implicate them some way. If Ethan took the animals back to town and returned them to the Army, the bait would be gone. Further, to take them back to Verity would be inconsistent with his role as a newspaperman. Why would a newspaperman even notice the Army brands or think it unusual that the horses were corralled where they were? No, they would have to stay there.

Ethan was fairly well satisfied that Old Man Curtain had nothing to do with the theft of the horses and, by implication, with the attack on the Army payroll. He seemed to have no idea that the animals even existed. His three sons, however, might have acted without their father's knowledge. Or one of them might have acted alone. Maybe they were involved in the actual robbery, or maybe they simply bought the animals or agreed to pasture them for a fee.

Ethan was about a half a mile from the entrance to Black Tail Canyon. He was riding through a broad meadow with just a few live oaks scattered every few hundred yards. Not much cover, he thought. He noticed some movement behind one of the trees on his left about thirty yards away, and as a reflex he pulled Rangeley up. Just then there was a shot, and Ethan was suddenly splattered with blood. The bullet had taken off Rangeley's left ear. He reared and screamed and then bucked Ethan heavily to the ground, then ran off kicking his hind legs and shaking his head as though trying to rid himself of the pain. He kept running and screaming, and soon disappeared leaving Ethan sprawled on the ground, slightly stunned but otherwise unhurt.

Another shot kicked up the dust a yard or so from where Ethan lay momentarily. Ethan rolled away, and then got to his feet and ran in a zigzag pattern toward a tree fifty yards away. Another shot threw dirt up to the right of him as he ran, and another to the left. *He's got me bracketed,* thought Ethan, *if he knows what he's doing.* The other man kept shooting, but kept missing and Ethan was able to get to the tree. He dove the last few yards and landed hard behind the trunk. A bullet knocked off some bark about three feet above Ethan's head. Another whanged off a rock to the side.

Ethan eased his head around the tree trunk. As far as he could tell, there was only one man shooting. There might be others around, but Ethan doubted it. They would have all opened up on him, if they'd been there. So, just one man to deal with. Ethan's rifle was in his saddle scabbard with Rangeley, wherever he was. Ethan had his two Schofields, but the range was too great for pistols. The shooter was probably a hundred yards away, excellent range for a rifle but nothing more than wishful shooting with a pistol. Ethan thought about firing a few annoyance shots, but then decided that it would be better to let this shooter wonder. In time, he would begin to think that maybe he had hit Ethan. With luck, he'd get impatient and finally decide to come and look, in which case he would have to cross the hundred yards or so of open country. And when he got within twenty yards, thought Ethan grimly, he would learn something.

Ethan waited there about thirty minutes. The shooter

kept up his fire but did no damage, except to the tree trunk. At the beginning Ethan wondered whether the sound of the firing would reach the Curtain ranch. But it was nearly four miles away. If anyone had heard it, they would have been here by now. Finally, Ethan heard the other man yell out. "Hey, greaser. You still alive? Hey. You hear me? All I want's the gold. Toss out that little sack of yours in front of the tree and I'll let you go." Ethan said nothing. "Hey, greaser! There's ten of us out here. You ain't got no chance. Might as well give up the gold." Ethan laughed. *What a cretin,* he thought. Must be one of the Curtains, maybe the one he saw in the window. "Hey, greaser, just toss out that gold and then run like hell outta here. I won't shoot. I mean, we won't shoot, you got my word on it."

All right, thought Ethan, that's as good a game as any.

"Señor," yelled Ethan. "I am badly hurt. You have shot me."

"Can you walk?"

"No. I am shot through both legs. The pain is something terrible, *señor.* Please help me. I will give you the money."

There was silence while the shooter considered. "Toss out the money bag. And then I'll come over there to help you."

Ethan threw the bag of gold coins out in front of the tree about ten yards. "There, *señor.* I have done as you asked. Now please come to help me."

"All right. I'm coming. But don't try nothing. Don't forget the other nine men has got you covered, if you try something."

"I cannot even move, *señor.* Please. I am bleeding to death. *Madre mia."*

Ethan watched as the other man slowly emerged from his tree. It was one of the Curtains, he assumed.

At any rate, it was the face he had seen in the window. The man came slowly toward Ethan's tree. He held his rifle ready but came cautiously. *This one's too dumb to live,* thought Ethan. He checked his loads in his Schofields one more time and waited.

"Don't forget," yelled Curtain, "that we got you covered. Nine rifles is pointed right at you, so don't think you can be tricky."

Curtain crept closer. When he got within twenty yards, he saw the money pouch on the ground and ran over to it. When he bent over to pick it up, Ethan fired. The bullet hit Curtain's rifle in the stock, and the force of the blast shattered the rifle and spun Curtain around and knocked him down. Ethan stood up and ran over to where Curtain was lying. Curtain wasn't hurt, but he was stunned and shocked at the turn of events.

"Those nine boys of yours must've run off, amigo," said Ethan. He was standing about five yards away and pointing both Schofields at Curtain's head. "Guess they figured you could take care of things on your own."

Curtain sat on the ground and looked up at Ethan. He was confused. "You ain't a greaser," he said finally. "Who are you?"

"Stand up," said Ethan. "Do it very slowly."

Curtain got to his feet carefully keeping his eyes focused on the two pistols pointed at him. He was a younger version of his father, beady-eyed and dirty. He had a black smudge of beard and his hair was matted and hung down over his ears. He was dressed in overalls, too, and the same sort of grimy undershirt his father wore.

"You and your old man must have the same tailor," said Ethan.

"What are you plannin' to do with me, mister?"

"What's your name?"

"Jereme. Jereme Curtain."

"Why'd you try to ambush me?"

Curtain shrugged. "For the money. Why else? You flash that kind of money around and things like this'll happen. What are you meanin' to do?"

"I'm thinking about it. You shot my horse's ear off."

"I didn't mean to, mister. Honest."

Ethan laughed. "No, you bastard, you meant to shoot me in the back. You just missed, because in addition to being as dumb as a mud hen, you're a lousy shot. Anybody misses at that range doesn't deserve to stay alive. It lowers the overall quality of the human race."

"You mean to kill me?"

"Well, I'm seriously considering it. Only thing that's stopping me is the chance that you can learn from all this."

The other man brightened up. "Oh, sure, mister. I already learned my lesson. I won't never do nothing like this no more."

"Hm. There are so many negatives in that sentence, I can't make out what you really mean. No, I think it'll be better if the lesson is based on something more than just your word. Here's what I'd like you to do. Take your left hand and raise it up slowly to the side of your head. That's it. Now take two fingers and pull that left ear of yours out just as far as you can from the side of your head. It won't take much, 'cause it already sticks out like a jug handle. That's right. Now, just hold that position. Keep pulling hard. You'll be glad you did, believe me."

"What are you going to do?" Curtain stood there tugging at his ear with his elbow straight to the side.

"I'm going to read you the lesson for today, which comes from Genesis: 'an ear for an ear'."

"What? That ain't in the Bible."

"No? That's funny. It is in my version."

"I told you I didn't mean to shoot your horse, mister."

"Just be glad you didn't accidentally shoot off his pecker, Curtain. My version of Genesis says something about that, too."

"You ain't going to cut my ear off are you, mister?"

"Nope. I'm going to shoot it off."

"No. Please don't do that, mister."

"Just hold steady, amigo. There's not much margin for error. Don't worry, though. I'm a pretty good shot, usually. But sometimes these Schofields tend to shoot a little to the left. It worries me now and then."

Ethan pointed the pistol in his right hand at Curtain's head and pulled the trigger. The sound of the shot reverberated through the canyon. Curtain spun around again and fell to the ground. Then he groaned and rolled over. He had his ear, some of it, in his left hand still.

"Oh," he moaned. Then he sat up and looked in his hand, and then dropped what was there and clapped his hand to the side of his head. "Jesus, mister."

"No, this is the Old Testament, remember."

"I'm bleeding."

"That's normal when you're shot. If it's any consolation, I think your looks have improved. Course, if you're not satisfied, I can even you up."

"No, please. I'm satisfied, honest."

"All right. Now that I have your attention and you realize that I am a serious man and that I will not put up with any horseshit of any kind from the likes of you, I think we're ready to have a little conversation. Let me know if you want me to speak up. Now, what's your game?"

"The gold. I thought you was a greaser. You ain't a greaser, though."

"Just the gold? I'm not sure I believe you."

"It's true, mister."

"What about those horses in Black Tail Canyon? That's your land, isn't it? Where'd you get those horses?" Ethan cocked his pistol and stuck it up against Curtain's right ear. "No lies, now."

Curtain looked blank. "What do you mean, mister?"

Ethan studied him. Curtain looked genuinely mystified. "Army horses. Where'd you get them?"

"Honest to God, mister, I don't know nothing about Army horses. I ain't been in that canyon in months. There's no reason for us to go there. There's no deer in there and it's too far from the house for grazing stock."

"How about your brothers? Where are they?"

"They went down to Mexico last night. They got women down there. But they'll be back tonight, and you can ask them about the horses, if you want to. They might know something, but I don't know nothing"

Ethan stepped back and looked at Curtain. He decided Curtain was too stupid and too frightened to be lying.

Ethan looked down momentarily to put his left-hand pistol into his holster, and as he did so Curtain reached behind his neck into his collar and drew out a skinning knife he had hidden there. He grabbed the knife by the handle and raised it to throw in one smooth motion, but Ethan saw the movement and pulled the trigger on his right-hand pistol. The bullet hit Curtain squarely in the chest and knocked him back three yards. He fell on his back with his arms stretched above his head. His mouth was open and he had a surprised look in his eyes. There was a small, bloodless hole in his chest. Ethan looked down at him and then rolled him over with his foot. A large hunk of his back was gone, and there was a bloody red crater where it had been.

"Damn," said Ethan. Once again it struck him that a forty-five at close range was very thorough.

He looked up into the sky and saw some ravens soaring there. He didn't have a shovel to bury Curtain. There was nothing he could do about it, and he figured the ravens and the buzzards knew their business, anyway.

He picked up the money pouch and started walking up the canyon in the direction Rangeley had run. His ear would need attention. Ethan figured he wouldn't have run too far. It wasn't like him.

Nine

Ethan walked to Black Tail Canyon. It was only about a half a mile away, and he had the feeling that Rangeley might have headed there. If not, he could at least get one of the Army horses to ride as he searched for his own horse. As he walked, he considered the problem. There were at least two possible explanations for the attack on the Army, aside from the Apaches. The first involved the Curtains in some way. They didn't seem smart enough to do a job like that by themselves, but they would have had surprise on their side, and they could have just gotten lucky. One of them, apparently, had taken the shot at Tomás Sanchez. That at least suggested that one or more of the brothers knew about the horses in that canyon and didn't want them to be discovered.

The second explanation involved the Mexican rustler, Lopez. Lopez had been paying off his vaqueros with twenty-dollar bills that were most likely stolen from the Army. Ethan would have to check to make sure the serial numbers matched the list of stolen bills; Captain Wilkes could supply that information later.

But Ethan was virtually certain that the bills came from the robbery. New twenties like that were rare. A well-organized and relatively small force of Mexican rustlers and bandits could easily slip across the border at Nogales and set up an ambush in the Santa Rita Mountains. It was only a matter of twenty miles or so. Then, they could go back the way they came.

And most likely the Curtains were somehow in league with Lopez, or else why would the horses be on the Curtain ranch? The ranch was close to the border, and the Curtains could easily coordinate with Lopez. Perhaps the stolen stock came up from the south, driven by Lopez's vaqueros first into Mexico after the robbery and then north back across the border to the Curtains's range. The fact that Old Man Curtain and Jereme didn't seem to know about the Army horses did not eliminate the other brothers. And maybe Ethan wasn't giving Old Man Curtain and Jereme enough credit for being good liars. Maybe they did know more than they let on. Maybe Old Man Curtain had sent Jereme to ambush Ethan; that way they could get the gold and still keep the horses.

By the time he got to the mouth of Black Tail Canyon, he had the beginnings of a plan in mind.

Rangeley was in the canyon standing up against the fence. The other horses were gathered there, too, on the other side of the fence, as though commiserating with him. His ear had stopped bleeding, but he shook his head occasionally for the pain was apparently still troubling him. He recognized Ethan and trotted over to him.

"Hello, buddy," said Ethan. "I figured you might come here to tell your sad tale. Well, I got him for you, if it's any consolation." He stroked Rangeley's nose and face. "And don't worry about your looks. You still look real handsome to me. For a one-eared horse."

Ethan got his wire cutters out of his saddlebags and took down a section of the fence. He took his rope and looped it over the head of the horse that had been wounded in the robbery and led him through the hole in the fence. Then he repaired the fence by twisting the wires together. It wasn't a good repair job, but it didn't matter. If the other horses broke through, they wouldn't go far. The water and good grass were right where they were already.

He mounted Rangeley and then, leading the other horse, headed back to Verity.

It was late afternoon when Ethan got back to town. He went immediately to the marshal's office. He had not met the town marshal yet, but he had figured that as a newspaperman with a particular story to tell, the marshal was the first logical stop.

The sign outside the office said: JAMES O'BRIAN, VERITY MARSHAL. U.S. POSTMASTER. TELEGRAPH OFFICE. O'Brian was only a town marshal. He had no jurisdiction outside the limits of Verity. All county business was the province of the Pima County sheriff's office, located in Tucson, so reporting a crime committed twenty miles from town was little more than a formality. But despite these limitations, O'Brian was the closet thing to law enforcement in the area and therefore the first person Ethan needed to tell about the shooting near Black Tail.

O'Brian was at his rolltop desk reading through some telegrams that he would be sending. He wore a derby hat tilted back and a soiled paisley vest over a collarless shirt. His brown woolen pants were tucked into a pair of boots that had needed new heels for some time. He did not look much like a lawman.

As a younger man he had been known as "Sweet Jimmy," because he was a lightweight prize fighter of some renown. But the years and the effects of too much food and alcohol had damaged him, so that now he was a fat, bleary, and red-eyed wreck. Further, despite his boxing skill, he had been hit too many times in too many fights, so that his face had lost much of its definition. His nose and mouth had been battered nearly out of recognition, and his eyebrows were gone, replaced by scar tissue. His ears looked like half-baked biscuits stuck on the side of his bald and scarred-up head. And his hands were gnarled from being broken against other fighters' heads.

When he was drunk, he was sentimental, sloppy, and fairly harmless, and he would sit in the saloon telling and retelling his tales of the prize ring, never caring whether anyone was listening or not. During the morning hours he was hungover and sluggish. But in the afternoon Sweet Jimmy could be a force to be reckoned with for, despite the ravages of time, whiskey, and boxing, his mind was miraculously unaffected. When sober, he was quick-witted and mean-tempered, or so Septimus Harding had told Ethan. There was a malignant light in Sweet Jimmy's eyes when he was not drunk, and his handling of passing cowboys or traveling salesmen could be brutal. Many a cowboy went away from Verity with a bloody face or head, the result of a pistol-whipping from Sweet Jimmy O'Brian.

Sweet Jimmy looked up from his reading and glared at Ethan.

"Hello, Marshal. I'm Ethan Jaeger."

O'Brian's expression changed. "Ah, the newspaper fella. Nice to know you. I read that piece that Sep Harding had me send. Good stuff. Tells it the way it is about the damned Apaches. Have a seat. What's on your mind. Another story to send, is it?"

"Not yet, although there will be one for certain. Thing is, I was riding around down in the San Rafael Valley this morning and someone took a shot at me."

"A shot?" O'Brian sat up. "You weren't hit, I guess."

"No, but it was a close call."

"What were you doing down there, I wonder. You may know that's where Tomás Sanchez was shot just last week. Geronimo more'n likely did it. Or one of his devilish relations."

"Well, that was the reason I went down there. I came over from Tubac with Tomás's brother, Jesús, and he told me about what happened to him. So I thought I would go and take a look. It seemed like an interesting story, the kind of thing people back East want to read about."

Sweet Jimmy grimaced and spat on the floor. "The people back East must be bloody fucking stupid if they want to read about that sort of thing. Murdering Apaches and all."

"Well, I suppose you have a point there. But anyway, Tomás gave me the directions and I was down there today in about the same area when someone shot at me from ambush."

"Did you see him at all? Was it an Indian?"

"No idea."

"Did you shoot back at him? You're carrying a couple of pistols, I notice."

"Yes, I fired a few shots in his direction, but I doubt I hit him. It was pure luck if I did."

Just then Sam Shelby came into the office. "Hello, Ethan. Hello, Jimmy. I thought that was your horse out there, Ethan. What the hell happened to his ear, and where'd you get that other animal?"

"Someone took a shot at me down in the San Rafael Valley, and instead of hitting me, he hit Rangeley in the ear."

"You don't say it! Damn. Was it Apaches, do you think?"

"Hard to say. But I'm pretty sure it was only one

man. When Rangeley got hit he ran like the devil, which was lucky because it got me out of range quickly. He must have run a couple of miles, but then he threw me. He kept on going, but the place where he threw me was the mouth of a canyon, and there were a dozen or so horses fenced in behind some barbed wire. I borrowed one of them to chase down Rangeley, and by the time I caught him again I was pretty far from the canyon, so I figured I'd just bring the extra horse back to town and see about returning him tomorrow."

"Did you not see the brand on the other horse?" said Shelby.

"No, I didn't notice. Do you know the owner?"

"It's an Army brand." Shelby looked like he was on the verge of a discovery. "Do you have any idea where that canyon is? Could you find it again?"

"I think so."

Shelby turned to O'Brian. "Look, Jimmy. We'll have to do something about this."

"Well, it's not in my territory, you know," said O'Brian.

"I know that. But we can't be sending a telegram to Tucson and waiting a week for them to respond and maybe another week for them to send a deputy. For sure that's an Army horse, which means that it was stolen. Maybe it was stolen during that raid in the Santa Ritas. Maybe not. But here's the point, Apaches don't act like that. They don't corral their stolen horses behind barbed wire and just leave them. They take them back to their camps and, as often as not, eat them. So the odds are that whoever stole those horses was white. Now, you tell me, Jimmy, is there a bunch of thieving bastards living down there in the San Rafael, polecats who'd be perfectly capable of stealing Army stock and taking shots at anyone who might just happen by and stumble on the stolen horses?"

"The Curtains."

"The very same. Ethan, we've been having trouble with those people for years. They are the worst sort of vermin. Every year before spring roundup they will go and gather up our unbranded calves and slap their own brands on them before we find them, and what's worse, they'll kill the cow because that's the only creature that can identify her own calf."

"I don't follow."

"Well, the bond between a cow and her calf is unbreakable. A cow won't nurse another calf, and they will always recognize each other, even to the point that a court of law will admit it as evidence of theft if a stolen calf is reunited with its mother and the mother accepts it, which she will only do if the calf is her own. So, if you want to protect yourself against the only witness who can prove that an unbranded calf is not yours, you kill the cow and maybe butcher her out like an Apache would do, and you're home free."

"And the rancher who owns the cow and the calf loses twice."

"That's it, and it's a hard thing to prove. But you know it when you see it. No legitimate rancher has a hundred calves and ten cows, do you see? So, these rustlers have to sell their calves quickly, and that's the tip-off. Oh, the Curtains are black as heresy, no doubt about that. And now they've taken to shooting at my men and at innocent people like you, Ethan, and they're stealing from the Army, too. It's time we did something."

"What do you have in mind, Sam?" said O'Brian.

"I say we get some of my boys together and we go down there and see what's what. We'll pay a call on the Curtains, and then we'll pick up the other horses that are in that canyon, if Ethan can find it again. You deputize us, Jimmy, and we'll go on down there."

"It wouldn't be legal—the deputizing, I mean."

"The hell with that, Jimmy. This makes two shootings in the last week, both in the same place and both by the same people, I'll wager. This is no time to worry about technicalities. We'll show them the badge and then bring them in. They won't be asking to read the warrant. Then once they're in town, you can arrest them for being vagrants or something. The point is, once we have them we'll find out what they've been up to. Then we can turn them over to the county sheriff or the Army or whoever wants their miserable hides after we're finished with them."

"Fine by me. I'll even go along with you, Sam. Things are a little slow around here right now."

"That's the right note, Jimmy. We'll do the county a favor, and maybe next election you can run for sheriff." Shelby laughed and slapped O'Brian on the back.

"Oh, I don't think so. I'm a modest sort of man, Sam."

"What he means, Ethan, is that he'd rather live quietly in Verity without notice until a little question about fixing horse races in New Mexico is forgotten, or am I wrong, Jimmy?"

"Ah, that business about fixing was a foul slander, you know that, Sam. Still, there are always gullible people who'll believe the worst of a man. So it's better for me, I think, to avoid the limelight, as well as New Mexico, for a while. Which reminds me, Mr. Jaeger, I don't have any urge to see my name in the papers. I had enough of that during my fighting days, do you see. Let others have their chance now."

Ethan smiled. "First off, you should call me Ethan. And second, I'll be happy to leave your name out of my articles if you want me to. I'm surprised, though, about meeting so many modest men in Verity. Nobody wants to see his name in print." Ethan glanced at Shelby, and all three men started laughing.

"Ah, well, modesty is a virtue," said Shelby. "And

it's good to have at least one. Now, what do you say we get started first thing in the morning? I'll bring the boys and meet you here about sunup."

"Sounds good, Sam," said Sweet Jimmy.

Ethan nodded. "See you in the morning."

Ethan went to the doctor's office to see if he would take a look at Rangeley's ear. There wasn't a vet in town. Most ranchers did their own vet work. But the doctor was on a call at a distant ranch, so Ethan bought some disinfectant and swabbed out Rangeley's ear. The blood had coagulated well, and so as far as Ethan could see, the wound didn't need stitching, so the best thing would be to let it alone to heal.

"I hope this new arrangement doesn't throw you off balance, amigo." Rangeley snorted and tossed his head as he felt the disinfectant. But he seemed to be fine otherwise. Ethan took him to the livery stable and ordered some extra oats for him, and then went over to the Big Steer. It had been a long day, and he was dry.

There was no one in the saloon as yet except Jesús Sanchez, who was discussing the cantina business with the woman behind the bar. Sanchez smiled brightly when he saw Ethan.

"Bueno, señor. I am glad to see you. This is my friend, Consuelo, who is a cousin to my Rosa. This is her cantina."

"Hello, *señor."* Consuelo was a fat middle-aged woman, heavily rouged and pleasant-looking.

"Hello, Consuelo. I am happy to meet you. Your cantina is very comfortable, and the company congenial, as a general rule."

"Thank you, *señor."* Consuelo was pleased with the compliments, although she understood that what Ethan had said was mostly out of politeness. "I think Sally Rose will be here soon, if you were wondering. And also Annie."

Ethan nodded and smiled. "Sally Rose in case I'm edgy. Annie in case I'm desperate."

"As you say, *señor,*" said Consuelo. "It is not good to be lonely." She had seen much and had no illusions, but she was not yet cynical.

"Well, I'll think about it, Consuelo," said Ethan with a tip of his hat. "Now, Jesús, if you have a few minutes to have a drink with me, there's something I'd like to talk to you about."

"With the greatest of pleasure, *señor. Cerveza?*"

"That would be good."

"I will get them and bring them to the table, *señor.*"

Ethan sat at a table farthest from the bar. Sanchez joined him bringing two pint mugs of beer.

"Salud," said Jesús.

"Y amor, pesetas y tiempo para disfrutarlas," said Ethan. Taken together the toast meant: "Health, love, money, and time to enjoy them."

Sanchez stared at Ethan. *"Bueno, señor.* I did not know your Spanish was so comprehensive."

"Comes from hanging around in cantinas."

"Speaking as the owner of a cantina, I applaud you, *señor.*"

"Tomás feeling better?"

"Yes, much better. I think he will be able to travel soon. That is my hope."

"That's good to hear. Now, the thing I wanted to talk to you about involves a man named Juan Lopez from Sonora. Do you know him?"

Sanchez whistled. "Of course, *señor.* Everyone knows Juan Lopez, if you are referring to the man of that name who is a well-respected cattle rustler and bandit."

"That's the one."

"Yes, I know him. Believe it or not, my Rosa's niece works on his rancho as a cook. She is a very good cook and very ugly. This is lucky for her, since otherwise her virtue would be at risk in such a place, I assure you. Lopez is a great man in my country, and he is used to having his way."

"I thought you said he was a bandit."

"He is. But he is well respected because his activities are on a grand scale. That is the source of his reputation. He also gives generously to the Church, which frees him from the necessity of attending and at the same time provides a sufficiency of absolution. But aside from that, it is the magnitude of his thefts that bring him such respect."

"I think I understand you."

"I am sure of it, señor. You know how the world organizes itself. If you steal enough, you cease to be a thief and become instead an honored citizen. Money buys much. The secret is not to be small-minded in your conceptions."

"You are a philosopher."

"No, señor. A man who is not blind must acknowledge what he sees. Nothing more. Consider my poor country. Not long ago the prancing Frenchmen stole it from the people and gave it to a foreigner named Maximilian. This was called the building of empires. If a poor man steals a burro, we call it theft, and we hang him, as we should. But if a perfumed European steals an entire country, they write songs and books about him. Personally, I would hang him, too. But no one asks me."

"I would furnish the rope, Jesús."

"Yes, because you have your eyes open, too, señor. Not everyone does. The more you steal, the less you have to fear, it seems. For a while at least. Of course, in Maximillian's case, Juarez's army captured him, and naturally they stood him against a wall and shot him, which is normal in the politics of my country. But the point remains, I think. Your pardon, *señor.* These are commonplace thoughts. You have had them, too, I am sure."

"Yes. Still, it is always good to say what is true, regardless. To think this way is one thing. To put the thoughts into words is something else. It gives them life."

"Yes, as long as one does not by accident put the right words into the wrong ears. But if you will excuse me for asking, *señor,* why are you interested in Juan Lopez?"

"I understand that he is an interesting character, and I am thinking of visiting him. It would make a good story."

Sanchez whistled again and rolled his eyes. "Ah, Chihuahua, *señor,* that is a bad idea. I think you have had quite a few bad ideas before, if you will pardon me for saying so. But this is one of the worst. Lopez is a very great man in his own country but he has a personal failing, because he does not like gringos very much. Not at all, if you want the truth. I think to go down there would be a mistake."

"Maybe he'd like to see his name in the paper."

"He sees it there on a regular basis, *señor,* whenever there is a report of cattle being stolen anywhere along the border, from here to Texas. That is nothing to him, believe me."

"Well, it was just a thought. But let me ask you, if I wanted to get a letter to him without other people knowing about it, could that be arranged?"

Sanchez considered the problem for a moment. "It is possible, I suppose. Perhaps my Rosa would enjoy a visit to her niece. I could take her there. And perhaps Tomás would come along. We could easily go there and so deliver your letter. But it would be an entirely different thing for you to go there, *señor.* You must believe me on this."

"I do, Jesús. It's just an idea. What about the Apaches?"

"It is something to be considered, but I do not think the danger is very great. The road to Nogales from Tubac is short and well traveled. The Apaches prefer the mountains to the east and to the south, although they are a wandering people and one never knows when they will have a different idea. But once we are over the border, we would be under the protection of Juan Lopez. His vaqueros rule the land south of Nogales. Under such an arrangement I would not tremble for our safety. And you know me, *señor,* I tremble easily. Still, I hope that our discussion is merely theoretical. I would not want to be responsible for putting you into the hands of Juan Lopez."

"It's just a thought, as I said. But I would appreciate it if you said nothing about it to anyone."

Sanchez held up his hand as though swearing an oath. "You can trust me, *señor.*"

"I know that, Jesús. How about another?"

"With pleasure, *señor.*"

Ethan went to the bar to get two more beers. He was watching Consuelo fill the mugs from the draft barrel when Tramp Ellis came in. Ethan watched as Ellis tried to decide how to act. Predictably, thought Ethan, he tried the bluff.

"Hello there, dude," said Ellis. "I hear someone tried to shoot you today."

Ethan stared at Ellis. He felt the anger rising in his throat. "Word travels fast."

"Well, he must have been a bad shot, whoever it was." Ellis was trying to sneer, but he was put off a little by Ethan's stare.

"Yeah, probably just some ignorant sawed-off chucklehead like you, someone who's only good at getting drunk and shooting at other people's backs."

"Who're you calling sawed-off?"

Ethan laughed. "Why, who do you think, Ellis? And I notice that you're not concerned about being called ignorant, just short. Now that says most of what needs saying about you."

"Yeah?" Ellis was losing control of his bluff.

"Look here, Ellis. Just let it go. You're out of your depth. And by the way, I don't like being called 'dude,' so don't do it again, all right? Happens again and I'm going to put one of these Schofields in your ear and pull the trigger just so I can see how much sawdust comes flying out." Ethan stared at Ellis for a second, waiting for him to respond, and when he didn't, Ethan picked up the two beers and went back to the table. Ellis turned away and stood at the bar hunched over his drink.

"That is not a good man, *señor*," said Sanchez.

"No, he isn't. But he's common. What's that Abe Lincoln said about common people, that God must be fond of them because he made so many? Well, Abe was a smart man, but he missed the mark on that one. I figure God makes people like Ellis just to practice up before working on a jackass. *Salud.*"

"*Y amor?*" said Sanchez.

"Yes. That would be welcome."

"*Y pesetas?*"

"Why not, although the truth is, I've got enough money already. I'll settle for the other two. And world enough and time to enjoy them."

"*Bueno, señor. Bueno.*"

* * *

Ethan and Sanchez made plans to meet for dinner. Ethan wanted to look in on Septimus Harding before he closed up shop for the day.

As usual, Harding was behind his desk wearing his green eyeshade and his sleeve protectors.

"Hello, Sep. What's the matter? Have another bad pepper?"

"Must've. My plumbing is rising up in vigorous protest again today, and that's the only explanation I can come up with. I don't know who designed the human system, but days like this could make a fellow doubt the existence of a divine plan. Not me, of course. I'm too goddamn religious, but other folks might wonder. What's on your mind?"

"Just a little information. On cattle rustling along the border."

"Thinking of taking up a new line of work?"

"No, not yet, anyway. It just seems like it'd be an interesting story."

"Well, fine. Do you want to know what I think about it or just what I know? 'Cause I have more opinions than facts, like most people in this business."

"Both."

Harding leaned back in his chair and took out a cigar from his pocket, bit off the end, and lighted it. "Care for a smoke?"

"No, thanks."

"Nasty habit, although it's real easy to give up. I do it all the time. Now, about rustling. The way I see it, the whole business goes back to the time of the war for Texas independence. I mean, the bad blood that exists between the people along the border is partly the result of that fight, I think, anyway. Santa Anna did some pretty appalling things to the Texans, and they all remember it. At least their relatives do. The ones that sur-

vived. Then, of course, there was the Mexican War, and
the amigos down there remember that, which is natural. So there's a pretty long history of bad blood, and
both sides regard the other as a kind of fair game. Go
across, gather up some cows, and sell them in your
own markets, and no one in authority is going to ask
any questions. As long as you're on the right side of
your own border, you're safe as houses. Of course, the
difficulty is getting the animals in the first place, and
for that you may want to put together a small army for
the raid. But once you're back, you're home free, liter-
ally."

"And that's the way this fellow Juan Lopez oper-
ates."

"He could write the book on border rustling. I don't
know for sure whether he can write, but he's the recognized authority around here."

"And yet he never comes up here to do his raiding.
That seems a little strange."

"Well, Texas is a better market, and if you check the
map you'll see it isn't really all that far from here. He
goes over there, steals the beeves, and then herds them
west into Sonora, and nobody bothers him about it.
The Texas Rangers and the Army, what there is of it,
can't chase him over here. And Lopez isn't the only
one. There's a bunch of these fellas, some of them gen-
erals in the Mexican Army, who run their territories
like war lords. Nobody bothers them down there."

"How about going the other way? I guess the
Americans raid down there, too."

"Oh, sure. The border's a big country, and cattle
need a lot of room, so there's always the chance to
gather up a herd and get it over the line before anyone
knows about it."

"Sam Shelby has said as much to me. But the thing
that I wonder about is this—if Lopez is such a power-

ful man in Sonora, how do Shelby and the others involved in this get away with it? Why doesn't Lopez come up here and raise hell?"

"Well, some day Lopez might do just that. But if you were Shelby or someone like him and you went down there to steal some cows, you'd make damn sure you got them to market as soon as you could, and even while you were waiting to ship them you'd be careful to put them in places where they wouldn't be found easily. It's a big country out here, like I said."

"Still, it seems like a risky business."

"It is. But it's profitable. You see how Shelby lives. Plus, he can raise his own cattle as well, so he doesn't have to depend on rustling. I expect he regards it as a supplement to his regular business. And for some reason, at least so far, Lopez and his kind haven't raided up here. They tend to work farther east in New Mexico and Texas. I guess the pickings are better there. That's the only thing I can think of."

"How about the smaller operators, like the Curtains down in San Rafael? Where do they fit in this picture?"

"Oh, they're just white trash, as we used to say back in Missouri. They're on the fringes of it all. They're crooked as a snake crossing the road and just as nasty, but they're small-time criminals. I wouldn't put anything past them, but they're generally too dim-witted to think in grand terms. There are lots of that kind around here, but most of their thievery is petty. Just enough to get them hung if they get caught. Nothing more."

Harding took out his pocket watch. "Well, what do you know about that," he said. "It's quitting time." He opened a drawer in his desk and pulled out a bottle. "Care to chase away the evil spirits?"

"No, thanks. There's a posse going after the Curtains tomorrow morning, and I'm going to tag along. It'll be an early start."

"The Curtains? What'd they do now?"

"Well, I guess it's an accumulation of things. Seems like Shelby is tired of having them steal the cattle he stole from Lopez."

"Yes, it's a sinful world."

"Plus, one of them took a shot at me today. Or that's the way it looks, anyway. So I have an interest in going along."

"You don't say. Missed, I guess. Well, like I said, they're a bad bunch. The territory will be a better place without them."

"Well, we're just going down to arrest them and bring them back for questioning."

Harding smiled slyly at Ethan. "You're going with Shelby, didn't you say? Well, if the Curtains make it back to Verity without leaking from a variety of holes and in condition to answer any questions other than indirectly—such as, 'Is a six-foot coffin sufficient?'—it'll be news for sure. Shelby's like a hunter who finds ducks on the pond. He'll yell 'Shoo' so he can say he didn't kill a sitting duck, but he'll start shooting while the duck is still looking around to see who's there."

Yes, thought Ethan. *That sounds about right.*

Ten

The sun was just rising the next morning when Ethan met the posse outside Marshal O'Brian's office. Shelby had brought eight men with him. Ellis and the foreman Rourke were there, along with a half-dozen Mexican vaqueros who worked on the Double S. They were all heavily armed and grim. Marshal O'Brian was wearing his derby hat and an old plaid jacket. He looked out of place, and he was in a sour mood.

"You sure this trip is worth it, Sam?" said O'Brian.

"I'm sure, Jimmy. If you don't want to go, just deputize the rest of us and we'll take care of it."

"Ah, so far as that's concerned, you can all consider yourselves deputy town marshals. Amen. Hallelujah. Congratulations. That and a dollar will buy you a quart of whiskey. But I guess it'll make things more official if I come along. And you know me, Sam. I like things to be done proper." He struggled into the saddle, groaning as he did so, and they all headed south. Shelby led, and Ethan rode alongside.

The Curtains' ranch was about twenty miles away, and they planned to arrive there around midday, when the Curtains might be there for the noon meal. If they were not, the posse would surround the house and wait for the Curtains to return. Either way, the Curtains would be trapped.

"I've been thinking about those Army horses you found, Ethan," said Shelby. "Even though that canyon's on the way, there's no sense trying to gather them up before we get the Curtains."

Ethan nodded. He had been thinking about how to explain Jereme Curtain's body, assuming they ran across it. The shooting happened a half mile or so from Black Tail Canyon, so it was possible they might not find the body when they went to get the horses. They might see a few flying buzzards around, but buzzards were a common thing. Then there was the possibility that Old Man Curtain would recognize Ethan. It seemed unlikely, though, since Ethan would only be one of a group of men, and Curtain would have no reason to associate the Mexican Army officer he met before with one man out of a posse from Verity. It was a risk, but a risk that Ethan felt he could handle. *Guess I'll wait and see how things turn out,* he thought. *Play it by ear.*

"What are you smiling at, Ethan?" said Shelby. "You look like an undertaker who just got a deal on shovels."

"Nothing, Sam. Private joke."

They reached the Curtain ranch around noon. The ranch house sat in a small valley, and there were plenty of trees on the hillsides around it to provide cover. Also, there was a small arroyo running parallel to the house about fifty yards away.

Looking down at the ranch house, Ethan said to Shelby, "The Curtains couldn't have picked a worse spot to defend."

"You're right," said Shelby. "Some animals protect themselves by fighting. Others by hiding. The Curtains are in the second category. But we'll flush them out."

There was no one moving around outside the house, but smoke was coming from the chimney, and Ethan could smell fatback frying, so it was possible the men were inside. Shelby gathered his men around and gave his orders.

"There's no more than fifty yards between us and the house. Everyone take your rifles. Rourke, you and Ellis circle around to the right and get behind that big boulder over there. That will cover the right side of the house. If we need to rush the place, you can use that arroyo alongside the house as cover. Julio, you take the other boys except for Manuel and move to the left. Station someone about every thirty yards or so and make sure you cover the left side and the back. We'll be shooting down on them, so there shouldn't be any danger of shooting each other. But watch your shots, anyway. Manuel, you take the horses back to the right. Make sure you take them far enough away. Ethan, you and I and Jimmy will stay here in front. We'll spread out on both sides of the trail. The best way in and out of this place is along this trail we just came in on, so if they're not here they're likely to come back this way. We'll just stay behind these trees and let them pass. Once they get into the front yard and off their horses, we'll have the drop on them. There's no cover, and they'll have to surrender. But I have a feeling they're inside. Someone is, anyway. Maybe all of them, if we're lucky. All right, get to your positions. I'll wait a few minutes and then call to the house. Don't shoot unless I give the word or unless you hear me shoot first. Okay, move out."

Shelby was very professional as he gave his orders. His experience in the British Army and with the Confederates had apparently served him well. Ethan did detect a hint of excitement in Shelby's voice, the excitement one feels at the beginning of a stalk. Well, that was natural.

Just then, Ethan heard voices from inside the house. The Curtains, at least two of them, were arguing about something.

"Ah," said Shelby. "The rats are in the trap. We'll scoop up all four of them."

Not quite, thought Ethan. He moved to his left about twenty yards from Shelby and hunkered down behind an oak tree. He chambered a round in his rifle and watched as the men circled around the house.

Shelby waited for his men to get into position. When he could see that the house was surrounded, he called out. "Old Man Curtain! Come out here!"

"Who's there?" came a shout from inside. But Shelby did not answer.

The front door opened a crack and Old Man Curtain poked his head out.

"Who's there?" he said again. The door opened wider and Old Man Curtain came out onto the front porch. He was holding a shotgun. He stepped warily off the porch into the yard. "Where are ya?" he yelled. Another face looked out the front door, and a third from the window.

"Up here," yelled Shelby, and at the sound Old Man Curtain raised his shotgun and pointed it toward the noise, although it was clear he did not see anyone.

"Show yerself," said Curtain.

Then Ethan saw Shelby raise his rifle and fire. Old Man Curtain doubled over and pitched headfirst into a pile of cow manure, and then the rest of the men opened up. Eight or ten shots rang out, some of them hitting Curtain's body and flipping him on his back, others kicking up small clouds of dust around his body.

The man standing at the door closed it quickly and yelled something to his brother, who slammed the shutters at the windows. The firing became general, and shots started hitting the house breaking off chunks of siding and splintering the door and shutters. Ethan watched as Shelby fired repeatedly. Sweet Jimmy was also firing and yelling curses as he shot and levered his rifle and shot again.

Two rifles poked out from the firing slits in the heavy shutters. They were shooting wildly in different directions. Ethan could see some tree branches being clipped off by the bullets, but none of the shots was aimed and none came close to any of the posse. Then a shot hit the tree where Ethan was hiding. It splintered the bark above him and showered him with bits of wood. It seemed to come from the right, not from the house, but he couldn't be sure. He hit the ground and then poked his head around the tree to see where Ellis and Rourke were hiding, but he could not see them. Then he saw their rifles pointed at the house and firing.

"Keep firing, men!" shouted Shelby. "Ellis! Rourke! Move forward into that arroyo. We'll give you cover."

Ethan watched as Ellis and Rourke ran down the hill and jumped into the arroyo. *Ellis has got more sand than I gave him credit for,* thought Ethan. But in fact there was little danger, because there were no windows on that side of the house and no way for the Curtains to fire at either man in the arroyo. The rest of the posse kept shooting. Most of the shots were aimed at the front door and at the shutters, since the walls of the house were made of cottonwood logs and could withstand anything short of artillery. The door and shutters were being blown apart bit by bit, and Ethan could imagine the potential damage from flying splinters. Ethan was not shooting, but it made little difference. Nine men with repeating rifles could throw up a tremendous amount of fire. Pieces of wood were flying in all directions. Bullets clanged off the tools and pots that were hung on nails on the front porch. The noise was terrific. The chinking between the logs of the wall was being torn up little by little. One of the posts holding up the overhang above the front porch broke in two, and the roof began to sag. The men stationed behind the house were firing at the shuttered windows in the back. The Curtains' animals were all in a state of panic. The cattle had run off at the start of the shooting, but the chickens were running around in complete confusion, and the pig that had been lolling in the mud near the outhouse was running in circles squealing hideously.

"Somebody shoot that damned pig," yelled Shelby, and immediately a half-dozen shots hit the animal, but none was fatal and he continued racing around the front yard spewing blood and squalling, until finally he ran into the woods.

"Rourke!" yelled Shelby. "Get up on the roof and stop the chimney."

Rourke poked his head above the rim of the arroyo. Then he dashed across the side yard and jumped on a stack of split firewood that lay against the side of the house. From there he lifted himself on to the roof, took off his jacket, and stuffed it into the chimney. Then he jumped down again and ran back to the arroyo.

"Hold your fire, men!" shouted Shelby. "We'll smoke them out."

The men in the house kept firing, but they could not see their attackers and their bullets flew wild.

After a few minutes, Ethan could see smoke seeping out from under the front door and through the cracks in the windows, but there wasn't much of it. He assumed that the Curtains had been able to put out their fire and so minimize the amount of smoke from the clogged chimney. The shooting had stopped on both sides now.

"Damn it," said Shelby. "Looks like we'll have to burn them out. Rourke, you got that coal oil with you?"

"No. It's back with the horses."

"Okay. I'll get it." Shelby got up and ran back into the woods where Manuel was holding the horses, and in a few moments returned with a can. Then he worked his way around the side away from the windows of the house to the place where Ellis and Rourke had made their dash to the arroyo. "Hold your fire, men," he yelled. Then he ran across the short clearing and jumped into the arroyo with Ellis and Rourke. "Okay, men. Cover me. If anyone pokes his head out a window, shoot it off." Then Shelby ran across to the side of the house, jumped onto the woodpile, and lifted himself up to the roof. He opened the can and started splashing coal oil on the shingles of the roof. Apparently, the Curtains figured out what was going on, and they started firing up through the ceiling of the house. Ethan could see the splinters flying from the shingles as the bullets passed through the roof, but none came close to Shelby. They were shooting wildly at the sounds on the roof. Shelby's men in the front of the house resumed their firing at the shutters and door. One of the shutters flew off its hinges and one of the panels on the door blew into the house. Shelby emptied the can, and then reached into his shirt pocket for a match, struck it, and lit the oiled shingles. Soon a flame appeared and started to spread across the roof. Dark, oily smoke began to rise from the roof. Shelby jumped down on to the woodpile, ran back to the arroyo, and dove in.

In a few minutes the roof was ablaze. Black smoke was mixed with flames, and Ethan began to feel the heat of the fire. The old shingles burned like kindling, and soon the roof was a mass of flame. Jagged holes began to appear in the roof as the shingles collapsed into the house. Ethan could see the rafters exposed and burning, and then some of the flames spread to the cottonwood logs of the cabin's walls.

They won't be able to stand it much longer, Ethan thought. All shooting had stopped, and the only sound was the crackling of the fire consuming the roof. The smell of the oily smoke was nauseating.

The front door opened, and black smoke came billowing out. Ethan could see the two men standing just inside the door. They were coughing and rubbing their eyes, trying to decide which way to run. Then they ran out on to the front porch and, firing wildly with their rifles, turned left and ran toward the arroyo. They staggered as they ran, unable to see clearly. Their clothes were singed and smoking, and Ethan could see the panic in their eyes. The men of the posse held their fire as they watched the two Curtains lurching toward the arroyo.

Bad choice, Ethan thought.

When they were about ten yards away from the arroyo, Ellis, Rourke, and Shelby stood up and opened fire. One of the Curtains pitched forward, and the other spun around and fell on his side. Both were still alive after the first fusillade. They tried to crawl away, but Shelby, Ellis, and Rourke kept firing, and soon both Curtains were still. They lay in the dust, their smoldering clothes torn to pieces by gunfire.

"Hold your fire, men. Look sharp, though. There's still one left somewhere."

Ethan knew better, but kept his mouth shut. The posse held their positions while the house burned. The heat was intense even at a distance of fifty yards. In a few minutes the roof collapsed, and it was then clear that if a fourth Curtain had been in the house, he could not have survived.

Slowly, Shelby and the other two climbed out of the arroyo. The other men came down from their positions.

Ethan joined them. They dragged the three bodies away from the burning house.

"Juan," said Shelby. "Go up and get the horses, and send some of the boys to catch three of the Curtains' animals from their corral. We'll pack up these three bastards while we wait for that fire to burn itself out. I want to see whether the last one is in that house."

"Whew," said Sweet Jimmy. "That's a sorry-looking trio of rustlers, I swear." The three men were lying on their backs. Their mouths were open and their eyes half open staring at nothing. The two Curtain sons looked a lot like Jereme Curtain, Ethan thought—scruffy, dirty, mean-looking mongrels. All three bodies were leaking black blood from a number of wounds, but the hard-packed ground wasn't absorbing the blood, and it collected in small puddles.

"Yes," said Ethan. "I'm sure they're very, very sorry about how this whole thing turned out."

Sweet Jimmy and Shelby both looked at Ethan quizzically. Then they laughed, but there was little mirth in Shelby's tone.

"I thought the idea was to bring these boys back to town, Sam," said Sweet Jimmy.

"We *are* going to bring them back to town," Shelby said. "They'll come easier this way."

One of Shelby's vaqueros came around from the corral leading three horses.

"Load these three on those horses, boys. I don't think we need to find a tarp for them. Just rope them on good and tight. Damn, I wish that fire would hurry up and burn itself out. I want to know whether that fourth Curtain is in there."

It seemed odd to Ethan that Shelby should be so concerned. Sweet Jimmy also seemed puzzled by Shelby's attitude.

"What's the difference, Sam?" he said. "If the fourth

one wasn't here, he'll come back sometime and see what happened, and when he finds out about these three, he'll start running and won't quit until he hits New York City. You're not worried about him coming after any of us, are you?"

"No. It's that I like a job to be clean. No loose ends, that's all. I want it finished properly. Besides, even though a Curtain's not the kind to get involved in a fair feud, he damned sure is the kind to take a shot at people or animals from ambush. It's like cleaning out a nest of snakes in your barn and leaving one behind."

Ethan decided then that he would lead the posse back through the place where he had left Jereme Curtain. For some reason that he didn't quite understand yet, he wanted Shelby's mind to be clear on the question of whether any Curtains were left.

Ethan sat down under a tree to wait. He watched as Shelby talked quietly with Ellis and Rourke, and he noticed Rourke looking at him every once in a while. His small ferrety eyes were never still, it seemed. Rourke had shown courage during the fight. Ethan felt that he might bear watching.

After a while Ellis came strolling over, swaggering a little. It was the reaction some men had to participating in a fight and living through it.

"I didn't see you doing much shooting, mister," said Ellis.

"You boys were doing all right without my help. Besides, I'd rather use my ammunition on people than on houses and livestock. I saw you shoot that pig, though, Ellis. That was heroic. Maybe I'll write an article about you. 'Famous pig shooters I have known,' I'll call it."

Ellis stared at him and considered what to say next. "You're lucky you didn't get hit by a stray bullet," he said, finally. "It's been known to happen."

"Really? You mean get shot by one of your own people? That would be unlucky. But now that you mention it, I remember that's what happened to Stonewall Jackson during the war. Were you there at the time, by any chance?"

Ellis sneered and then grinned. "Not me, mister. Things happen, though, like I say." Then he swaggered away, apparently satisfied with the results of the encounter.

They waited an hour or so until the flames died down, and then Shelby, Ethan, and Sweet Jimmy searched through the smoking rubble of the house looking for a body. There was very little left of the house, just a shell of log walls and a blackened chimney. They poked around in the burned rafters and shingles that had collapsed into the house, but they found nothing resembling human remains.

"Well," said Shelby, "I guess the fourth Curtain wasn't here. We might as well get started back toward town. We'll pick up those Army horses on the way. Ethan, why don't you take the lead and show us where those horses are, if you think you can find it."

"I think I've got an idea where it is. Those mountains to the north and east make pretty good reference points."

They left by the same trail that Ethan had used when he came to the Curtains the first time out. They rode in silence, walking their horses. All of the men seemed tired, as the emotion of the fight and its aftermath drained away. They rode along in single file. The packhorses bearing the three Curtains brought up the rear, led by one of the vaqueros. In a half an hour or so they came to the meadow where Jereme Curtain had ambushed Ethan.

"This looks like the place where that fella shot at me," said Ethan. "We must be close to the horses, now."

"Look," said Sweet Jimmy. "What the hell's going on over there under those trees?"

Three buzzards were standing under the tree where Ethan had left Jereme. They had their wings raised halfway as though preparing to take flight. A coyote was snarling and dashing at them, protecting his find.

"Might as well take a look," said Shelby. "You boys take a break," he said to his men. He and Jimmy and Ethan rode to the trees. The buzzards took off, and the coyote slunk away looking back over his shoulder now and then. He did not go far, just far enough to be able to watch the men and wait for them to leave.

"Damn!" said Jimmy when they found the body. "What a mess." The buzzards and ravens had done much of the work. Then the coyotes had come. There was very little left of Jereme Curtain. But his clothes, although ripped and shredded, were still there. The rifle that Ethan had shattered with his first shot lay on the ground next to the body.

"Do you recognize him, Sam?" said Jimmy.

"Recognize what? There's not enough left of him to have a wake for."

"Maybe there's something in his pockets," said Ethan.

"I'll look," said Jimmy. He poked around gingerly in the pockets of Jereme's ragged overalls. "No, there's nothing here."

Ethan dismounted. He went over to the rifle and picked it up. The stock was splintered, and the receiver bent beyond use, but the rest of the rifle was intact. Ethan looked at the wooden forward grip that lay under the barrel.

"Well, looks like your questions are answered,

Sam," he said. He brought the rifle over to Shelby and handed it up to him. "Look at the name carved on that fore end."

It said J. CURTAIN. 1876.

"Well, well," said Shelby. He was smiling broadly. "Jereme Curtain. Looks like somebody got to him before we did. Could this be the man that shot at you, do you think, Ethan?"

"I suppose it's possible. But I don't think so. I never did get a clear shot at the man, whoever he was. I didn't even see him. It could have been Curtain here. If it was, he's the unluckiest man ever born, to get killed by a chance pistol shot."

"Well, he don't look too lucky right now," said Sweet Jimmy. "So it could have been him."

"More'n likely he got killed by the same one who ambushed me. Maybe Apaches. They left his rifle because it's ruined."

"Well, I guess we'll never know. But at least the story of the Curtains is over. I'm glad of that." The tension that Shelby had been showing was gone now. His dark mood had disappeared. "I guess we might as well bury him right here. Now that I think about it, we might as well put the whole family in the ground here. There's nobody left to claim any bodies, so there's no sense hauling these back to town, now. What do you say, Jimmy. You're the law here."

"Bugger that, Sam. I'm no more the law out here than you are, but far as I know the Curtains don't have any other relatives. This is as good a place as any."

Shelby nodded and then waved his men over. "Get the shovels out, boys," he said. "We'll bury these sonsabitches all right here."

Eleven

Shelby was in a jovial mood as they rode back to Verity.

"Well, Ethan," he said. "You see how justice is done out here. It's a little rougher than back East, I suppose, but it is swift and sure. The thing is, if you let fellas like the Curtains get away with thievery, there'll be no living in this country. You've got to be on the alert all the time."

"As somebody once said, 'The sword of justice has no scabbard.' "

"Now that's a fine phrase. Whose was it, do you know?"

"Some Frenchman."

"It figures. They're good at talking. Almost as good as the Irish. Speaking of which, I don't suppose you're thinking about reporting all this in your paper."

"I'd like to, Sam. It would make a good story, but as I promised you before, I won't use your names. Something along the lines of, 'A posse of leading citizens went to arrest a group of known criminals and were forced to fight it out with them when the criminals opened fire. Final score: upstanding citizens, four, criminals, zero.' "

Shelby laughed. "Well, that would be the truth of it, wouldn't it?"

"Close enough. And as we used to say back when I was a Naval gunnery officer, close enough is generally good enough." Ethan smiled at Shelby to show that they were of the same mind about all of this and that Shelby need not worry about what Ethan would write.

"Ah, you're a good fella, Ethan. Say, I'm going to have to take a herd over to Willcox to the train depot. It's a fair distance over there, and when you're trailing cattle, you want to take it slow so that the silly beasts don't lose their flesh before you weigh them out and sell them. Anyway, I'll be gone about a week or so. We'll be leaving first thing tomorrow. Maybe you'd like to go along. See a little bit of the cattle business, first-hand."

"I appreciate that, Sam. I do, indeed. But I'm way behind in my work. If I don't send something to my editor, he'll wonder why he's paying me. And this little fight will be good material."

"I understand. Well, if you change your mind, let me know."

"It's not likely. But there is one thing you could do for me, if you wouldn't mind. I'd like to borrow a couple of your dogs and maybe do a little more quail hunting. That was a good day we had, and I'd like to go out again, if I get my work done."

"Oh, absolutely. I'll tell Danielle that you might be coming by. She knows the dogs as well as I do, and she'll set you up."

"That would be great, Sam. I appreciate it." That, at least, thought Ethan, was true.

* * *

It was well past sunset when they reached town. Ethan said good-bye to Shelby and Sweet Jimmy, stabled Rangeley, and then went to his room. He quickly wrote the story that he would ask Sweet Jimmy to send the following day. He assumed that Sweet Jimmy would make a copy of the story to show Shelby when he returned, and so he wrote it just as he told Shelby he would. It didn't matter. It would never be printed anyway. Then he went to the Big Steer.

The saloon was crowded. A traveling salesman was standing at the bar trying to interest a group of cowboys in some tonic that would restore hair. Since the salesman himself was bald, his story lacked credibility.

"Whyn't you use the stuff yerself?" said one of the cowboys.

"I would, friend, in a heartbeat, but supplies are limited, and it is expensive to transport this precious fluid all the way to the West from London, England, where it is manufactured and where Prince Albert himself uses it on a daily basis. The famous Prince Albert beard is the direct result of this formula, I assure you. And if you have ever seen any pictures of His Royal Highness, you know that the hair on his head is luxurious, yes, luxurious. Yet, before he started using this formula, he was as bald as a cue ball."

"How much?" said another cowboy.

"One dollar. And cheap at twice the price."

"I'll take some."

The salesman was delighted. He reached into his carpetbag and retrieved a pint bottle, and gave it to the cowboy, who opened it and poured it over the salesman's head.

"No need to thank me, friend," said the cowboy. "This is just a little Arizona hospitality." The other cowboys hooted, and then two of them grabbed the sputtering salesman and lifted him by the seat of his pants and his jacket collar. "Don't come back before yer hair's luxurious, mister," the first cowboy told him. "Otherwise, we might think you was tryin' to put something over on us simple cowboys. If you don't mind, I'll just go ahead and owe you that dollar till then." Then they threw him out the door of the saloon.

Ethan stood aside as the salesman went through the door. Then he went to the bar and ordered a beer. Squirrel Tooth Annie was in the corner sitting on a stool and playing her concertina. She grinned at Ethan, stuck out her tongue, and made an elaborate show of pumping the concertina while she fluttered her eyes. "Oh, I'm only a bird in a gilded cage," she sang. The sound was appalling. Sally Rose was not there tonight, or maybe she had already left with a customer. The other tables were filled with men playing cards, and the air in the room was dense with cigar smoke. Then Ethan saw Sanchez sitting by himself in the corner opposite Annie. He went over to join him.

"Evening, Jesús. Consuelo must be happy. There's a good crowd tonight."

"Yes, señor, although as you have seen, the crowd is now smaller by one traveling salesman. It is sometimes a difficult thing to be in business."

"Well, you've got to take the rough with the smooth, I guess. I'm glad to find you here, Jesús. I've been thinking about what you said about Juan Lopez, and I've got an idea."

Sanchez shook his head and looked sorrowful. "I know your ideas, señor. I will be happy to listen to this latest one, but I am afraid it will be like the others."

"First of all, let me ask you a question. You have heard my Spanish. Do you think I could pass for a Mexican?"

"Ah, Chihuahua, señor. I see where this may lead. But to answer your question, yes, you could pass for a

Mexican, but only as long as you did not open your mouth to speak." Ethan laughed. "I say this to be honest, *señor,* not to discourage your ideas, which I understand I cannot do. But tell me I am wrong. Tell me that you are not thinking of going alone into Mexico to see Lopez posing as a Mexican vaquero."

"No, not alone. I was hoping that you and I could go together, perhaps with Rosa and Tomás."

"Ayee, your ideas grow worse."

"Maybe. But I don't think so. Hear me out. You said you were willing to go there, just the three of you. Well, if I go along that will be one more man in case we run into trouble. I would pose as one of your wranglers, and I would keep my mouth shut if we run into any of Lopez's men on the trail. When we get there, you could deliver the letter for me. In the letter I will propose to talk to Lopez, and if he agrees, I can then explain that the letter came from me. If he does not want to meet me, I will remain in disguise, and we can all return to Tubac. This way is more efficient than my waiting for you to go there and then return with an answer. And I would not reveal who I am until after Lopez has agreed to the meeting."

Sanchez considered the plan and nodded glumly. "Yes, it could work, I suppose. Unless, of course, Lopez takes it into his head to resent my bringing a gringo into his country. That would be an awkward thing if it happened."

"There is that possibility. But only if Lopez rejects the proposition and if I am discovered somehow. That is unlikely. I am experienced in this kind of thing, Jesús. But since there is that risk, perhaps we should not take Rosa along. The girl working there is your niece, too, in a way. It would not seem unusual if you went there to visit her, would it? Perhaps you could be carrying a message for her from Rosa, asking her to come to Tubac for some reason. Perhaps Rosa would need her help in the cantina for a while."

Sanchez stared at Ethan as though reevaluating him. "You are adept at creating these stories, *señor*."

"It's part of the job, Jesús."

"Yes, I begin to see that." He sighed. "Well, *señor*, I think you are right about leaving Rosa behind. There is no sense risking a woman who has such skill in making tortillas, and if she is going to become a widow, she would be happier doing it in Tubac where she has friends and the cantina to support herself. *Madre mia*."

"This would be a very great favor, Jesús. And my paper would be happy, of course, to pay you and Tomás well for your help. Forgive me, I should have mentioned that before."

Sanchez nodded and seemed pleased. "Ah. I see. Well, money is a good thing when it is honestly earned, and so I will help you with this deception that you are proposing. But, *señor*, I will have to see whether Tomás would be able to join us. He is able to travel, yes, but this adventure is something more than travel, I think. Having been shot so recently, he may be reluctant to risk it again so soon. I will have to ask him. It may be that he will need time to forget before doing something bold again, the way women need time to forget about giving birth before they become receptive to the suggestions of their husbands. Do you think so?"

"You are a sensible man, Jesús."

"No, *señor*. If I were a sensible man, I would be sitting in my own cantina, not here listening to the ideas of a man who proposes such risks just for the sake of writing words for strangers to read."

Ethan went back to the rooming house. The salesman who had been thrown out of the saloon was sitting in the lobby. His shirtfront and suit coat were stained with hair tonic. He looked up expectantly when Ethan walked in.

"Good evening, friend," he said. "I wonder if I could interest you in a tonic that . . ."

"I have enough hair, amigo." He lifted his hat.

"Ah so I see. But this tonic is not just for hair restoration. It also is useful in fighting the ague, rheumatism, and gout, as well as heart and liver ailments."

"I'm all right in those departments, too, mister."

"Yes? Oh, well, that's too bad. This is a hard town to do business in," said the salesman glumly.

"I imagine it is," said Ethan. "You might try calling on the editor of the newspaper, though. He's allergic to peppers."

The salesman looked confused. "If he's allergic to peppers, why doesn't he just stay away from them?"

"Hard to say. But people sometimes do things that aren't good for them. He'd probably be interested in what you're selling, especially if you wanted to place an advertisement. Tell him I sent you. Name's Sam Grant."

"Well, thank you, Mr. Grant. I'll do that."

"Don't mention it."

Ethan went up to his room. In about thirty minutes Sally Rose knocked on the door.

"Hello, honey," she said. "They told me downstairs that you were looking for me."

"It's terrible the way people lie to young girls."

Sally Rose giggled. "Well, they didn't actually say it in so many words, but I figured you'd be looking for me if the idea ever occurred to you."

"That kind of logic is hard to argue with. Come on in, honey. Make yourself at home."

* * *

In the morning Ethan woke to the sounds of cattle moving through the fields behind the town. It was Shelby trailing a herd to the railway at Willcox. Ethan looked out the window, and despite the dust he could see Shelby and Rourke at the head of the herd and a number of the vaqueros who had been at the Curtain fight strung out along the sides of the herd. He did not see Ellis. The noise and dust were thick in the air, but the wind was blowing away from town. There seemed to be about a thousand head of cattle, as far as Ethan could judge. They were bellowing and protesting, and the vaqueros were snapping their ropes at any that tried to break away.

Sally Rose got out of bed and came to the window. She wasn't wearing anything, and she looked a little blowsy. Morning light did not suit her, Ethan thought.

"I don't like cows," she said. "They're smelly and they drool all the time."

"I know some people who answer to that description, too," said Ethan. "Now, how about doing me a favor."

"Anything you want, honey."

"Get dressed and get out of here. I've got some things I need to do today."

"Sure, honey. After last night I didn't think you'd want anything else from me." She smiled at him with something like affection. "Fact is, I'm tuckered out anyway." She gathered up her clothes and dressed. "Will I'll see you tonight?"

"Hard to say."

"All right. Well, like I said last time, you know where to find me." Ethan nodded and Sally Rose left.

Ethan went to Hop Sing's and once again paid extra for clean water. Then he dressed with more than his usual care. By the time he was finished Shelby's herd was gone, but the cloud of dust was still visible above the horizon to the east. He took his story over to Sweet Jimmy's office. O'Brian was not there yet, so he left the story with a note asking him to telegraph it to his editor at the *New York Herald*. Then he got Rangeley from the livery stable and headed west toward the Double S.

There wasn't much going on at the ranch when Ethan got there. Most of the vaqueros were on the trail drive. Octavius was working on the wagon tack, and he nodded and waved as Ethan rode up to the house. Ethan did not see anyone else around.

"Hello the house," he said.

She came to the front door and stepped out on the veranda. She was wearing a simple dress, and her hair was loose around her shoulders, as always. She wore no makeup or jewelry, and to Ethan she looked as fresh as the morning air. She smiled warmly when she recognized Ethan.

"Hello, Ethan. Sam told me you might be coming by, but I did not expect you this soon."

"Morning, Danielle. I finished the article I was working on last night, so I thought I'd come by and borrow a couple of your dogs and do some hunting, if you don't mind."

"Of course. Please come in. I am just finishing some things, and perhaps you would like some coffee. Unless you are in a great rush."

"No, the birds will wait." And, Ethan thought, they can wait until they die of old age as far as he was concerned.

Ethan followed her inside. She was wearing just a trace of perfume. It smelled like spring flowers or like the desert after a rain. Ethan could not decide which.

"Come and meet a friend of mine," she said. There was a black boy, about ten years old, sitting on the leather couch in the main room. He had a book spread out on his lap, and he looked at Ethan with a calm sort of reserve, as though he would decide later whether this man were a friend or not.

"This is Moses, Ethan. Moses, this is Mr. Jaeger."

Moses stood up and when Ethan offered his hand, he took it and held it, but his grip was soft, as though he was not sure exactly about this business of shaking hands.

" 'Lo, there, Moses," said Ethan. The boy nodded.

"Moses is Octavius' and Juno's grandson," said Danielle. "I am teaching him to read. Moses, Mr. Jaeger is a writer for a newspaper in New York City."

The boy's eyes widened. "I like newspapers," he said.

"Well, that's good to hear," said Ethan. "I always like to meet customers. Do you read the Verity paper? The editor's a friend of mine."

"Oh, yes. Mr. Harding said someday I might go in there and work for him and learn the business. I have to get better at reading first, though."

"That's a good plan, although I've run into a few newspaper people who can't read or write for that matter. Not much anyway." Ethan smiled at the boy, and Moses suddenly grinned. He had made a decision about Ethan, it seemed.

"Well, Moses, I think we are finished for today," said Danielle. "We'll start from here tomorrow. But be sure tonight to practice what we learned today. *D'accord?*"

"*D'accord,*" said Moses. Then he looked at Ethan. "I'm learning French, too," he said. Ethan nodded approvingly. Moses put his book back on the bookshelf. "I guess I'll go and pick some apples, Miss Danielle. Grandma said she's gonna make a pie tonight."

"Reading, writing, and apple pie," said Ethan. "You must be living right, Moses."

"Yes sir. I am." He grinned again and left.

"Would you like some coffee, Ethan?"

"That would be good." She poured some from a pot that was on the side table.

"Where are Moses's parents?" Ethan asked.

Danielle shrugged. "I don't know. About six months ago he arrived on the stage from Fort Worth. His mother went off with someone, apparently, and she sent him here to his grandparents. As for his father? Who can say? So, you are going shooting again, today. But quail this time, I think, not thieves."

"I guess Sam told you about that fracas with the Curtains."

"A little. Not much. He said they will not be a problem again."

"That is certainly true."

"I suppose it is for the best. This is a violent country."

"Not the sort of thing that happens in France, is it?"

"I don't know," she said. "I have never been to France." She looked at Ethan and smiled.

"Oh, I thought Sam said that you . . ."

"That I am the daughter of a nobleman who owns a vineyard in Bordeaux? Oh, yes. He is fond of telling that story." There were traces of both contempt and humor in her voice. "It is a little game that he plays, I think."

"I see. But you are French."

"Oh, yes. And my father is in the wine business. He is a merchant in New Orleans." She looked at Ethan seriously. "Do you think I am disloyal for telling you this? I do not like these stories, you see."

"I understand that. It's surprising, though, hearing this. How did you meet Sam?"

She shrugged again and pursed her lips. Ethan had noticed before how she expressed her moods often by the movement of her lips and mouth. "My father is a good man but he has no head for business, unfortunately. Do you know what it is to be poor, Ethan?"

"Well, I guess not, really. We were not exactly wealthy people, but there was always enough. And nobody else had any more, which is the way you measure, I suppose. If we were poor, we didn't know it."

"Ah, that is the difference, exactly. There are many kinds of poverty, but the worst is the poverty of the *gentil*. You have this word in English, I think."

"Yes. Genteel."

"Yes. That's it. When you have the genteel poverty, you have all the disadvantages of having nothing but none of the advantages of being honest about it. A poor man who acknowledges his poverty is happier than the poor man who must hide it, although both are miserable, of course. The honest poor man expects nothing and so is not disappointed, but the genteel poor man is always surprised at his condition and ashamed of it. And worse, a poor gentleman can usually get credit, so he adds debt to his list of miseries. A poor man who is not genteel can never borrow, so he is better off in that sense, I think."

"I understand you."

"Yes. My father borrowed heavily from a bank in New Orleans. Sam was a director at the bank, and that is how we met."

"And is your father out of debt now?"

"Yes, I think so. As Sam said at the time, there are usually ways to work these things out. He bought my father's notes and then destroyed them, after we had made our arrangements."

"And now you are the lady of the house."

"Yes. I am the lady of the house. And we receive regular shipments of wine. Quite nice, *n'est-ce pas?*"

"I see."

"You do not seem very surprised."

"Well, I am, a little, I suppose. But many men invent themselves. That is never surprising to see. And some inventions are more elaborate than others. Sam isn't very different from most other men. At least not in that way."

She looked at him with great seriousness. "Is that true, Ethan?"

"I think it is, Danielle."

"And is that a good thing, do you think?"

"No, although in most cases it's harmless. Sometimes reality's a little hard to take, like in the case of your father, I guess. Sometimes you need a little armor."

She nodded her head as if in resignation to something. Then, after a moment, Ethan saw her decide to change her mood.

"And do you wear armor, too, Ethan?" The tone of playfulness was back in her voice.

"Usually. But today it's at Hop Sing's, getting polished."

She laughed gaily and reached out and touched his arm, as she had done the night of the dinner. It was an intimate gesture, or so it seemed to Ethan. But he could not tell if she meant it that way.

"Well, enough of philosophy," she said. "Come. I am keeping you from your shooting. Let's go have a look at the dogs, and you can decide which ones appeal to you today."

"I wonder if you'd like to go, too," said Ethan. He realized that he had been planning to ask her all along. "Sam told me you were a great shot, and I'd be happy to have your company."

She seemed delighted and surprised. "Truly? Why, yes. I would enjoy that very much. You are sure you would like it?"

"Nothing I would like better."

"Well, then, I must change. And I will ask Juno to get some lunch for us to take along. It won't take me long."

"No hurry. Do you mind if I look at these books while I'm waiting?"

"Of course not. There are some others in Sam's study, too. I'm sure he wouldn't mind if you looked at them. I'll only be a few minutes." She left to find Juno.

The books in the main room were all bound in leather. Many of them were in French, and they appeared to have been well used. The English volumes were in many cases unread. The pages were not cut. There were novels by Dickens and Trollope and volumes of history by Macauley. Mill's Essays. A volume of Carlyle's essays, however, had apparently been read several times. The book fell open to a well-thumbed page, and Ethan read a passage that someone, Shelby probably, had underlined:

No man lives without jostling and being jostled; in all ways he has to elbow himself through the world, giving and receiving offence.

Ethan replaced the volume. He glanced at the rest of the books on the shelves in the main room, but they offered no particular insights. Then he went into the next room, which was Shelby's study. Here again, one wall was filled with shelves. Many of the shelves contained articles and mementos of Shelby's past. Ethan recognized insignia from the Civil War, both Union and Confederate. A cavalry saber hung on the wall below a Confederate battle flag. Several Union cavalry pennants hung next to the battle flag. Some sergeant's and corporal's chevrons sat on one of the shelves next to a Union campaign hat. Brass buttons, officers' shoulder straps, Minie balls, and canister shot were arranged on another shelf, collar insignia and cavalry spurs and two Army Colt pistols on still another. In the corner of the room, a McClellan saddle with a saber attached sat on a small table, the stirrups draped over each side. The room was a museum of Union and Confederate articles. There were also trophies from some of Shelby's hunting trips—a wood duck mounted as though in flight and a small bobcat snarling and reaching out with his right foot, claws extended.

Shelby's desk was against the opposite wall. It was finely polished wood with leather inlays on the top and brass handles for the drawers. On one side was a pile of books. Ethan read the titles: *A History of the Crimean War, The Complete Poetical Works of Tennyson,* and *The Anglo-Irish.* On the other side of the desktop was a pile of blank bills of sale as well as some correspondence from Shelby's bankers and business associates.

Ethan went back to the main room, and in another minute Danielle returned. She was wearing a tweed outfit with a long skirt that was cut up the middle to make loose-fitting trousers, so that she could ride astride and not have to use the sidesaddle. The jacket was fitted, and showed her form in a way that made Ethan's throat tighten. There was a leather patch on the right shoulder of the jacket, a place for mounting her gun. She had on a black Stetson hat that was slightly faded from the sun. She was flushed and smiling, and he saw once again that her eyes were the color of cornflowers and that the color was intensified somehow by the dark brim of her hat. It was all that he could do to prevent himself from gathering her up and running off with her.

"I am ready, Ethan," she said.

"I am, too. Danielle."

She paused for a moment and looked at him, as

though trying to decipher something, to decide whether he had meant something more than the obvious, and perhaps, whether she had, too.

"Our lunch is ready, too," she said finally. "It is outside on the veranda. And Octavius has picked out two dogs for us, and I think we can just let them run from here. There's no need to take the wagon, and besides, Octavius has some things he needs to do this afternoon. Is that all right?"

"Sounds fine to me."

"Good. Well, shall we go?"

Ethan nodded and they went outside. Octavius had brought Danielle's mare around. He had saddled it and put a shotgun in the scabbard and tied it next to Rangeley.

"Oh, *mon Dieu,*" she said when they went to the horses, "What has happened to your poor horse's ear?"

"Some fella shot it off, I'm afraid. He was aiming at me, though, so Rangeley's not taking it too personally. Although he is not happy about it."

"Poor Rangeley." She went up to the horse and stroked his nose. "Oh, poor Rangeley." The horse nickered and raised his head slightly at her touch. "Well, *monsieur,* you are still quite handsome, I think, despite the lack of an ear. I will have to warn my mare to keep her head today. Was it one of the Curtains, Ethan? During the fight with them?"

"Yes, it was one of the Curtains, although it happened before the fight, when I was riding down in the San Rafael Valley. I guess he was trying to rob me, but we got away."

"And so Rangeley has been avenged."

"Yes."

She nodded. "Good."

"Speaking of handsome horses, Danielle, that's a nice-looking mare you have. What's her name?"

"Palfrey," she said smiling. "It's a little joke between us."

They mounted their horses and went out through the main gate. The two English setters, Mollie and Maggie, ran in front of them. They had already begun to hunt.

Ethan and Danielle rode west into the oak-lined canyons. The November day was cool and clear, and there was just a trace of wind, just enough to let the dogs scent, and they ran with their noses into the wind, zigzagging across the grass-covered floors of the canyons and up the grassy sides where the quail spent their mornings. Now and then they would stop and smell the breeze, as though considering some problem, and then they would run again, overlapping each other in a way that looked well thought out and carefully planned. The sun reflected off their white coats and the flags of their tails as they went about their joyful business, immersed in the moment.

"Those are wonderful dogs," said Ethan.

"Yes, truly. The greatest thing about the chase is watching them. The shooting is something secondary, I think."

They rode for about an hour travelling in a more or less straight line, moving from one canyon to another, farther and farther away from the ranch. But during that time the dogs did not find any birds.

Then, at the opening of a small canyon, Maggie became agitated. She hunted around the base of an oak, moving back and forth, her nose next to the ground. Then she froze. Mollie, who was on the other side of the canyon, noticed the point and came creeping over slowly, not wanting to flush the birds that Maggie had found. Mollie crept up behind Maggie and then went on point, too.

"Whoa, Maggie. Whoa, Mollie," said Danielle. "You whoa there."

Ethan and Danielle dismounted and took their shotguns from their scabbards. The dogs were standing just where the hillside met the floor of the canyon.

"They'll probably fly uphill," said Ethan. "You go ahead and shoot. I'll back you up." He could see the excitement in her eyes and in the way she moved as she approached the dogs. She cocked the hammers on her gun. Ethan stood behind her, and he did not cock his gun. He did not intend to shoot this time, because he wanted to watch her and did not want to be distracted by the possibility of a shot. Just a yard or so behind the dogs Danielle stopped, apparently to enjoy the moment, the picture of the dogs, and then she turned her head back toward Ethan and smiled radiantly at him as though punctuating the perfection of the tableau. And as she turned the covey went up. Six birds flew more or less straightaway. She raised her gun and fired two quick shots. Two birds went down in a puff of feathers. The other four birds beat their wings rapidly to gain altitude and speed, but then set their wings and glided across the canyon and landed in the grass there, out of range. Danielle broke open her shotgun and reloaded.

"Good shot, Danielle," said Ethan. "Sam wasn't lying."

She smiled again, a look of pure joy on her face. "I don't usually get two," she said. "You bring me luck."

Maggie chased after the fallen birds, and was in the process of retrieving one, but Mollie was still hunting in the same area, and suddenly she went on point again. Then she pounced and landed on a bird that had been hiding in the grass. Her pounce broke the wing of the quail, and Mollie picked it up and brought it to Danielle.

"Mollie!" she said. "Bad girl. Your job is to find

them, not catch them. Give me that." Danielle took the bird and held it in her open hand. It tried to flutter, but could not.

"Look," she said. "A young one."

"Yes, from this year's brood, I would guess."

"Pauvre petit oiseau," she said. "Poor little bird. What shall we do with him, Ethan?"

"Well, a bird with a broken wing will not last very long out here."

"I will take him home," she said. "And when his wing is healed, he can go and take his chances. As it is, it is too unfair." She put the bird into her saddlebag. "I think he will be all right there." Then she looked at Ethan. "Does it seem strange to hunt them and then to save such a one as this? It is ironic, I think."

"I am never surprised by irony, Danielle. It is the way of things, usually."

Maggie retrieved the other dead bird, and Ethan put them both in his vest pocket.

"Well, let's see if we find some more," he said.

"The next time is for you, Ethan. It is your turn."

They rode for another hour or so, but they did not find any more birds. They decided to ride up a long wash that was dotted with cottonwoods and sycamores.

"I think there is some water farther up this wash," said Danielle. "It would be a good place to stop for a while."

They came to a small spring at the base of some sycamores. Mollie and Maggie jumped into the water and lay on their bellies lapping up the spring water and cooling themselves after their long runs.

"I'm famished," said Danielle. "Would you like to have lunch here? It is a pretty place, I think."

"Yes. And the dogs could use a rest."

They dismounted, and Danielle took down a small basket that had been tied to her saddle. She spread a cloth in a sunlit spot beside the spring. There was a bottle of wine and a loaf of bread along with some cheese and fruit in the basket, and she laid out the food and some plates and two glasses for the wine. Ethan watched as she broke some pieces of bread and cheese and sliced the apples and arranged it all on the plates. She opened the wine and poured some into the two glasses.

"*Voila*. Luncheon is served, *monsieur*," she said with mock formality.

Ethan sat on the ground and took his wine and raised the glass to her.

"What is it you say? *À votre santé?*"

"Yes. *Santé*. Your health." She smiled at him, and then took a slice of apple and some cheese, and then she took a sip of wine. "This is a Côte du Rhône. Quite nice with this food, don't you think?"

"Yes, I do. Very nice."

They ate in silence for a while. To Ethan the combination of tastes, of the bread and fruit, the cheese and wine, was exquisite, as perfect as the weather that day, the cool air and sunlight there in the canyon filled with oaks and sycamores beside the spring. He watched her as she ate. She seemed to relish the food, and he noticed how the tip of her nose was sunburned and how it moved as she ate. And he noticed that the color of her mouth was the same deep red as the apples. After a while she took off her hat, shook her hair loose, took another sip of wine, and then looked at him.

"Are you married, Ethan?" she said.

For some reason the question did not surprise him. "I was. She died."

"Ah. I'm sorry. Was it long ago?"

"Yes. Many years now."

Danielle said nothing but continued to look at him.

"She was very beautiful," he said. And he suddenly

felt the story coming out of him. "Her name was Maria, and we lived in California. In the south. Our house was on Point Loma, near San Diego, and we could see the bay and the ocean from our windows. We could see the whales from there. And the ships standing out to sea or coming home. She and her family had come there from Mexico, during the troubles with Maximilian. To me it was like paradise, because I came from Maine, where the winters are very gray and long, so that California was a revelation to me. And of course she was there with me, so for a while it was the way you hope that life will be. I was on a merchant ship, so that I was gone many months at a time, but when I was at home the times were very good to the point that I began to relax and think that maybe this would last, that it was true, but then one time I came back, and she had died."

Danielle leaned toward him slightly, her expression one of unguarded seriousness. She started to reach for his arm, but stopped.

"And I can't remember saying good-bye to her that last time or how she looked," he said. "I don't know why that is. For a while I went to the places where we would go, as though expecting to see her there. I knew it was impossible, but I went to those places anyway. But then, after a while, I went away. And I have not gone back there." Ethan paused, still lost in thought. "She was very beautiful, Danielle," he said finally. "Like you." He paused again. "I'm sorry," he said. "I should not have said that."

"It's all right, Ethan."

"That was a long time ago. Sometimes it does not seem like so long ago. But other times, it seems like it was from some other life."

"And so from there, where did you go?"

"I went to where I've been until I came here, Danielle." Ethan smiled at her, finished his wine, and stood up. "Well," he said, as though casting off the other mood, "if we're going to get any quail, I'd better shut up, and we'd better get packed up. Those dogs have had enough rest, I think."

"Yes," she said. "Yes."

They headed back in the general direction of the ranch, and during the afternoon they found three more coveys of quail. Ethan shot two from the first and two from the third, and Danielle got one from the second.

"You shoot very well," she said after he made the double on the last covey.

"You seem surprised." He knew why she was surprised, but he did not say more about it.

"No, not really." Ethan noticed that when she said "not really," it came out "naw treally." Her accent was not obtrusive, but just noticeable enough to give color to the way she said things, and Ethan loved to listen to her.

About four o'clock they decided to head back, and they reached the ranch just as the sun was going down. Ethan took the birds from his vest and laid them on a bench next to the front door. Danielle took the live bird from her saddlebag and examined him. "He seems all right," she said.

"I expect he'll make it."

Then they stood in the dusk and wondered what to do next.

"Would you like to come in for a moment, Ethan?"

"I would like to. But I'd better be getting back. I have a few things to do before tomorrow."

"What is happening tomorrow?"

"I have to take a little trip for a week or so. Maybe two."

"Oh. But then you are coming back. Yes? So, you will come and visit again. Perhaps we could go shooting again."

"I'd like that, Danielle. Today was a good day."

"Yes. I will treasure it."

She smiled at him, and he thought he saw a trace of sadness in her eyes. Then she went inside.

Twelve

When Ethan got back to town, he went to his room and dropped off his shotgun and hunting gear. Then he put on his gun belt and went to the Big Steer. He was looking for Sanchez. And after the day he had had, he felt like having a drink. Maybe more than one.

The salesman was at the bar again. He was reading a newspaper. It was early still, and there were no other customers. Consuelo was behind the bar, and she nodded pleasantly at Ethan. He ordered a beer. The salesman looked up from his newspaper.

"Hello, friend, could I interest you in ... Oh. It's you. Sorry. Say, I stopped in to see that editor friend of yours, but he said he doesn't know anyone named Sam Grant."

"I'm not surprised to hear it. He suffers from memory lapse. Your tonic good for that?"

"Well, it couldn't hurt, I suppose."

"Well, I suggest you try again. Chances are he won't remember your first visit anyway, so you can start fresh."

The salesman grinned and nodded. "That's the way

it is every day, friend. When you're in commerce every day is a new beginning. A new opportunity."

"Yes, I feel the same way."

"Really? And what is it you do?"

"I'm an undertaker. As you said, every day brings a new opportunity."

The salesman looked uneasy. "You don't look like an undertaker, friend. You look more like a gunman. No offense."

"None taken. In fact, you're partly right. You see, if you're in my line of work, you can either sit around waiting, which is bad business practice, I think, or you can go out there and create your own customers. That makes more sense to me."

The salesman looked at Ethan quizzically, trying to decide whether Ethan was joking. "Yes, I see that," he said finally. "Well, it's been interesting talking to you. But I'd better be going. Tomorrow's likely to be a busy day."

"Don't you want to finish your beer?"

"No, thanks. I've had enough." He nodded ingratiatingly and then left.

A few minutes later Sweet Jimmy O'Brian came in.

"Hello, Ethan," he said. His tone was very friendly. "I sent that article you left at the office. Damn, it was good." He started laughing. "I liked that part about a posse of concerned citizens trying to make a peaceful arrest and having to respond with gunfire when they were ambushed by the desperados. I think that's how you put it. That was good. And no names."

"In my experience vigilantes generally like to remain anonymous, especially when they have to defend themselves with deadly force. No sense complicating the issue."

"No, you're right. Well, that'll give the folks back

East a little thrill to go with their morning coffee and marmalade."

"That's the whole point, Jimmy. Have a drink?"

"I wish I could, but I still have a few things to send out. I just came over here to get some more sweetener for my coffee." He gestured to Consuelo, who got a fresh bottle of whiskey and put it on the bar. Jimmy paid her and winked at Ethan. "Coffee just isn't the same without a little sweetness."

"Just like life, Jimmy."

O'Brian laughed again, and patted Ethan on the shoulder. "That's what I like about you writin' fellas. You and Harding, both. You're a couple of philosophers."

"Yep, and seekers after truth, as you can tell from that article."

O'Brian laughed again. "Well, one thing's for certain. Regardless of exactly what happened, the Curtains won't be writing any letters to the editor to complain about being misquoted, by God. And that's the important thing. Well, back to the grindstone."

Ethan got another beer and went over to the table in the corner where he usually sat. He figured Sanchez would be in by and by, and he had exhausted his store of small talk with the salesman and O'Brian. What he wanted now was to think about Danielle Shelby. What he needed was not to think about her. In either case, he wanted to be by himself until Jesús arrived.

Gradually people drifted into the bar. Mostly they were cowboys, and they stood at the bar drinking and talking quietly. Then Squirrel Tooth Annie came in with her concertina, and the noise at the bar increased, as the cowboys bantered back and forth with her. She saw Ethan sitting in the corner and waved at him, but he did not respond. She came over anyway.

"Hello, honey. You know what somebody just told me? That Stonewall Jackson is dead."

"Really? That's funny. I'm a little tired, but otherwise I feel fine."

"Oh, sure. That ain't your real name. Stonewall Jackson was a general and he's dead. What's your real name?"

"Rutherford B. Hayes."

"Like the president? You any relation?"

"He's my brother."

Annie considered the situation for a minute. She seemed to have doubts.

"Wait a minute. If he's your brother, how come you're both named Rutherford?"

"My mother was partial to it. All my brothers, all six of us, are named Rutherford B. Hayes, although the B stands for something different, so she could tell us apart."

"Well, I guess that makes sense. What's your B stand for, honey?"

"Bob."

"I knew there was something funny about that Stonewall business. I can always tell. You interested in a little company, Bob?"

"Not for the foreseeable future."

"All right. But I'll be at the bar if you change your mind."

Ethan nodded, and she went back to drumming up some business with the cowboys.

Finally Sanchez arrived. He saw Ethan and came over to the table. "Good evening, *señor.* You are well?"

"Guess so. How's everything, Jesús?"

"Things are progressing. Tomás is well enough to travel, and I think we will leave for Tubac tomorrow.

There is a wagon train of miners heading that way, and I have asked to join them."

"That's good."

"Yes. We will go the long way around the mountains. The road is safer, and with that many men, I do not think we will be troubled by the Apaches, although of course one never knows with them."

"That suits my plans, too, Jesús, assuming you still are willing to go down to Sonora with me. To Juan Lopez."

Sanchez shrugged. "Yes, I will go with you. I had hoped that you would forget this idea, but as I see, you have not. But I will go. I am afraid, though, that Tomás is of a different mind. He has no interest in this trip. It is as I suspected. Having been shot once, he is not very interested in having it happen again. I am not either, for that matter, but the reality of Tomás's experience is more forceful than my own imaginings, colorful as they are."

Ethan nodded and smiled. "That is much the same as I have said to you before, Jesús. Reality may be better or worse than we imagine, but it is usually different."

"Yes. That is why you must go to places, to see them. I understand that. I just do not think it is prudent. But I will go along, because I have promised. There is also the question of payment. One can always use a little extra."

"I am happy to hear that, Jesús. My plan is to go back over the pass the way we came. I will then meet you in Tubac. I will probably be there the day after you arrive. We can go to Juan Lopez from there. Can you be ready to leave on such short notice?"

"Oh, yes, *señor*. My Rosa runs the cantina with great efficiency. In truth, she does not need me. For that, at least. I will assemble my things and be ready to leave when you arrive. But of course I must ask you, why do you go back through that pass? Why not come with me and Tomás and the teamsters?"

Ethan just looked at Sanchez and smiled.

"Ah, yes, I understand, *señor.* It is because that is the way you do things. I knew it made no sense to raise the question, for I already knew the answer. Still, one feels a responsibility to ask these questions when a friend persists in putting himself in the way of danger for no reason beyond adherence to a way of doing things. But that is your way. I understand that. And so I will see you in Tubac in two or three days, assuming all goes well."

"Good. Where's your dog, by the way? I haven't seen him around."

"Some things we can know. Other things we can never know. The whereabouts of Nariz is generally in that second category, *señor.* In short, I have not seen him since the incident of the roping. I think he is sulking somewhere. He is passionate in his resentments."

"Well, maybe I'll run into him up in the mountains."

"It is possible. He has great affection for them. If so, I hope for your sake that he has not found another skunk. He seems to be drawn to them."

"Well, we all do things that aren't good for us."

"Perhaps, but this business of skunks is not good for anyone else either. No one in his vicinity, at least. That is a difference."

In the morning Ethan watched from his window as the small wagon train of miners along with Jesús and Tomás set out on the road west. He went downstairs and had breakfast, and then he went to the newspaper office.

Harding was at his usual spot behind his desk.

"Morning, Sep. How's your stomach today?"

"Hello there, Ethan. The answer to your question is, my stomach and related plumbing is remarkably fine. There's a fellow here in town selling some new tonic, and damned if it isn't just what the doctor ordered, so to speak. Fixed me up right smart. Feel like a new man, or like an old man with a new set of innards."

"I'm glad to hear it."

"You know what Ben Franklin said: A mature man's three best friends are an old wife, an old dog, and ready money. But he left out the most important: good digestion, which comes just after ready money and just before an old dog, with the old wife bringing up the rear. I'd trade any number of old dogs and old wives, for that matter, just for the promise of good digestion."

"No more bad peppers."

"No, indeed. That tonic's a miracle. I think the drummer selling the stuff is a little touched in the head, though. Told me that an undertaker named Sam Grant sent him. And even though he's been by to see me three or four times, he always introduces himself as though we've never met before. Damnedest thing. Still, it's not easy to come by good stomach tonic. What's on your mind?"

"Well, I'd you to make me up a little handbill. And I'd also like you to forget it afterwards."

"Well, my memory ain't what it used to be, so that should be easy enough. What've you got?"

Ethan took out a draft of the bill he wanted printed. It was a wanted poster showing a drawing of a man's face. And under the picture it said: WANTED. JOHN WESLEY HARDIN. $5000 REWARD. SUSPECT IS WANTED FOR MURDER AND ROBBERY IN THE STATE OF TEXAS. CONSIDERED EXTREMELY DANGEROUS.

"Hm," said Harding. "John Wesley Hardin. Texas

gunman. All-around bad hombre. But you know, the funny thing about this poster is that this picture looks just like you."

"Life's full of coincidences."

"And you want me to print this up so it looks legitimate and then forget I did it."

"That's right. And, Sep, it's important. And it's also okay. You can trust me on this."

"Well, I think I can figure out more or less what you're up to. Where're you heading, Mr. Hardin?"

"Mexico. I hear there's an opening for an experienced man down there. But I would not want that to get out either, Sep."

Harding nodded. "Don't worry. We newspaper boys have to stick together. And I understand that sometimes it's easier to gather up a story when people don't know what you're up to. How soon do you want this poster?"

"Soon as possible. In fact, it'd be good if you could do it now."

"All right. I'll do it myself. My devil's not in yet, and anyway he doesn't need to see this. Fewer people know about it, the better off you'll be, I suspect. This shouldn't take too long. There's nothing complicated about the drawing."

"Thanks, Sep. I appreciate it. Could be that'll come in real handy where I'm going."

"I believe it. Down there something like this is as good as a passport. Maybe better. But there's one thing about your idea. I thought they caught Wes Hardin last year and threw him in prison. Did he get out somehow?"

"Not that I know of. But you know those Texas jails. Some of them are real flimsy. That'll go some way to explaining how he got to Mexico in the off chance that some people down there also heard he'd been caught."

"I understand. Well, give me an hour or so."

* * *

Ethan went back to his room, packed up his gear, and took it over to the livery stable. Priam was in his stall calmly chewing hay.

"Well, Priam, you've been doing nothing the last few days but standing around looking ugly. It's time to get back to work."

Priam looked at Ethan noncommittally, although his squint gave him an air of skepticism.

"That mule's the gentlest mule I ever saw," said the stable man. "He only tried to bite me once."

"That's high praise, friend. I'm sure he appreciates it."

Ethan packed his gear on Priam. It was a complicated job, and Ethan was careful. He did not want any trouble with the packs on this trip. Then he saddled Rangeley and went back to the newspaper to pick up his poster. He shook hands with Harding and left town, heading northwest for the pass over the Santa Ritas.

They made good time across the grasslands on the way to the trailhead, and they reached Box Canyon, the place where the Army patrol had been attacked, by early afternoon. Everything looked the same. Evidently no one had been to the site since Ethan and Sanchez the week before.

As they continued to climb toward Madera Canyon, where the trail led up to the summit of Mount Wrightson, Ethan noticed that both Rangley and Priam were getting a little skittish. They seemed uncomfortable for some reason, so when they reached a point in the trail that gave Ethan a good view both ahead and behind, he stopped and climbed up a small promontory to have a look. There was nothing ahead that he could see, but when he looked backwards he spotted a rider about two miles away. The man was going cautiously, apparently not wanting to catch up with Ethan. Ethan studied him for a minute or so before recognizing him.

"It's Ellis," he said. "Now, boys, what in hell do you suppose he's up to?"

Ethan remounted and picked up the pace. He wanted to get to his campsite on Mount Wrightson in plenty of time to arrange a reception for Ellis if the man was following him. He loped to the trailhead of Mount Wrightson, which was about four miles away. He unsaddled Rangeley and tethered him loosely in the same glade, where there was grass and good water. The glade was well off the trail, and although there was a chance that Ellis might discover Rangley, Ethan did not think there was any danger. If Ellis was following Ethan, it was not because he was after his horse. Most likely Ellis would have to leave his own mount at the trailhead and follow on foot to the top. Ethan took his rifle from Rangeley's scabbard, and untied his shotgun case from the saddle and secured it in amidst Priam's packs.

"Our work's not over yet, Priam. Let's go." Ethan took the mule's lead and started walking quickly up the trail. Priam was surefooted and paid no attention to the narrowness of the path. He picked his way expertly up the four miles or so of difficult trail, although there were places where the loose rocks caused Ethan to stumble. The pathway narrowed to just a few feet in spots, and to the right there was nothing below for hundreds of feet except rocky gorge. But after little more than an hour, they reached the plateau and campsite where the heliograph was hidden.

Ethan unloaded the packs from behind his saddle and quickly made camp. It was getting close to twilight. He set up his tripods and his hammock in the center of the plateau. He put his bedroll in the hammock, and then covered it over with a tarp and placed his hat on top, where his head would have been. He hobbled Priam near a patch of grass. He built a fire and brewed some coffee, and then took his rifle and shot-gun, hid behind a rock about ten yards from the ham-mock, and settled down with his coffee to wait for Ellis.

The wind was brisk. It would muffle the sounds of anyone coming up the trail. But Ethan had a good hid-ing place. No one could circle around behind him, and he figured that Ellis, if he came, would announce him-self in some way or another.

It was dark by the time Ethan heard the noises. Someone was walking up the trail. Ellis, assuming that's who it was, was treading carefully, but he could not be entirely silent on such a loose and rocky trail. Priam pricked up his ears and nickered nervously. Then Ethan saw Ellis. He was crouching and maneuvering toward some rocks about fifteen yards away. Ethan watched as Ellis found a hiding place. He could see him remove his hat and then peer over the rocks to reconnoiter the campsite. The fire was still glowing and the light threw Ethan's hammock into sharp relief. He could see Ellis smile as the man saw what he thought was an ideal sit-uation. Ellis slowly raised his rifle and then fired three quick shots into the hammock. The first shot knocked Ethan's hat into the air, and the other two tore into the hammock and tarp about where Ethan's chest would have been. Ethan was surprised at the quickness of the three shots and by the noise, which in this rocky plateau reverberated wildly. Priam brayed at the sound and tried to buck, but settled down as soon as the echoes died away. Ellis waited behind the rock, looking for signs of movement, and then slowly stood up and came cau-tiously over to the hammock.

"Well now, dude," said Ellis. "Looks like you're the one with the sawdust leaking out his ears, ain't you? Dude." Ellis was sneering and chuckling.

When Ellis was between Ethan and the firelight,

Ethan stood up and cocked the hammers on his shotgun.

Ellis froze. He heard the clicking of the hammers. He knew he had made a mistake.

"Hello, Ellis. I thought I told you not to call me that."

Ellis swung around to the sound. Ethan fired one barrel into Ellis's left foot, and the man went down. He dropped his rifle and yelled in pain.

"Don't shoot again! Please, don't shoot me again." He was rolling around on the ground clutching his foot. "God!" he said. "Goddamn."

"Yes, I can imagine that's painful." Ethan left his hiding place and went over the to the man on the ground. He stuck his shotgun in Ellis's ear, and Ellis froze again.

"No," he said. "Please."

"Roll over on your belly and put your hands behind you. Do it slowly." Ellis groaned as he rolled.

Ethan clamped on a pair of handcuffs and checked to make sure there was no room for Ellis to wriggle out of them. They were tight. Then he pushed Ellis over onto his back with his boot.

"Now let's have a look at that foot. Hmm. Well, it's kind of a mess right now, but I don't believe it'll kill you. You should live long enough to hang. Course, your fandango days might be over, but they were over one way or the other anyway, so I wouldn't fret."

"Who are you? Some sort of lawman?" Ellis was gritting his teeth. His eyes were wide with fear.

"No. I got these manacles off a sheriff who didn't need them anymore. Thought they might come in handy one day, and turns out I was right. Now you just rest right there for a minute while I take care of a little business."

Ethan went over to his packs and got a rope. He tied

one end to the trunk of a tree, and then tossed the rest over a limb that was about ten feet above the grassy spot where Priam had been grazing. He made a loop.

"I don't have time to make a proper noose, but I believe this'll do, " he said to Ellis.

"What are you going to do?"

"What's it look like? Attempted murder's a hanging crime. And I can't see that it makes much sense to haul you back into Tucson for trial. It's too far away. So we might as well take care of things right here."

"You wouldn't hang me. Not in cold blood."

"Sure I would, Ellis. It'll teach you a valuable lesson. You try something, you take the consequences when it fails. That's the way it works. Besides, what makes you think my blood's cold?"

"No." He started struggling and managed to get to his feet, but his wounded foot would not support him and he toppled over onto his face. He started whimpering.

Ethan led Priam over to the tree and placed him under the branch. He then grabbed Ellis by the handcuffs and dragged him over to the mule. Ellis was not a big man, but he was struggling. He smelled of fear. Ethan pulled out one of his Schofields and hit the man behind the ear. Ellis went limp. When he came to, he was sitting astride Priam with the noose around his neck. He looked around wildly, but then realized where he was and became very still.

"That's a good policy," said Ethan. "Priam's a particular mule, and he doesn't like to be kicked. Makes him jumpy, so I would sit real quiet if I were you."

Ethan had no intention of hanging Ellis. He had tied the other end of the rope to the tree with a slipknot, so that if Priam bolted or walked out from under Ellis, Ellis would have merely fallen. But Ellis did not know that.

The mule was grazing. When he reached out for some fresh grass, the rope tightened.

"Ahhh, I can't breathe. I'm choking."

"That's the general idea."

"Please, mister. I'll do anything."

"Well, that's neighborly, but right now I can't think of anything I want you to do."

"My foot's killing me," wailed the other man.

"No. The rope's going to do that job."

"Please."

"Don't beg like that, Ellis. It's not dignified. Course, I might be willing to trade you your miserable hide for a little information. And I emphasize the word 'might.' "

"Anything. Anything."

"Well, that's sensible. First off, who sent you? Somebody must've. You're too dumb to be working alone."

"Rourke. He told me to come after you." Priam stretched for some grass "Ahhhh!"

"Rourke? Why?"

"I don't know. Honest, mister. I don't know. Please believe me."

"Well, I'm sure most people would, but I have a skeptical nature. It's a bad flaw, but I've learned to live with it. So, let me ask you again, why?"

"He thinks you're a lawman. You've been asking a lot of questions and looking around."

"What's he got against lawmen?"

"He's on the run. He's wanted in New Mexico for horse stealing and shooting a man."

"I can believe that. But something doesn't make sense. If he's the one on the run, why'd he send you after me? Why not do it himself? And why'd you agree to do it? Your story doesn't hold water, Ellis, and I hate being lied to. I guess I better just go ahead and slap that mule on the rear."

"No, no. Wait. I'm on the run too. We both are. For the same thing."

"How'd you decide who would come after me?"

"We tossed a coin for it. Whoever lost was to go on the trail drive. One of us had to."

Ethan laughed. "Now that I can believe."

"What are you going to do with me?"

"I haven't decided yet. Why don't you just sit there for a while and think about your sinful ways. I'm going to try to catch some sleep. Priam looks like he's pretty well settled in for the night, so I don't think he'll wander off. Course you can never tell about mules. If he moves out from under you there, just give a yell. And in the off chance that your friend Rourke followed you, be sure and wake me, because I guarantee you that mule will start bucking around if he smells anything unusual. Don't worry, though, I'm a light sleeper."

Ethan settled down behind a rock. He didn't want to risk sleeping in his hammock in case Rourke had somehow left the trail drive and circled back and was lurking around somewhere. He put his hat over his eyes.

"You ruined my good twenty-dollar hat, Ellis. It's enough to make a fella grumpy."

"Please, mister."

"Good night."

"What about my foot? I could bleed to death."

"It's possible. All the more reason to sit quiet."

Ethan did not intend to sleep; he wanted to make sure that Ellis had been alone. He could hear Priam cropping grass and Ellis groaning and whimpering. Far off in the distance, Ethan could hear some coyotes yipping and howling. The stars had come out and the moon was up so that Ethan had a good view of the trail. He watched and listened for thirty minutes or so, but there were no other sounds. Then he went back to the mule. Ellis was sitting as straight as he could, and the rope was taut.

"Ellis, I can't sleep. Must have been that coffee."

"Please, mister."

"I've been thinking things over, and I've decided to give you the benefit of the doubt. I don't think I'll hang you after all. Not tonight anyway."

"Thanks, mister. Thanks." Ellis's voice was barely a whisper. "Water. Please."

"Sure. Just sit there a second while I untie that rope." Ethan detached the rope from the tree, and as soon as Ellis felt it go slack, he fell off the mule and landed on his wounded foot. He groaned, but then lay quiet. Ethan took the noose off his neck, sat him up, and gave him some water from his canteen.

"Now, Ellis, I'm giving you a chance to live a few more days until the law decides how best to get rid of you. Don't bother to thank me. But in return I'd like to make sure that you've told me the whole story about you and Rourke."

"I have. There's nothing else to tell. I swear to you."

"Yes, and I'm sure your word is your bond. But I was impressed by your shooting last night. You got off three quick shots and hit the target each time. And I remember you were pretty handy down at the Curtain ranch. You even managed to hit the tree just above my head one time. That was you, wasn't it? What's more, you tell me you're wanted for robbery and murder in New Mexico. So I started thinking about those soldiers who were killed not far from here. Someone who could shoot that well, along with maybe a couple of other handy fellas like your friend Rourke, could have wiped out those eight men before they had a chance to pull their weapons. What's your opinion?"

"The Apaches killed those men."

"Maybe so. Maybe not."

"We didn't have nothing to do with that."

"Well, since you say so, I'll believe you, of course. Still, I might want to revisit this subject with you a little later on."

"What are you going to do with me?"

"I think I'll take you on down to Tubac tomorrow. There's a nice little storehouse there that'll serve as a jail until I come back for you. How do you feel about Mexican food?"

But Ellis did not answer. He had fainted. Ethan dragged him over to the hammock and lifted him in. He took the rope and wound it round and round the outside of the hammock so that Ellis was trussed up with just his nose and mouth exposed. Then he took the tarp and spread it over the hammock to cover the ropes and placed his hat over Ellis's face.

"Let's hope for your sake that Rourke really is on that trail drive and not sneaking up the pathway here."

Ethan got a sleeping bag and returned to his hiding place. He lay on his back on top of the bag and watched the stars. He thought about Ellis's story, and he could not decide whether to believe him or not. Perhaps Rourke had sent him; that did seem plausible. Both Rourke and Ellis had come from New Mexico, and maybe they had crossed Ethan's path there without Ethan's knowing it. Maybe one of those imaginative stories in the Santa Fe newspaper had come to their attention. Maybe someone in Santa Fe had pointed Ethan out as a detective. Or maybe Rourke just had a sixth sense about lawmen. None of that connected them with the robbery of the Army payroll. Perhaps they didn't have anything to do with it. There were plenty of other candidates, and the money that had shown up down in Mexico was a strong argument for the involvement of Juan Lopez in some way or other. Maybe he had been in business with the Curtains. Now that the Curtains were all dead, they could not answer questions about how or why the Army horses were on their land. But Lopez could. That was why Ethan had to go there. He would drop Ellis off in Tubac and lock him in a storehouse there until he could take him back to Tucson. Then he could deal with Rourke. But all of that must come after his visit to Juan Lopez.

Ethan checked on Ellis one more time. The man was securely trussed in the hammock, and he appeared to be asleep. Ethan went back to his sleeping bag and crawled in. He listened to the night sounds; the howling of a pack of coyotes, the screech of a rabbit caught by some predator, the wind in the branches of the oak trees and junipers. The night air was cold and had no scent. The moon had set, and so in the absence of its light, the stars seemed more profuse than at any time in Ethan's experience, even during his days at sea. *Must be the altitude,* he thought. And yet despite the myriad stars, the sky seemed even emptier than usual to him, as though the hard pinpricks of light merely served to emphasize the blackness around them. Then, as always before sleep, Ethan thought of Maria and tried to remember her clearly. But he could only recall a vague image of her smiling at him, as though she were standing in the mist some distance away. He remembered that once in California they had camped out on a mountaintop on a night like this. The sky had not seemed empty then. And then he thought of Danielle Shelby, as he had been doing the past few nights, since he had seen her. Her image came to him clearly, like a photograph, but that did not do him any good.

"Damn," he said. "Damn."

* * *

He woke at daybreak and stirred up the fire and put on some coffee. He got some bacon from the packs, and fried it in an iron skillet and ate it with his fingers. He heard Ellis mumbling and groaning in the hammock.

"Mornin', Ellis. I expect you'd like a drink of something." He removed his hat from Ellis's face and poured some water into Ellis's mouth. Ellis drank greedily. "How's your foot?"

"It burns like hell." Ellis's eyes were feverish.

"It's something you'll have to get used to, I imagine. I'll take a look at it later. Right now I've got some chores to take care of, so you just lie there and relax." Ethan replaced his hat on the other man's face, so that he could not see. Then he went to where the heliograph was hidden, and uncovered it and set it up in the opening to catch the morning sun. Captain Wilkes had agreed to have a man stationed at Fort Lowell each day at two o'clock to receive Ethan's signals. But he had also said he would have someone check the site on Mount Wrightson each day every hour on the hour, so that if Ethan needed to send a signal before or after the assigned time, the man could see the flashes and send someone to the station to receive and acknowledge Ethan's message. At eight o'clock the sun was high enough to catch, and Ethan began sending his recognition signal. He signaled for ten minutes, but there was no answer. Then after another thirty minutes, there was a return flash from the fort's signaling station in the mountains. Wilkes's people had apparently seen the first flashes and had gone to the station to reply.

Damn, he's a good man, thought Ethan. Ethan returned the recognition signal and then began to send a series of messages. There were several questions that Ethan needed answers to. Wilkes would need time to do some research, so Ethan finished his signal by saying that he would be gone for a week or two but would return either to Mount Wrightson or to Tucson and that he hoped Wilkes could have the information by then.

Ethan put the heliograph back in its hiding place and covered it over. Then he went to the hammock and unwound the ropes. Ellis was barely conscious.

"Now let's have a look at your foot, Ellis." Ethan cut the man's boot off and peeled back the sock. The foot was swollen and red. Blood had coagulated over the dozens of small wounds in the ankle and on top of the foot. "Well, I've seen lots worse. You're missing a couple of toes, and I think your ankle's broken, but that's not surprising. That was double-aught buck in that shotgun charge, so you should be glad there's anything at all left of that foot. It won't be your best feature, though, after this."

"What are you going to do, mister?" Ellis's throat was dry and his voice was weak.

"I told you last night. Take you down to Tubac. There might be a doctor there who can dig out that shot and patch you up. Till then I think I'll wrap your foot. It stopped bleeding, so you should be all right for the time being."

Ethan poured some water and some whiskey over the wound. Ellis writhed and yelled when the whiskey seeped into the wounds. Then Ethan bandaged the ankle.

"You're lucky I always carry a medical kit with me, Ellis. You should do the same, seeing as how you appear to be accident-prone."

Ethan then turned the hammock over and dumped Ellis on the ground. Since Ellis's hands were still cuffed behind his back, he could not break the fall and landed hard on his face and chest.

"Sorry, Ellis. Getting out of a hammock is lots harder

than getting in. Now you just lie there while I get packed up. I think that mule is capable of carrying the packs and you, too, although the ride won't be that comfortable. Better than having to hop all the way down that trail, though."

When Ethan had Priam loaded up, he led him over to a rock. He picked Ellis up by the handcuffs and seat of the pants and took him over to the rock and helped him up. From there he could get on Priam.

"Just hop on in front of those packs, Ellis. I'd uncuff your hands, but I know you're an experienced cowhand, so you don't really need your hands to ride. Besides, we'll be taking it slow down this trail."

Ellis said nothing, but glumly swung his wounded leg over Priam and settled in behind the mule's neck. Priam didn't care for something about the arrangement, but after tossing his head and snorting, he settled down.

"Priam objects to your smell, I think, Ellis. Probably reminds him of a goat. Well, let's go."

Ethan took Priam's lead and started walking down the trail. The first several hundred yards were fairly easy going, but soon they got to a stretch that was steep and narrow and slippery from the loose rocks. There was a cliff on one side, not high, but about eye level, and on the other side the trail dropped off into a deep rocky canyon that was studded with boulders and yuccas. Priam had not objected to this part of the trail on the way up, but something was bothering him now. His ears started twitching, and he began tossing his head as though trying to rid himself of an annoying insect. They came to a turning in the trail, and just ahead there was a small ledge on the right covered with manzanita bushes. Priam stopped suddenly and extended his neck and started braying.

"What's wrong with this mule?" said Ellis. He was

looking at the drop-off on his left, and he was frightened. "I don't like the way he's acting. Maybe there's Apaches around."

Just then Ethan saw movement in the manzanitas, and he pulled his pistol. A mountain lion poked his head through the bushes and snarled. Ethan held his fire, not wanting to spook Priam, but it was too late. The mule saw the lion and jumped straight into the air, and then landed and kicked out with his back legs. Ellis managed to hold on during the first jump, but the kick threw him over Priam's head. He landed on his left shoulder, and the momentum of the fall propelled him off the pathway and over the side of the cliff. Ellis yelled something as he fell, but he hit the first boulder about twenty yards below, and was silent after that as he rolled and tumbled from one rock to another, leaving a trail of dust and small stones, until he came to rest in the canyon bottom about a hundred yards below. Ethan held onto Priam's lead as the mule continued to buck and bray. The lion turned and ran up the side of the canyon, jumping easily from boulder to boulder, and Ethan did not bother shooting at him. It was all that he could do to hold on to Priam's lead.

Gradually the mule calmed down. The packs had loosened because of Priam's gyrations, but they were still on the packsaddle. Ethan tightened up the knots as soon as Priam had settled down.

"Well, Priam, I can't say I blame you, but you've lost me both a witness and a suspect." Ethan looked over the side of the cliff, and saw Ellis arranged in a position that no living body could assume. "I guess I better go down there and make sure. But from here I'd say he's about as dead as he's going to get."

Ethan tied Priam's lead to a flat rock. He thought about hobbling him. But he wanted the mule to be able to fight if the lion did come back. If that happened, Priam would need his front hooves free.

Ethan struggled down the side of the cliff, angling from rock to rock, moving back and forth like a ship tacking into the wind. Long before he reached the body he could see that Ellis was indeed dead. He was lying on his back. There was very little left of his face; it had been scraped and battered by the rocks and yuccas. There was a dark patch forming on his chest, and his legs stuck out in different directions. Ethan straightened out his legs, and then turned him over on his stomach and unlocked the handcuffs. He looked in Ellis's pockets, but there was nothing there.

"Well, Ellis, this is a shame. Just when we were getting better acquainted. I suppose the decent thing would be to bury you right here. But I haven't got a shovel, and besides, this ground's pretty hard, which I guess you learned on the way down." Ethan considered trying to haul Ellis back up to the trail, but there was no way he could do it alone. Then he thought about covering Ellis up with rocks, but he knew that that would only be a cosmetic gesture and a minor inconvenience to the coyotes who would dig him up in short order. "I guess you might as well stay right there the way you are, Ellis. It'll save everyone a lot of trouble. It's a poor funeral, but it's the best I can do. Amen. I'll take care of your horse, though."

Ethan took his hat off and wiped the sweat away. He looked up and saw the ravens gliding overhead. They were black against the dark blue sky, but as they soared, the sunlight glanced off their wings now and then and turned them silver.

"Well, boys," he said. "Here's another one."

Thirteen

When Ethan reached the glade where Rangeley was grazing, he found Ellis's horse, still saddled and tethered to a tree.

"Looks like Ellis didn't expect to stay the night. Well," he said to the horse, "whatever your name is, you're currently unemployed. Best thing to do I guess is take you down to Tubac. If I turn you loose you'll just go back to Verity, and there's no sense letting those people know about Ellis's sad demise sooner than they need to."

Ethan saddled Rangeley and then tied a lead to Ellis's horse. Then he mounted and, holding the leads to Priam and the other horse, headed down the mountain toward Tubac. They had about a six-hour ride ahead of them.

It was dark when Ethan reached the little town. He took the animals to the livery stable, and stored his packs there, too.

"I am happy to see you again, *señor,*" said the livery

man. "I see you have acquired another horse." Ethan noticed the man looking at the Double S brand on Ellis's horse.

"Yes, I found him wandering around up in the Santa Ritas. I'm afraid his owner may have had some accident."

The livery man looked at Ethan. "Yes, it's possible, I think. Accidents are common in this country."

"Well, maybe he'll turn up." Then, taking his rifle and shotgun and his spare clothing, Ethan went to Sanchez's cantina.

There was a group of rough-looking characters sitting at one of the tables. The skinny prostitute was sitting with them, and she looked up and smiled with her bad teeth when Ethan walked in. Sanchez was behind the bar polishing glasses, and he nodded and grinned when he saw Ethan.

"*Bueno.* I am very glad to see you here safely, *señor.* Did you meet with any trouble on your way?"

"No. It was uneventful. How are you, Jesús?"

"Well. And so is Tomás. And there is further good news, of a kind. Nariz has reappeared. In fact he was here when we arrived."

"I am glad to hear it."

"Yes." Sanchez sighed. "But no sooner did he return than he disgraced himself again. He killed and ate two piglets from a new litter of Rosa's favorite sow, and she has banished him after beating him with a stick."

"He is getting too lazy to hunt, perhaps."

"Yes, I suppose so. It happens to all of us as time passes, I think. But Rosa does not accept this argument. Would you like some food? And perhaps *cerveza?*"

"Yes, although not in that order."

"*Bueno, señor.* Rosa has prepared a pot of *menudo.* A bowl of Rosa's *menudo* along with her tortillas and a mug of cool beer, and a man feels that life is worth living again, even after a long day of traveling." Sanchez drew some beer and placed it on the bar. Then he leaned over the bar and whispered. "And speaking of traveling, I don't imagine that you have changed your mind about the trip we discussed."

"No. I hope you have not changed yours."

Sanchez shrugged resignedly. "No. I am ready to leave tomorrow if you wish it. Wait here and I will get the *menudo*."

Ethan stood at the bar and drank his beer. Then he looked around the room and noticed a man sitting alone at a table in the corner. The man was middle-aged and expensively dressed. He wore a dark suit and well-polished boots. His gray hair was parted in the middle and brushed carefully on each side, and he had a well-tended cavalry moustache. His nose was long and straight, and he had clear gray eyes and a fair complexion. He seemed very much out of place and perfectly at ease. The man nodded at Ethan and beckoned him over to the table.

"Would you care to join me, sir?" said the man. "My new friend Jesús Sanchez told me he was expecting you, that you were a journalist from New York, although I have to say you don't look like any of the journalists I have ever met." The man was smiling pleasantly, and Ethan knew from his accent that he was English.

"That's been said before," said Ethan. He went over to the table, and the man stood up and extended his hand. His grip was limp, as though he was not used to this kind of ceremony.

"I'm Antony Wentworth," he said. Ethan could smell his hair pomade.

"Ethan Jaeger. Nice to know you."

"Please join me," said Wentworth.

"All right."

"I just arrived last night from Tucson. I was glad to hear that someone from the East was coming this way. This is a hell of a place, I must say. It's good to have someone to talk to." Wentworth spoke slowly and distinctly, as though he was used to being listened to.

"What's an Englishman doing out here?"

The other man nodded as if appreciating the fact that Ethan did not need to question the obvious fact of his origin. "I represent some investors in London. We're looking for some cattle-ranching opportunities. I have been in Wyoming and Colorado, and I came to Arizona last month. Quite an odyssey. Nearly over, thank God."

Ethan nodded. He knew that there were a number of Englishmen who owned ranches in the West.

"This is a rough time to be travelling around out here," Ethan said. "The Indians are in kind of a bad mood."

The other man laughed. "Yes, I know. Fortunately, the Army has pretty much settled the Sioux and Cheyennes in the north, but I understand that this part of the country is still a little nervous about the Apaches."

"Nervous is one word for it."

"My clients tend to have a long-term perspective. You know, the best time to invest in anything is when everyone else is afraid to. There is always risk, but 'fortune favors the brave.' "

"I have heard that. Virgil, wasn't it?"

"Bravo. An educated man. But more to the point, fortune favors the wealthy. And fortunately my clients are brave enough to send me here and wealthy enough to wait for the Apaches to become Methodists or whatever else might be their wretched destiny."

"Well, they haven't converted yet, so I hope you're not traveling alone in this country."

"Oh, no. I have several men, good men, with me. That table of scoundrels over there is my bunch. What they lack in sartorial splendor they make up for in marksmanship. But to be honest, we haven't had too much trouble on this trip. Just one scrap with the Utes up in southern Colorado. They wanted our horses, and we wanted to keep them. Very basic sort of dispute. We settled them, though." Ethan found himself warming to this man. Despite his elegant clothes Wentworth seemed to be very competent, and there was nothing of the braggart about him. He had the easy and ironic air that Ethan had always found appealing among some Englishmen he knew, the ones who were confident about themselves without being insufferable. He knew some of the other kind, too, however, and therefore took each one on his own merits, as he did with everyone else.

"I suppose you know that there's one of your countrymen who owns a big ranch on the other side of this mountain range," Ethan said.

"Yes. I'd heard that. Fellow named Shelby. One doesn't know him, though. But I understand he's done well."

"Yes, from the looks of things. And there's some beautiful grassland over there. I don't know if any of it's for sale, but it's pretty country. It's a much higher elevation than this desert country, so the landscape is very different. And there seems to be plenty of water, judging from the windmills."

"Yes, that's what I understand. I'm heading in that direction tomorrow, as a matter of fact. Do you know Shelby?"

"A little."

"Good man?"

"Seems to be. He's actually Irish, I think, although he was in the British Army for a while. I guess he was the younger son of a lord over there, and he spent some time in the Army and then came over here and got started in Texas. He came to this part of the country after our war."

"I see. Shocking business, your war. I spent some time with the Army of Northern Virginia as an observer. I was in the British Army, too, at the time, and our government's sympathies were with the South, as I expect you know. It was self-interest rather than sentiment, of course. We needed the cotton. Too many mill workers with nothing to do. Leads to unrest, do you see? But your war was dreadful. Unbelievable carnage, some of those battles. Quite astonishing what men will do."

"Yes. It is."

"Were you involved?"

"Yes, in the Union Navy."

Wentworth nodded in approval. "So this fellow Shelby was in the British Army? Well, then, we will have some things in common."

"Yes, I think he told me that when he left home he joined the Heavy Brigade of cavalry. Fought in the Crimea."

The other man raised his eyebrows and looked surprised. "Did he actually say that? That he joined the Heavy Brigade? That's odd."

"In what way?"

"Well, you know, the British army is composed of regiments. A man joins a regiment, not a brigade. Brigades are tactical organizations, so to speak. But the allegiance is to the regiment. I think the Inniskillings and the Scots Greys were part of the Heavy Brigade. But I can't remember if there were others. I was in the Household Cavalry, myself. Very smart. Had to resign, though, after a fracas involving a major's wife. A diabolical mess, I assure you. Not the sort of thing to advance one's career." He laughed at the memory. "Well,

I suppose it was worth it. Barely. Charming figure, although she was very silly. Wrote me some girlish letters filled with romantic imaginings and some extravagant compliments which her husband somehow got hold of and naturally resented. Well, no man likes unfavorable comparisons, of course. Very embarrassing. He wanted to challenge me but thought better of it. He was a desperately poor shot, which is a liability for a soldier or an outraged husband. Got himself killed in Africa. No loss, really, although he was a splendid horseman. But dull-witted. His wife then married a bishop. Fellow with no chin but lots of money. I listened to one of his sermons once. He couldn't pronounce his R's, so when he said it was time to 'wead the wesponse,' I started laughing and had to leave. Have another?" Wentworth tossed off the rest of his drink. "This tequila is dreadful stuff. But one grows accustomed to it with practice."

Just then Sanchez arrived with Ethan's food. Wentworth peered into Ethan's bowl. "What's that stuff?"

"Menudo, señor," said Sanchez. "Very good."

"It's tripe and chilies," said Ethan. "It also requires some practice to get used to."

"Good," said Wentworth. "I'll have some, too, if you please, Jesús. And do not spare the chilies. They are impossible to find on Pall Mall, I assure you."

Ethan waited while Sanchez brought another bowl. He watched as Wentworth tentatively scooped his first spoonful. Wentworth paused for a moment and then smiled.

"Wonderful stuff. I suspect one would not want to see it being prepared, but the result is very fine. You know, English cooking is shocking. Very bland. I will probably starve to death trying to get accustomed again to mutton and potatoes after months of eating your various national dishes. I have grown very fond of jerky, for example. Especially elk meat. Properly done, it is quite good, although I have not decided yet what wine would be best with it. Something red, but exactly what, I can't think."

"You might raise that issue with Shelby. He tells me his father-in-law has a vineyard in Bordeaux."

"Does he indeed? This fellow is blessed, it seems. Next you will tell me that he has a beautiful young wife."

"I'm afraid that's true, too." Ethan's expression and tone of voice betrayed him slightly.

"Ah," said Wentworth. "I see. Well, dammit, man, that's very hard. Perhaps he'll insult me and I'll have to shoot him. Just to even things up a bit. You said he was Irish anyway, I believe. That's little better than an Apache, in my books. There are quite enough Irish in the world as it is. Need thinning out. Can't have them monopolizing the best wines and women."

Ethan laughed. "Well, it's hard to hate a man for having good luck."

"No, it isn't. It's the easiest thing in the world, especially for an Englishman. We're experts at it. But, then, different cultures are good at different things, I suppose. The Germans, for example, make excellent sausage. Have another?"

"No, thanks. I'm still working on this one."

"Well, then, tell me. How's the writing business? I once knew a fellow who wrote for the *Times*. Very brainy, but dull. His wife ran off with a clergyman, and he was rather gloomy after that. Started calling for the dissestablishment of the Church, although he always claimed there was no connection. Hard to believe, if you ask me. But there it is."

Wentworth poured himself another glass of tequilla and drank it in one motion without grimacing.

"Sounds like things are pretty spicy over there in England," Ethan observed.

"Oh, decidedly. It's how we compensate for the blandness of the food, I suspect. Got to have a little something to liven up one's day. Our weather is diabolical, too, so that contributes, I think. Nothing like a bit of crumpet to make you forget the day is foggy and the outlook is for rain. What are you writing about? Indians? Cowboys? Road agents? That sort of thing?"

"Yes, as a matter of fact. But my assignment is rather broad, so anything that might seem interesting to the readers back East is fair game."

"Ah, yes. Got to give them a little adventure with their morning tea. Or should I say coffee? You know, the coffee in this country is appalling. These men I am traveling with actually think they have made coffee if they scatter a few grounds in the pot and pour some hot water over them. I won't miss that, I assure you." He paused for a moment and studied Ethan. "I don't mean to offend you, but I notice that you have some holes in your hat. Is that the style among newsmen?"

"Not really. The moths are very bad this time of year."

"I see. Well, that explains it. Where do you go from here?"

"I think I'll look around here for a while," he said. "Maybe see the border country. Jesús is quite familiar with the area, and he's agreed to be my guide."

"Ha, ha. That's good. Let Jesús be your guide. Sounds like a Baptist hymn. Ha, ha. Bloody good. I once knew a Baptist. Very clean woman, as you might expect. But with an unfortunate tendency toward shrewishness. I pitied her husband. Anyway, this particular Jesús seems like a fine fellow. Have you seen his wife? Very fat. It's remarkable that he has retained his affection for her, but he seems to have managed it. Personally, I lose interest in a woman once they reach a certain poundage. One would rather not be suffocated.

Which reminds me, I heard a story about your General Custer when I was in Wyoming. No one knows exactly how he died, of course, but a Cheyenne I ran across told me that they discovered him on the battlefield and he was still alive, so they sent for the fattest woman in the village and she lifted her skirts and sat on his head until he expired. Rather a poor ending, it seems to me."

Ethan chuckled ruefully. "Yes, and if that story's true, I'm sure his final moments were filled with regret."

"No doubt, no doubt. Rather a harsh lesson. Poor beggar. But he had it coming to him if you ask me. By all accounts he displayed very bad judgment in attacking that village. Of course, that's hindsight." Wentworth paused and then went into a fit of laughter. "Ha. Ha. That's good! Hind sight. Exactly what happened to him. Bloody good! You should use that in one of your stories."

"That's not how the readers want to think about George Custer."

"Yes, I understand. On the other hand, thoughtful people would then fully realize the extent of his brave sacrifice. Think of the headline: Custer Faces Death. Ha, ha. But I understand your point. Too much truth is bad for the weak-minded. Of course, you could take a different tack. Track down the fat Cheyenne and get her side of the story, learn how she felt about the episode. Now, how about another bowl of this excellent stew. What is it you call the stuff? *Menudo?* Damn good."

The two men ate in silence for a minute or so. Wentworth seemed to be puzzling over something.

"I've been trying to place your accent, Mr. Jaeger. I know you're a Yankee, but that's as far as I've got so far. You know, we English are keenly aware of accents. It's one way to tell who's who and what's what. For such a small island, we have an astonishing variation in speech. And I can determine whether a man is a gentleman merely by the way he forms his words. Nothing else is required. And I can usually tell where he comes from. I'm working to be able to do the same thing in this country, but my experience is still limited."

"Well, you were right about my being a Yankee," said Ethan. "I'm from Maine."

"Ah, yes. That would explain it. I haven't met many men from Maine. Haven't quite got the accent down. But that makes sense. Also explains the Navy, I would imagine. Maine is near the sea, I recall. I once considered joining the Navy, but those fellows are gone for months and months, and at the time I was involved with a young lady who was quite attached to me and could not bear to have me away from her side, which was a bit awkward because her husband was rather a wide-awake type from the City. Banker of some sort, I should imagine. Very rich. He was a nasty beggar who confronted her with his suspicions one day—all quite true, of course—but not the sort of thing a gentleman does, you know. Well, he thought about challenging me to a duel, but thought better of it when he heard I had already shot two men for similar misconduct, so he tried to have me beaten by some ruffians, but I settled them. The things we do for love, don't you know. Had it not been for her, I might have been an admiral by now. Their uniforms aren't as dashing as the cavalry, of course, but they do get to see a bit of the world. Well, now that I have located your accent, I have another question for you. I have been admiring your side arms. Would you mind letting me look at one?"

"No, not at all." Ethan handed Wentworth one of his pistols. "These were designed by an Army man named Schofield. Originally the Army version had a seven-inch barrel, but Wells Fargo recently ordered some of these with the five-inch barrel, and I managed to get hold of a couple. They are very fast loading." Ethan showed Wentworth how the gun opened.

"Ah, I see. Breaks open like a shotgun. Very good. Much faster than the Colt Army issue, I can see."

"Yes, very fast."

"Odd that a journalist should worry about speed of loading, though." Wentworth's eyes were twinkling. "Even odder that he should carry two pistols."

"Well, the pursuit of news is sometimes hazardous."

"Yes, apparently so. You did mention the problem with moths earlier on. I see that you only load five chambers. Very sound practice. I've known several men who have dropped their pistols and had them go off. A friend of mine once shot his own servant that way. Just winged him, fortunately. Well, this is a fine gun. Perhaps you'd like to see mine?" Wentworth reached into his jacket and pulled a pistol from a shoulder holster. It was a short-barreled Colt. "They call it a Lightning. Double action, you see. You don't have to cock it each time. Just keep pulling the trigger and the thing will blaze away. Quite good."

"Yes, I can see that."

Wentworth replaced his pistol. "I haven't had to use it too often, but tomorrow's another day. Speaking of which, I am leaving in the morning for Verity. I've been told that the best way to get there is to go south from here almost to the border and then to turn east so as to go around these mountains. Is that what you would advise?"

"I think so. Unless you're in a hurry, there's no sense going through the Santa Ritas. It's a bit shorter, but there's a greater chance of running into Apaches than if you stick to the road. You know they call themselves 'the mountain people.' "

"Yes, I see. Not much different from the Highland

Scots, it seems, although I doubt the Apaches make as good a whiskey. On the other hand, I don't believe Apaches play the bagpipes, so that's in their favor. I have mixed feelings about the Apaches. I'd like to meet one, but not at the cost of being tied down on an anthill, which is one of their favorite ways of treating captives, I understand. Rather one-sided sport, if you ask me, but then so is fox hunting. It's as Jane Austen said, 'One half of the world cannot understand the pleasures of the other.' Do you know Jane Austen's books?"

"As a matter of fact, yes."

"Rather good, I think. I don't suppose you'd like to ride along tomorrow? If you're headed down to the border, we could at least travel together for a while. It's good to have someone to talk to. My men are useful in many ways, but their store of conversation is limited. Also, I had it in mind to stop and have a chat with Pete Kitchen. Do you know him?"

"Not personally. But he's a famous man in these parts. He's been ranching down near the border since before the Civil War, which means he's been fighting Apaches for a long time."

"So I've heard. I thought he might be a useful source of information. And, you know, he might be a good story for you. Just the sort of thing to fascinate your readers."

Ethan considered the suggestion. On the one hand, he didn't want it known in Verity that he was heading into Mexico, and he assumed that Wentworth would discuss meeting Ethan with the people he met there, including Shelby. On the other hand, it wouldn't hurt to travel together through the country between Tubac and the border. Seeing Pete Kitchen would be a good excuse to be going that way.

"Well, that might work out. Pete Kitchen would

make a good story. I think Jesús knows him, and we were planning to leave in the morning."

"Splendid. That way I, too, could let Jesús be my guide for a while, at least. I shall have to write and tell my mother. She will be pleased. She has become very devout recently. I expect to do the same when I am her age. It's as St. Augustine said when he was a young man, 'Oh, Lord, give me chastity but not quite yet,' or words to that effect. He was one of the few interesting saints. Most of the others were very gloomy. Comes from a poor diet, I suspect. Well, I think I will retire. The rooms in this cantina are rather comfortable, don't you think? Not exactly Mayfair, but serviceable. See you in the morning, then."

Wentworth went over to the table where his men were sitting and gave them their instructions for the morning. He was obviously used to being in command and like all experienced and competent commanders, he did not make a show of giving orders. He merely told the men what he expected, and then went on about his business in the perfect confidence that he would be obeyed. He waved at Ethan and Jesús behind the bar, and went to his room.

Ethan thought about Wentworth for a while. He envied the man's easy approach to life, his ability to hold it at arm's length and laugh at it. He just didn't seem to care. Ethan knew he could be wrong about that, though. You never really knew what was in another's mind and heart. On the other hand, he thought, you could get a pretty good idea from the way someone behaved.

Sanchez came over to Ethan's table to remove the bowls. *"Senor,"* he said with a conspiratorial whisper. "I wonder if you would do me a favor. I have decided to take Nariz along with us, if you do not object. He is sometimes useful despite his occasional mishaps. But as I said, Rosa has banished him, and so I have hidden him in your room, so that in the morning I will be able to find him and persuade him to accompany us. Would you mind sharing your room with him tonight?"

"He hasn't brought home any more skunks, has he?"

"No, *señor*. His aroma is strong but not unpleasant, I think. I threw him in the river after the incident with the pigs, so he is clean."

"Well, I guess I can put up with him."

"Thank you, *señor*. Someday he may be of service to us. It cannot hurt to have him along, assuming he can resist his urges."

"That's a big assumption about anyone, Jesús. But it's fine with me if he wants to travel with us."

"Gracias, señor. I will see you in the morning, then. Buenas noches."

"Yes, good night."

Ethan went to his room. There was no light on, and he could hear low growling coming from under the bed.

"Dammit, Nariz, shut up or your hunting days are over as of tonight."

The dog must have recognized Ethan's voice, and he came crawling out from under the bed and rolled on his back and let his tongue loll out. Ethan sat on the floor and patted the dog's stomach.

"I've seen uglier dogs, I guess, but I don't remember when."

Nariz wagged his tail and licked Ethan's hand.

"But good looks aren't everything and, looking on the brighter side, there are still plenty of skunks left to kill. We'll get you out of here tomorrow so you can get started."

* * *

Ethan woke early to the smells coming from Rosa's kitchen. He dressed quickly and shaved, and then went to the livery stable to see about the animals. He packed up his gear on Priam, and then saddled Rangeley and led both animals back to the cantina and tied them to the rail. Then he went in for breakfast. Wentworth was up and out seeing to his men and animals as well, so Sanchez was the only one in the cantina.

"Good morning, *señor,*" he said. "I hope you slept well and that Nariz did not bother you."

"He snores like a buzz saw, but other than that he was all right. I left him in the room so you could find him when we got ready to go."

Sanchez nodded. "That was wise. I have packed my mule with plenty of food. Rosa does not understand the purpose of this trip, but she does understand the purpose of money, so she asks no questions."

Ethan ate a quick breakfast and then went outside. Wentworth was waiting. He was sitting on his horse with one leg thrown over the pommel of his saddle. He was smoking a cheroot and seemed to be enjoying the day. He was dressed more appropriately this morning, and could have been mistaken for a cowboy were it not for the perfection of his mustache, which was brilliantly waxed. He wore a broad hat and flannel shirt and jeans. His pistol was in his shoulder holster, and he had another large Army Colt in his belt. His horse was a beautiful bay, very well cared for and equipped.

"Good morning, Mr. Jaeger. Splendid day for a ride. I have sent my men ahead. If there are any Apaches waiting in ambush, perhaps they will attack them and leave us alone. Ha, ha. By the way, have you noticed that your horse is missing an ear?"

Ethan had to laugh despite the soreness of the subject. "Why, yes. We newsmen are trained observers."

"Quite so. Did he come that way or did he lose it somehow?"

"A fella took a shot at me and hit Rangeley by mistake."

"I see. What happened to this 'fella'?"

"Last time I saw him he was getting real popular with the buzzards."

"Ha, ha! Serves him right, too. Who was the man? An author objecting to one of your reviews? A jealous husband? A noble savage?"

"No, just a common thief, I imagine. We didn't have a chance to exchange biographies."

"Ha, ha. Very good. The term 'noble savage' reminds me again of the Highlands where the country is invested with savage nobles. Or, as Dr. Johnson described the place—a savage land wracked by savage weather inhabited by savage people tending savage sheep. Or something like that. Isn't it interesting how things are connected? You travel around enough and you come to realize that men everywhere are pretty much the same. All rather contemptible. Certain exceptions exist, of course, such as myself and, I hasten to add, you; one would not want even accidentally to insult a journalist who is so well armed. Women, however, are another story. Rather good, as a rule, as long as they are discreet. Where is Jesús?"

"He's getting his horse and pack mule from around back."

Sanchez came around the corner. He was riding his horse and leading a pack mule. He had Nariz tied to a rope, and the dog was dragging his feet and snarling.

"Nasty-looking brute," said Wentworth. "His geneological chart must look like a spider's web."

"Yes, *señor,*" said Jesús. "His ancestry is very colorful. As you can see, he sometimes objects to taking suggestions. But once we are out of town, he will become more agreeable, I think."

"I've known quite a few men like that," said Wentworth. "Well, shall we go?"

They headed south to the border. The morning was still cool, and there were just a few wispy clouds to the west. Mare's tails, they were called. The rest of the sky was so brilliantly blue that it seemed to tint the air. The road south ran through a broad valley. Stark mountain ranges lay along both sides, and the mountains of Mexico were just visible ahead. The Santa Cruz River lay on their left, and although it was a small stream, it supported a line of cottonwoods that stood along its banks and stretched as far as the men could see. To the right, where there was no water, the country was dotted with mesquite trees and cactus. Ahead about two miles they could see the dust from the horses and mules of Wentworth's men.

"Rather easy to see why the old Spanish missionaries came this way," said Wentworth as they rode along slowly. "Just wander north along the valley looking for converts. The river's very convenient for baptisms. No sense climbing around in the mountains when they had this nice flat trail. Think what an accident of geography that is. The Indians who lived in the valley, the Pimas and Papagoes and whatnot, in exchange for a lifetime of labor on the mission farms, get to go to heaven, while the Apaches up in the mountains are apparently destined for hell. All because of geography. Well, it seems a bit hard on the Apaches, although no one told them to live in the mountains, I suppose. What's your opinion, Jesús? Is that fair?"

"I think the Apaches will go to hell in any case, *señor*. Baptism would not help them."

"Perhaps not. But what if the Apaches had lived here in the valley and the Papagoes had lived in the mountains? What then?"

"Then there would not be anyone at all here in this valley. The Apaches would have killed all the priests before they had the opportunity to explain the benefits of baptism. That is what I think."

"Maybe so. It's an interesting question, though. It's like wondering what history would have been like if the French had lived in Germany and the Germans in France. Would French wines be as good with the Germans looking after them? Personally, I doubt it, although a good Moselle is nothing to sneeze at. But would French cooking consist of cabbage and pork? Would German women be fashionable? Hard to imagine. Perhaps there's another world where everything is reversed. What do you think, Jesús?"

"I think you have been travelling a long time, *señor,* and I think you should remember to keep your hat on in this hot sun."

"Ha, ha. Quite so."

When they were about two miles south of town, Jesús released Nariz. The dog immediately dashed off ahead of them and disappeared. Jesús looked at Ethan and shrugged. "Perhaps he intends to meet us at Pete Kitchen's," he said ruefully.

Several hours later they reached Pete Kitchen's ranch. Wentworth's men were camped at the base of a small hill. The ranch house sat on the top of this hill. It was made of adobe bricks and stone, and there were parapets along the sides of the flat roof. The house had obviously been built for defense. The valley surrounding the hill was green and fertile, and Kitchen's cattle were grazing in a meadow near a small creek. Ethan noticed that the man tending the cattle was heavily armed with two pistols and a rifle.

When they rode up to the house, Pete Kitchen came out the front door and greeted them warmly. He was an average-sized man with a small mustache and thinning hair. He was friendly, but there was no lightness about him. He gave the appearance of having seen a great deal.

"Hello there, Jesús. Gents. Welcome to El Potrero. Please step down and come on in. The day's getting warm."

Jesús introduced Ethan and Wentworth, and they went inside. The main room of the ranch house looked like an arsenal. There were rifles and shotguns propped in every corner, and there were heavy shutters on each of the windows. The shutters had firing slits in them, but they were open now, and the sunlight was streaming into the room. The floor was made of heavy Mexican tile. The ceiling was beamed and sturdy-looking. There were some comfortable chairs arranged around the stone fireplace.

"Have a seat, men," said Kitchen. "I imagine you'd like a drink of something to cut the dust." He got out a bottle of tequilla and some glasses and put them on the table. "Help yourselves. Now, what brings you down here?"

"Señor Jaeger is a writer for the newspapers," said Sanchez.

Pete nodded and smiled. "Well, we could use a little help back East, Mr. Jaeger. There's too many people there in the government making policy about things they don't understand."

"That's nothing new, I'm afraid," said Ethan.

"No, that's a fact."

"And Señor Wentworth is visiting this country from England to look for ranch land."

"I see. Well, there's plenty of it around here, Mr. Wentworth. Only trouble is staying alive long enough to raise your beef. Or keeping your beef alive long enough to sell it. And it isn't just beef. I've got some of the finest pigs you'd ever lay an eye on, and the damned Apaches just love to shoot them full of arrows. Waste of arrows and a damned sure waste of pigs, but that's their way."

"Yes, I understand." Ethan noticed that Wentworth had dropped his bantering tone and had become serious. "I've been thinking of looking to the east in the Verity area. What's your opinion of that country?"

Kitchen considered the matter for a moment. "Well," he said finally, "it's good country. Better in some ways than around here. But you'd better be damned sure of the titles to any land you buy. There's one hell of a mess right now around here because of various claims from the old Spanish land grants. Takes years to get some of them sorted out. But aside from that, Verity's a good place to be. They've got it settled pretty well by now, and ever since they put the Chiricahuas on the reservation up in San Carlos two years ago, things have quieted down a little. It's not like the old days, although it's still no place for the faint-hearted. The Apaches break out every once in a while and raise hell. I expect you know Geronimo and Juh are out now. Could be anywhere. And Victorio's still raising Cain over in New Mexico and Chihuahua. Word is he's killed over a thousand people in the last year. Could be an exaggeration, but not by much if I know anything about it, which I do."

"How will it end, do you think?" said Wentworth.

"They'll quit or we'll kill 'em all," said Kitchen. "There's no other answer that I can think of."

"Do you think the Apaches had anything to do with the attack on that Army payroll a little while back?"

said Ethan. "I've been following that story, and people seem to have different opinions about who did it."

"It's possible, although the way I hear it, those soldiers weren't scalped or otherwise bothered, aside from being killed, that is. That's unusual. But it's hard to say."

"Do they always scalp their victims?" asked Wentworth.

"That's been my experience. I expect you saw our little cemetery on your way in today. There's a lot of good people buried in there who were torn up pretty badly, all the result of Apache attacks. I've been fighting them for twenty years, so I know their ways." He paused as though remembering the people he had buried and what they looked like. When he spoke again, it was with a faraway tone in his voice. "A while back a bunch of them came through here on a raid and killed my son. He was my only son. They scalped him, and he was just twelve years old." Kitchen's eyes were dead-looking. He paused for a moment. "His name was Santiago."

The four men were silent. Sadness enveloped Kitchen like a fog, but it was a fog that he had lived in for years and he was accustomed to it.

"So," he said finally. "I don't know who killed those soldiers. In this place it could have been just about anyone."

"Surely all the Apaches aren't alike," said Wentworth. "Haven't you ever run across a good one?"

"You might as well ask if I ever ran across a good mountain lion. Good and bad are white man's categories. They don't apply to Apaches. I guess General Crook would disagree with me. He's used some Apaches for scouts and seems pretty pleased with the results. But I'd sooner rely on a coyote. Speaking of which, Jesús, I saw that dog of yours a little while ago.

He was running like his tail was on fire, heading south."

"Yes. I am not surprised."

"I hope you fellas will stay to dinner and spend the night. Our cook is something special, I promise you."

"We'd appreciate that, Mr. Kitchen," said Wentworth. Jesús and Ethan nodded.

Just then a girl of about ten came running into the room. "Uncle Pedro, Uncle Pedro, there's an Indian on your target hill!"

Pete Kitchen jumped from his chair and ran to the front door. He stepped out on the porch and shielded his eyes as he looked toward the top of a hill about three hundred yards from the house. The other men followed him.

"Son of a bitch," said Kitchen. "Look at that bastard."

The Indian saw the men on the porch, and turned around and lifted his breechcloth, bent over, and slapped his bottom. Kitchen reached inside the front door, grabbed a Winchester, and taking a very quick aim, fired. The Indian pitched forward and fell on the other side of the hill.

"My God, that's a good shot," said Wentworth.

Kitchen nodded grimly. "What that fella didn't realize is I use that hill for target practice on a regular basis. He picked the worst spot he could have to show his ass to me."

The other men had drawn their guns, and were looking to see if there were other Indians around. "I expect he was alone," said Kitchen. "The young ones will do things like that every once in a while. Makes 'em feel important. But that one is finished. I'll lay you odds that bullet went up his ass and came out his ear hole. Tell you what, though, I'd better go on up there and check."

"Mind if I go along?" said Ethan.

"Suit yourself. But the rest of you probably ought to stay close, just in case. There's no sense taking chances. There might be others around. Mr. Wentworth, maybe you could get your men to come up to the house. My boys know what to do when there's shooting, so the ones who are close by will come in, too."

"Yes, I'll go get them," said Wentworth.

"And I will stay here," said Sanchez.

Ethan got his rifle and followed Kitchen. They walked cautiously toward the base of the hill, stopping periodically to listen. But there were no sounds except the rushing of the water in the small creek. They climbed the hill. Each man took a different path to the top. When they reached the summit they found the Indian sprawled on his face, blood seeping from between his legs. They crouched down beside the body watching and listening for several minutes.

"Looks like he was alone, like I figured," said Kitchen finally. "If it was a raiding party, they wouldn't have announced themselves like this." He stood up and examined the body more closely. "About eighteen years old I would guess. Old enough to get some crazy idea in his mind and then act on it by himself. Probably was up on the reservation one night and just took it into his head to go out and raise a little hell and maybe steal a mule while he was at it."

"Apache?"

"Yep." The Indian was lean and brown. He wore a red bandanna tied around his head. It was the same sort of bandanna that Ethan had found at the burned-out Army wagon. That was his only garment aside from his breechcloth and knee-length moccasins. Ethan could smell the wood smoke in the Apache's hair, and he wondered whether it came just from last night's campfire or was the accumulation of a short lifetime of fires.

The wood smoke was mixed with the smell of blood and exposed viscera. It was the kind of smell that got in your nostrils and stayed there for a while.

"Well," said Kitchen. "I hope he enjoyed his joke."

There was a short bow and a quiver of arrows lying on the ground nearby. Kitchen gathered them up. "More stuff for the collection," he said.

"What shall we do with him?"

"Leave him here for the time being. If there's any more around they'll want to get his body, for sure. If he's still here in the morning, we'll know he was alone. Then we'll bury him."

"What about the coyotes?"

"I ain't sentimental, Mr. Jaeger."

"Call me Ethan."

"Okay. And I'm Pete. But I still ain't sentimental. Well, let's get on back to the house and let the people know that it's pretty much all clear. I'll post a guard on the roof just in case, but I don't think there's any more around."

The two men started down the hill.

"You know, Pete, I was looking around at that place in the mountains where the Army patrol was attacked, and I found a red bandanna like the one that Apache was wearing."

"Really? Well, you could see it's just red cloth. Could have come from an Indian, or it could have been off a soldier's neckerchief. Hard to say."

"I suppose. While we're on the subject, have you heard any rumors about Juan Lopez operating north of the border? I mean, could someone like Lopez have been involved in that robbery, do you think?"

"Lopez?" Kitchen thought about it for a minute. "Well, like I said, anything's possible, but I doubt Lopez would take the chance. I know him a little. He doesn't like gringos, but I'm married to a Mexican woman and all my hands are Mexicans, so I'm only half gringo in his eyes, and he's always left me alone. There's no doubt he's an old bandit and worse. And a few years ago he would have been a prime suspect. He used to be a terror on the Spanish Trail stealing horses in California and driving them east. He once ran a herd of over a thousand head from Los Angeles all the way to Santa Fe. And he was involved in the slave trade, too, buying or kidnapping Paiute and Navajo children and selling them off down in Sonora and Chihuahua. He was partnered up with the Utes in that business for a while. The Utes were famous slavers in those days, you know. But since the war Lopez has stayed pretty much south of the border. I hear he raids into Texas and New Mexico now and then, but generally he takes the cattle back down to Mexico and sells them there. I doubt he'd pull something like the payroll job. He's too rich and respectable now. But you never know. Army payroll is pretty tempting, and like I say, he doesn't care much for gringos. But I haven't heard any rumors to that effect, and I imagine I would have if he'd been involved. Word gets around. Tell you what, though, you want to know about Lopez, just ask your friend Jesús." Kitchen smiled slyly and nodded at Ethan. "That old boy knows more than most about the doin's of Juan Lopez. He may be a little fat and a little old now, but he wasn't always that way."

Fourteen

The next morning Wentworth was ready to leave for Verity.

"Well, gents," he said to Ethan and Jesús, "I have enjoyed knowing you, and I hope that we'll meet again sometime. Perhaps in the hereafter, but perhaps before that. One hopes so, at any rate. And Ethan, if I can find a way to shoot this fellow Shelby for you, I will be happy to do it. Open up the field, don't you know. And I promise to stay away from the wife. As I said before, I wouldn't ever want to offend a newsman who carries two pistols and wears a moth-eaten hat." Wentworth winked and laughed and then rode off after his men, who had already started down the road to the east.

"I think Señor Wentworth is a little crazy," said Jesús. "Half the time I have difficulty understanding him. The other half I do not understand him at all."

"He's an Englishman," said Ethan.

"Yes. I suppose that is the source of the trouble."

The two men said good-bye to Kitchen and then headed south. When they had ridden a couple of miles, Ethan pulled up and dismounted.

"I think it's time to get into costume, Jesús. If I'm going to be a Mexican, I'd better start looking like one."

"Yes, that is wise."

Ethan dug into his packs and pulled out an old serape and a straw sombrero. He put his other hat into the pack. "This won't do my hat any good, but it's looking a little used anyway."

"Yes, *señor.* I noticed the bullet holes, but I did not want to say anything about them."

"Yes, it's a strange country, Jesús. People go around taking shots at other people's hats. If I weren't such an easygoing fella, I might resent it."

Jesús nodded glumly. "I wonder what happened to the man who made those holes, *señor.*"

"He's seen the errors of his ways, Jesús."

"You are a strange man, *señor,* if you don't mind my saying so."

"It's been said before, Jesús. Well, how do I look? Will I pass?"

"Yes, *señor,* as long as you let me do the talking."

"Bueno. Vamos!"

Sanchez rolled his eyes. *"Ay, madre mia."*

In less than an hour they were in Sonora. The country ahead looked mountainous and very dry, for they had left the river valley, which veered off to the east. The road was little more than a trail, but it was relatively flat and easygoing.

"How long do you think it will take us to get there, Jesús?"

"About two days, *señor.* There is a little village about halfway, and there is a cantina. At least there used to be. I am hoping that we can spend the night there."

"Sounds good. It beats sleeping outside. You know, Pete Kitchen said a funny thing when we were checking on that Apache. He said you know more about Juan Lopez than you let on. What do you suppose he meant by that?"

Sanchez sighed resignedly. "Well, *señor,* a man does many things when he is young, and when he is no longer young he sometimes looks back on those things with regret. It is difficult to be good always. Sometimes a man's unfortunate urges take control of him, and he falls into bad ways. So it was with me."

"I see. Well, well."

"Yes, *señor.* But I have reformed, I assure you."

"I believe that, Jesús. But what does this mean? Did you ride with Lopez in those faraway years? Were you a bandit?"

"I was his cook, *señor.* Lopez is a man who enjoys his pleasures, and even on the outlaw trail he was careful to eat well. He believes that it is the secret to contentment. 'Women and money,' he used to say 'are very good things, but a man can do without them and still be happy. But an empty stomach will always make him miserable.' That was his philosophy, *señor.* Of course, he always was careful to have the women and the money, too, so his theories were never put to the test with any thoroughness. But we knew each other from when we were boys, and he knew that I was a good cook, so he asked me to go with him on some of his trips, and I did. I thought of myself as a cook only and not a bandit. It is true that now and then I may have helped him and the others collect some horses and cattle that did not belong to us, but I regarded this as just being helpful. I know now of course that this was wrong, but at the time it did not seem that way. But I never hurt anyone, *señor,* because as I have told you, I am a poor shot unless the person is willing to stand still, and the people who chased us now and then were always riding very fast after us, and I always missed. For that I am grateful. Now you know my secret, *señor.*"

"Yes, well, it seems you're a deep one, Jesús. But I think this is actually good news, assuming that you and Lopez are still on good terms."

"Oh, yes, *señor.* When I collected enough money to buy my cantina, I went to him and asked his permission to leave, which he granted happily. He said he would miss my *frijoles,* but he understood that a man must follow his ideas. That was many years ago, but that should not matter. And as I have said, my Rosa and I have visited her niece who took my place, although she does not go on his trips for business. So I have seen him a few times since my retirement. He was always very happy to see me. I did not think it necessary to tell you this, *señor,* because I hoped you would forget the idea of this visit. But since we are going there now . . ." Sanchez shrugged and smiled. "Well, *señor,* what do you think of your friend now?"

"I think that foxes come in many shapes and sizes, Jesús."

They rode along in silence for a while as Ethan considered this new information. Now and then Sanchez would glance at him as if trying to gauge his mood. After a few more minutes of thinking about what Sanchez had told him, Ethan made his decision.

"You know, Jesús, I was raised a Presbyterian, but one of the things that always appealed to me about your religion is this notion that confession is good for the soul."

"That is true, *señor.* I feel better that you know about my past and that you do not think worse of me for it. At least that is my hope."

"No need to worry about that. And since my own soul could maybe use a little brightening up, I'm going to make a confession, too. You see, I'm not really a newspaper man. I'm a detective, a Pinkerton, and I'm looking into this robbery of the Army payroll."

Sanchez's eyes grew wide, and then he smiled broadly. "Ah, I see, *señor.* That explains many things. Such as why you insisted on going through the pass where the attack occurred. I understand it now." Then his mood suddenly changed. *"Madre mia.* I am taking a detective to Juan Lopez! This is not a good thing for either of us, *señor.* In fact, it is very bad. Juan Lopez does not like gringos—excuse me, Americans—to begin with, and he especially does not like the police, except those who are on his payroll, which is a considerable number here in Mexico, but not across the border. And if you think that he was somehow involved in this attack on the Army, then it is especially bad to be coming into his country. I think we should turn around while there is still time."

"I understand your point, but I don't think there's any danger. Let me tell you what my plan is, and if after that you still want to go back, well, that is your decision."

Sanchez looked gloomy, but shrugged. "As you wish, *señor.* But I feel bad things will happen."

"There's not much doubt about the fact that Lopez was involved somehow. Some American money that was probably part of the payroll showed up down here. He used it to pay off some of his men, and one of them came through Verity and spent it there. So, the question is, how did he come up with that money? The second thing we know is that the Curtains were also involved in some way, because the Army horses that were stolen in the raid showed up at their ranch, which is right on the border. And they shot Tomas because he stumbled on the horses hidden in a valley on their land."

"It grows worse and worse, *señor*. It is obvious that Lopez stole the money and the Army horses and sold them to the Curtains on his way back to Mexico."

"Or maybe the Curtains were involved in the raid."

"I doubt it, *señor*. As I said, Lopez, because of his unreasonable attitude toward Americans, would never associate with people like the Curtains. I do not mean to speak ill of the dead, but the Curtains were exactly the kind of gringos that Lopez despises. He would not work with them, although he might be willing to relieve himself of the encumbrances of the horses as he made his escape back to Mexico. That would be like him."

"Yes, that's possible. But the Curtains were dirt-poor. Petty rustlers. Where would they come up with the money to buy the horses? Why would Lopez bother to sell them, when he could bring them back to Mexico and sell them here? He is used to driving stock long distances, and there was no one on his trail at the time."

"I cannot say, *señor*."

"No, it doesn't make sense to me either. But one thing is clear, we have to find out how Lopez got ahold of that payroll money."

"I notice that you use the word 'we,' *señor*."

"Yes, I hope that you will help me, Jesús."

"*Madre mia*. But suppose the money did not come from the Army? Suppose Lopez came upon it through some other means? Perhaps he robbed a bank. He often used to talk about robbing a bank in Texas. It was one of his ambitions. Why attack the Army, in which there is a chance of being shot, when he could simply ride into a Texas town with his men and steal everything there in comfort and safety?"

"That's a possibility. But I have to be sure one way or the other. And there's no other way to do it than to go there and look around. Since he knows you, you might be able to find out where the money came from."

"Me! *Chihuahua, señor.* This looks worse and worse."

"Well, that may not be necessary. Have you ever heard of a man called John Wesley Hardin?"

"Yes, *señor.* He is a bad man from Texas. A *pistolero.*"

"That's right. He's in jail now, so I am going to adopt his name and present myself to Lopez as a man who wants to join him. Hardin is well known as a man who hates the government. He made his reputation killing soldiers just after the war. He is exactly the sort of man who would look to Lopez as a patron, and although he is a gringo, his reputation might make him acceptable to Lopez."

"But suppose Lopez knows this Hardin or has seen him."

"It's a possibility, but I don't think it's likely. In the meantime, I'll travel along with you in this disguise until we get to Lopez. You can tell him that I came to Tubac and heard that you used to ride with Lopez, and asked you to take me down to him and that I paid you for it, so you took the job simply to make a little easy money. You have no other stake in the matter. Surely he wouldn't resent that."

Sanchez thought about it for a minute. "No," he said finally. "I do not think he would resent it if I brought some gringo *pistolero* to him. He could always kill you if he wanted to, and it would not matter to me, having been paid. He would know that I understood that when I brought you."

"That's right."

"But suppose that is what happens, *señor?* What then?"

"Then you go back to Rosa and have her say a prayer for me." Ethan smiled, but he was serious and Sanchez understood that.

"What if Lopez knows that this Hardin is in jail?"

"People break out of jail all the time, Jesús. What better reason to be coming to Mexico?"

Jesús nodded. "Well, *señor,* I suppose your plan could work. But I fear for myself. Not that I will be in danger from Lopez, because I do not think he would harm me for bringing this Hardin to him. But for the possibility that I might do something that will place you in danger and lead to some sad ending. Suppose I am faced with a terrible choice and I somehow betray you? What then?"

"That does not worry me, Jesús."

"No. But it worries me, *señor.*" Jesús shook his head and looked doubtful. But then, after a few moments, he started chuckling ruefully.

"What's the matter, Jesús?"

"Nothing, *señor.* I was just thinking about what you said before about foxes. And I was also thinking that I hope these two foxes do not fall prey to the hounds."

"Me, too."

They rode along through the desert, and Ethan continued to refine his plan and explain his ideas to Jesús. By the time they reached the outskirts of a small village where Jesús knew of the cantina, they had worked out how they would proceed.

The village was little more than a collection of adobe huts. There was a small white church at the end of the street, and a cistern filled with water in the middle of the small square. The cantina sat in the square opposite the church. There were chickens scratching in the dust outside the cantina, and some small boys were playing in a mud puddle near the cistern. Aside from that, the village was quiet. Ethan and Jesus tied their animals to the hitching post outside the cantina, and were about to go inside when there was a sudden commotion. A woman was screaming somewhere behind one of the houses, and a second later a dog came running around the corner. The woman was chasing him. She was holding a stick in her hand and running as fast as she could, but the dog easily outpaced her. The dog had a chicken in his mouth, and did not pause when he saw Ethan and Jesús, instead dashing out of town leaving a trail of dust and a distraught Mexican woman in his wake. The small boys left their puddle and took up the chase, and soon there was general shouting and chaos in the village. A man, probably the woman's husband, came around the corner with a shotgun and fired at the dog. The shot kicked up some dust well behind him. The man fired again and missed again, and then started swearing and shaking his fist.

"Madre mia," said Jesús. He watched the dog disappear to the north. "He is a very fast runner even carrying a chicken. It is a good thing he did not stop to say hello, for I would have had to deny him." Jesús looked sheepish, but Ethan started laughing.

"He's getting lazy, though, Jesús. He's given up hunting in favor of stealing."

The shots brought another man running out of the cantina. He had a pistol in his hand, but soon understood the situation and put it away. He too started laughing, and then went back inside.

Jesús looked surprised when he saw the man, and he whispered to Ethan. "I know that man, *señor.* He is one of Lopez's vaqueros."

"That's good. It'll give us a chance to try out our act, and maybe we can pick up a little information."

Jesús nodded, but he looked a little doubtful. "Well,

I suppose if we are going to be exposed, it is better that this man should do it than Juan Lopez. That I am sure of."

They took their animals to a small corral behind the cantina, for there was no livery stable in the village. They unsaddled their horses and removed the packs from the mules. A small boy was watching them as they unpacked, and Ethan offered him a dollar if he would watch their things that night. The boy accepted eagerly.

"I do not think we have to worry too much about our packs, *señor,"* said Jesús. "The people in this town are pretty honest. You can tell that from their poverty. The two things often go together. And besides, Juan Lopez has the lock on dishonesty in this country. He would not welcome any competition even on a small scale."

"I understand. Still, it won't hurt to have someone keeping an eye out. He can give a yell if he sees something."

They went into the cantina. It was just one room with a low ceiling made of saguaro spines. The floor was dirt packed down hard by years of wear. There was a small bar at one end of the room, and a tired-looking bartender stood behind it gazing at nothing. The only light came from a small kerosene lamp on the bar. There was no one in the cantina except the vaquero, who was sitting at one of the two tables. He had a bottle of tequila and a glass in front of him. He was a big man dressed in an embroidered jacket and white shirt and pants that had silver disks running down the outside of the leg. He wore heavy Spanish-style spurs with rowels the size of silver dollars. His gun belt was well polished and expensively inlaid with silver. His hair was long and combed straight back from his face. He was clean-shaven except for a wispy mustache. He looked up when Ethan and Jesús walked in. At first he did not recognize Jesús, but then he jumped to his feet and grinned and held out his arms.

"Jesús! Have you come back to us? What's the matter? Has Rosa spent all your money?" He hugged Jesús and slapped him on the back.

"*Olla,* Joaquin. I am happy to see you. No, Rosa is better at saving than spending. I am here on a little business, that's all."

"*Bueno.* Come sit with me. Have a drink." He looked at Ethan. "Come, both of you." He called to the bartender. "José, bring two more glasses. Now, Jesús, what sort of business are you doing here? And who is your friend?"

Ethan could see Jesús pause, as if he were unsure of his lines. But then he seemed to change suddenly, to fall back into an old habit of speaking and thinking. The friendly, somewhat shy, cantina owner disappeared and the bandit that he had been took his place.

"The two things are related, Joaquin. This man is the business. I am taking him to meet Juan Lopez. His name is Wes Hardin."

Joaquin looked at Ethan. "A gringo. Why would you take a gringo to see Juan Lopez?"

"Because he paid me."

Joaquin nodded. "Does he speak Spanish?"

"Why don't you ask me that question?" said Ethan.

"Ah, *bueno,*" said Joaquin. "Your Spanish is very good, although your accent is terrible. Who taught you? An Apache?"

"I just picked it up."

"I see." Ethan watched as Joaquin decided how he would proceed. He was a little drunk, and that made him more unpredictable. Jesús was watching, too.

"Señor Hardin is a well-known *pistolero* from Texas," Jesus said finally. His tone was matter of fact, as though well-known *pistoleros* were not that uncommon. Joaquin stared at Ethan but said nothing. If the name meant anything to him, he did not show it.

"If you are such a famous *pistolero,* why are you dressed like a peon?" he said finally.

Ethan stared back at him. The other man's black eyes were clear despite the tequila he had drunk. "Why is a rattlesnake the color of stones?"

Joaquin smiled and nodded. But there was no merriment in his smile; it was more like a snarl, and Ethan could feel a sense of growing menace. The other man poured some tequila for himself. Then he filled Ethan's and Jesús's glasses. Then he looked at Ethan. "You know, that sombrero makes you look like a farmer. A peasant."

Ethan said nothing. Joaquin thought about something for a while. He drained his glass and slammed it on the table. Then he refilled it. "I hate gringos," he said finally. "What do you think of that?"

"I don't like 'em much myself," said Ethan.

"Eh? But you are a gringo."

"I make an exception for myself. And my mother."

"Ha, ha. A gringo with a sense of humor. That is good. But you know, Señor Pistolero, what is even worse than a gringo is a Tejano, a gringo from Texas. I hate them worst of all. What do you think of that, Señor Tejano?" Joaquin was leaning forward. His face was just a foot or so away from Ethan's. "I said, what do you think of that?"

Ethan paused before he answered. He was staring at the other man, and he knew that his eyes were dead-looking because he saw it in the other man's reaction. Ethan could see the sudden flicker of doubt.

"Here is what I think, Joaquin," said Ethan quietly. "I think that your hands are on the table wrapped around a tequila glass and that mine are under the table wrapped around a pistol butt." The other man's eyes grew wider, and he leaned away. "Now, listen to this sound carefully," said Ethan. He pulled back the hammer. *Click.* The hammer was at half-cock. *Click.* Now it was fully cocked. "So, Joaquin, now it's your turn to tell me, what do you think of that?"

Joaquin thought about his predicament for a moment and then smiled sheepishly. "You know, *señor,* I think that some Tejanos are better than others. In fact, I am growing very fond of one in particular."

"That's good, because I imagine that you're also pretty fond of your *cojones,* and it would be a shame for you to have to leave them in that chair when you go home tonight."

"I agree wholeheartedly, *señor.*"

"Bueno," said Jesús. "I think we understand one another now. There is no reason that we cannot be friends, I think."

"None whatever," said Joaquin. "I only wish I had more time to spend with you, *señores,* but unfortunately I have to be going soon. In fact, almost immediately." He smiled and shrugged resignedly.

"That is a shame," said Ethan. "We were hoping that you could tell us a little about Juan Lopez's business. I am going there to offer my services, and it would be useful to know more about what he is doing these days. It has been a while since Jesús rode with him."

"Ah, I see. Well, *señor,* the business is much the same as it has always been. You remember how it was, Jesús. You gather from one place and sell to another. It is a simple formula. And it works regardless of what your product is—cattle, horses, sheep. Even pigs, although they are difficult to drive."

"How about money?" said Ethan. "Does the formula work with money?"

"I can see you have something to learn, *señor,* with all due respect to the pistol pointed at my *huevos.* The object is to get money. If you already have it, you do not need to worry about gathering products in one market and selling them in another, do you see?"

"You mean you don't get involved in stealing money directly?"

"Oh, from time to time when the chance offers itself, if someone wanders by, well, yes, we will lift a purse now and then, but that is not our specialty. We are in the horse and cattle business. Even in the days when Juan Lopez was selling Indian slaves, it was the same principle. Gather stock in one place, drive it somewhere else where there is demand, and sell it. Is that not so, Jesús? You were there in the old days in California. It has not changed much."

"It has always been that way, yes," said Jesús. "But the times are changing, and I thought perhaps Juan Lopez was changing with them. He always spoke of wanting to rob gringo banks. That is why I thought he might want to meet Señor Hardin."

"Well, you understand how that is. A man has ambitions, yes, but when business is already very good, it is hard to find the time to go into other fields. What would be the point? Aside from the mere fact of doing something different. Besides, you will not believe this, Jesús, but Juan Lopez is growing mellow. He talks often about even marrying so that his children can become legitimate. Of course, his problem is deciding which woman to marry, for he cannot marry them all. He is not a Mormon, after all. Still, it is something that he would not have considered in the years past. And he is not working so many hours. He is letting others do the work, such as myself. It is a good thing. He has even taken up fishing. You are surprised. But it is true, I assure you. You know that stream that is near the hacienda? Well, it is full of trout, and every day he is out there. That shows you how things are. You will find him somewhat changed, I think, Jesús. But of course, underneath he is the same. Not a man to underestimate."

"I am glad to hear this, Joaquin," said Jesús. "As you can imagine, I had some reservations about bringing an American to him, knowing his attitudes."

"Oh, in his heart he still feels much the same way. But he has had more dealings with gringos during the last few years, and he has learned to tolerate them. I do not think he will resent your coming, Señor Hardin."

"That is good to hear," said Ethan. "But I am disappointed about the banks. I had hoped he was interested in that business, too."

"Well, perhaps you can convince him. He is a reasonable man. Well, amigos, I must be going." Joaquin stood up, and Ethan brought his gun hand out from under the table and, still holding the pistol, rested his hand on the tabletop. The Schofield was still cocked. Joaquin looked at the pistol and smiled.

"That is a large pistol, *señor.* I am very glad we were able to understand each other before something unfortunate happened."

"I am, too, Joaquin. It is always good to make a new friend."

"*Adios,* Jesús. And to you also, Señor Hardin. With luck, we will meet again. As amigos, I hope."

"Yes. *Adios.*"

Joaquin left the cantina. Ethan swiveled his chair around so that his back would be against the wall and he would be facing the doorway of the cantina.

"I understand your precautions, *señor,*" said Jesus. "But I do not think you need to worry about Joaquin. He is not the sort of man to come rushing back in here firing off his pistol. It is not his way."

"What is his way? To shoot at us from an alley?"

"Oh, no, *señor.* He would regard that as cowardly. He is actually a friendly sort. He was just a little drunk. But he is famous for not liking gunfights. I don't think he has ever fired a gun at someone except when he was absolutely sure of hitting him, although many times he has been shot at by posses, especially across the border. But he is a strange man in this way. He practices many hours with his shooting, and he is a very good shot, but he is also a perfectionist, and I have seen him many times aim and aim and aim at someone but never pull the trigger because he hates to miss. He is not a coward. Far from it. I have seen him cut off a man's hand with a bowie knife and then kick the unfortunate to death. Give him a knife and he will fight like a tiger. But he has this strange reluctance to shoot if he thinks he might miss. In this he is the opposite of myself, for I shoot often and rarely hit, while he shoots rarely but never misses. But he would regard dueling with you as a very poor set of odds. I know him, *señor.*"

Ethan let down the hammer on his pistol, but he left it on the table. "Still, it doesn't hurt to be cautious."

"No, *señor,* you are right about that."

They drank their tequila in silence. Something apparently was bothering Sanchez. He was lost in thought and he looked sorrowful, suddenly.

"What's the matter, Jesús? You look gloomy. You remind me of Sep Harding after he's had a bad pepper."

Jesús smiled wanly. "There are no bad peppers, *señor,* only those that are not so good. In that they are like tequila and women. All three have a bite, but the overall effect is generally a good one, unless, of course, a man has too many. Too many peppers, too much tequila. These are bad things."

"How about too many women?"

"Less bad, *señor.*"

Ethan laughed. "And to think I am listening to a married man."

"Yes, well, it is not possible to have too many women, because God has given men a regulating feature to help us against too much temptation. A man can eat two dozen peppers, but no man has two dozen women at one time."

"What would Rosa say about this philosophy of yours?"

"She would agree, because she is aware of the regulating feature from experience. And as the years go past, the regulating becomes more noticeable." He let out a long sigh.

"Well, at least she is not jealous."

"Yes. She used to be, but happily, she has progressed from jealousy to tortillas. It is natural. Women have these stages, like men. That is what is bothering me. The thought of Juan Lopez going fishing instead of raiding is a depressing one."

"There's nothing wrong with fishing, Jesús. I like it myself."

"Truly? I thought of it as a sport for old men. Of course, there is not much opportunity in the desert, so I know nothing about it. But the idea has no appeal. And then there was the business of Nariz stealing the chicken. Once he was a great hunter, but now he is progressing from skunks to pigs to chickens. The next thing you know, he will find some she wolf and have a litter of pups and then spend the rest of his days lying in the dust outside the cantina. It is a sad prospect. It reminds me of myself. Once I followed the bandit trail, as a cook, granted, but still, as an active man. Now I while away the days polishing glasses. It makes me melancholy to notice all these things. It seems the road of a man must always go downhill after a point."

"Maybe. But we've still got some miles left in us,

Jesús. After all, you're helping me investigate a crime. That's as good as cattle rustling, I think."

Jesús brightened up a little. "Yes. That's true. And you know, *señor,* I think our plan will work. You were very convincing in your act. And your Spanish was better than I thought it would be, although your accent is very bad, as Joaquin said. I hope you will forgive me for saying so. But what you said was very convincing. It was hard even for me to tell that you were not serious about shooting off Joaquin's *huevos.*"

"But I was serious, Jesús. That's the secret of good acting."

Jesús nodded glumly. "Well, if Joaquin should see Juan Lopez before we do, I am sure he will prepare the way for us. And now that I know Lopez has taken up fishing, I am less worried about our plan."

Fifteen

The next day they continued south. The road was flat and dusty, and the heat was oppressive. The sun glanced off the rocks and sand and radiated upward into their faces. Dust devils swirled like miniature tornadoes on both sides of the road. Giant saguaro cactus were scattered everywhere along the hillsides and beside the road. Some of them were twenty feet tall, with contorted arms that pointed in all directions like madmen giving directions. Here and there were thickets of mesquite bushes. And now and then Ethan would notice a longhorn staring malevolently out at them from the thickets.

"Juan Lopez's cattle," said Jesús.

"I wouldn't want the job of rounding up those critters."

"Nor me, *señor*. The life of a vaquero is full of such unpleasantness. Running a cantina may be dull, but it is relatively safe, as long as when people get drunk and fight they only kill each other."

"How far do you figure we have to go, Jesús?"

"By this evening we should be near the turn to Juan

Lopez's house," said Jesús. "He lives at the base of those mountains that we can see to the southeast, in the foothills where it is cool and where there are trees and water. The grass is very good there, too. In many ways it is like the Verity valley."

"It will be good to get away from this heat. And I expect the animals will be glad to get off this hardpack." Ethan turned to check on Priam. He was plodding along without effort, it seemed.

They rode in silence for a while. Jesús was obviously thinking about something.

"I wonder what became of Nariz," he said finally. "I don't think that peasant hit him with the shotgun, but perhaps a pellet or two kicked up and got him in the backside. If so, perhaps he has become discouraged with our project and has returned home."

"Well, so far he hasn't been much use to us."

"I do not mean to disagree with you, *señor,* but you must remember that if Nariz had not stolen the chicken, we would not have noticed Joaquin until we went into the cantina, and we might have been caught off guard. Who knows what could have happened? As it was, things went perfectly."

"You figure Nariz stole that chicken just to create a diversion?"

"No. Perhaps not. But I do think that there are causes and effects, and this good effect was partially the result of Nariz. I do not wish to give him too much credit, for I know he has been of only marginal value lately. But there is no denying that he has been of some help to us." Jesús sighed and shook his head. "I wish you had known him in the old days, *señor.* He had no equal then."

"Well, there's still nobody quite like him, Jesús."

"Ah, thank you, *señor,* for saying so."

They reached the turning in the road about midafternoon. From there the road began to climb gradually out of the desert into the foothills. They left behind the saguaro and mesquite thickets and came into the grasslands, vast meadows of yellow grass dotted with live oaks and cut here and there by washes and small grassy-sided canyons. There were animals grazing wherever they looked, longhorns, mostly, but there were some other breeds that looked like variations on the longhorn theme, as well as horses of every possible color, all well conditioned and sleek-looking, and a few scruffy gray burros mixed in here and there.

"Looks like Juan Lopez doesn't favor any particular kind of stock."

"No, *señor*. When it comes to cattle and horses, his only requirement is that they start life as someone else's property. Beyond that, he has no prejudices."

They rode for another hour or so, and then stopped to rest and water the animals near a small spring. There was some shade from a stand of cottonwoods, and the water was clear and very cold.

From there they could see something white gleaming on a mountaintop about five miles away.

"Juan Lopez's hacienda," said Jesus. "Very beautiful. Now, *señor*, I have been thinking. The best way to introduce you to Juan Lopez would be for me to go to him alone and explain the situation. You could wait here. If I can find him immediately, I will come back for you. If not, or if he is too busy to see me, I will stay the night and come back for you in the morning."

"It's a good plan, Jesús. I'll wait here with the pack animals. You know what to say to Lopez, I think."

"Yes, *señor*. We had a good rehearsal with Joaquin. Now I am confident of my lines. I worry, though, about leaving you here with the possibility that some vaqueros could discover you."

"I can take care of myself, Jesús. But if it'll make

you happy, I won't build a fire if I have to stay here tonight."

"Yes, that would be best. But I hope I can return tonight, and if I am to do that I had better leave now." Jesús mounted up.

"Just one more thing." Ethan went to his saddlebags and retrieved the wanted poster he had Sep Harding print. "Here. This might help the story."

Jesús stared at the poster. *"Madre mia,* this man looks just like you, *señor!* How is this possible, that such a coincidence . . . Ah, I see. *Bueno.* Yes, this will help. I will be back as soon as I can. *Adios."*

"Adios, Jesús. Good luck."

Sanchez did not return that night. Ethan unpacked Priam and Jesús's mule and hobbled them, but he left Rangeley saddled, although he loosened the cinch. "Sorry, old boy, but we may need to get out of here in a hurry." He did not bother to put up his hammock. He stretched his sleeping blanket on the ground and then lay down. He chewed on some jerky and listened to the animals grazing and to the sounds of the little spring creek. There was a hatch of mayflies just coming off the creek. The delicate insects had struggled to the surface of the water, and now were flying into the evening to begin their mating rituals, and even as they were pairing, violet green swallows were darting in among them and plucking them from the air. In the distance Ethan could hear a Gambel's quail calling to the others in his covey to come together for the night. And then he heard the howl of a coyote who had also been listening for quail. "The hunters and the hunted," he said out loud. Then he allowed himself to think about Danielle Shelby and their day of hunting, and he wondered where she was at that moment and what she was doing.

Maybe she and Shelby were entertaining the Englishman, Wentworth, right then. Ethan could picture her in her white dress. He thought of the way her diamonds looked around her throat, and remembered the scent of her perfume. *Maybe Wentworth really will find a reason to shoot him,* he thought half seriously. *That'd be lucky. Course then I might have to fight Wentworth for her. But by God it would be worth it.* In one sense he was joking to himself. In another, he wasn't.

Jesus returned early the next morning.

"Buenos dias, señor," he said. "I am sorry to leave you here last night, but Juan Lopez has some guests staying there. Some high officials. So I was not able to see him until this morning. Happily, he is an early riser."

"How did it go?"

"Very well, *señor.* He was very glad to see me. Even more so than he would have been in the old days. This is because of the mellowing that Joaquin told us about. It is quite true, although he is still a serious man. That I can assure you."

"What did you tell him about me?"

"Just what we agreed, that you were John Wesley Hardin, a famous *pistolero,* and that you were on the run—I showed him the wanted poster, and he was impressed—and that you were coming to him with some ideas which you would only discuss with him, that I was paid for bringing you here but that I thought you were someone he should see, even though you are a gringo."

"Bravo, Jesús."

"Yes. Anyway, he is willing to see you, *señor,* today at noon."

"That is good. Just right. Thank you, Jesús."

"You are welcome, but I must tell you, *señor,* that I enjoyed myself. It was good to see Juan Lopez again, and also good to be playing a part. It was like the old days before I was an honest owner of a cantina. It was a fine feeling. But there is something I would like to recommend."

"What's that?"

"I think you should see Juan Lopez alone—without me, I mean. It will strengthen the impression that I have merely brought you here for a price. That is something that Juan Lopez understands. If I appeared to be your sponsor, though, he would wonder, and we do not want him to wonder, *señor,* believe me."

"That makes sense. Maybe you can visit with Rosa's niece while I see Lopez."

"That was my idea, too. It will seem natural, yes?"

"Yes. You know, you're getting good at this kind of thing, Jesús. Next thing you know, you'll be a full-fledged confidence man."

"Thank you, *señor.* It is kind of you to say so. And now I think we should build a fire and have some breakfast. We are under Juan Lopez's protection, so there is no danger from his vaqueros."

After breakfast they loaded up their animals and headed for the hacienda. Juan Lopez's house stood on the top of a foothill near the base of some mountains that were part of the Sierra Madres. The house was white with a red tile roof. It was surrounded by a high wall, also painted white and obviously built for defense. Men with rifles were sitting on the wall at various strategic spots. Ethan and Jesús rode through the main gate and into the courtyard and dismounted. Two boys dressed in loose white shirts and trousers took their horses and mules and led them to the corral outside the main wall.

The courtyard was made of gravel and it was well swept and smooth. There was a well in the middle, and a fountain. These were decorative, but Ethan knew their real purpose was to provide water to the house in the event of a siege. The veranda was made of sautillo tiles that were highly polished, and it was covered by a tile roof that was supported by thick wooden beams. The main door to the house was heavy mesquite wood, and it looked as though it could withstand a cannon shot. The walls of the house were thick and the windows small and shuttered. The shutters had firing slits in them, and they too were made of heavy mesquite.

"This place is a fortress," said Ethan.

"Yes. In the old days the Apaches were even worse than they are today. And a man in Juan Lopez's business sometimes makes enemies. So it is good to have a well-made house."

Jesús knocked on the door, and an Indian woman opened it.

"Hello, Lupe," said Jesús. "This is Señor Hardin who is going to meet with the Patrón at noon today." The woman nodded and gestured to Ethan to come inside. "I will leave you now, *señor,* as we discussed," Jesús said. "I will be close by, however."

Ethan followed the woman into the main room. It was rather dark, because most of the shutters were partially closed. The room was very large and cool. The ceiling was high and made of heavy beams and dark, grooved boards. The walls were white and clean and covered here and there with tapestries and paintings, dark renderings of Biblical disasters and martyrdoms, all framed in heavy gilt. There was a fireplace at one end of the room, and above the fireplace the massive

head of a buffalo. The furniture was all leather and
dark wood and very well made. The floor was tiled and
polished and covered in places with Navajo rugs. There
were bookshelves along one wall filled with dusty-
looking volumes as well as some artifacts—Indian arrows, beadwork, a stone knife, and a few pots with
black geometric patterns. On one of the shelves was a
small wooden box of the kind Ethan recognized. On the
outside of the box were the words "House of Hardy,
London." Ethan opened the latch. Inside were several
dozen trout flies, flies that were similar to the ones
Ethan had used as a boy in Maine, and he felt a surge of
homesickness, just looking at them. There were stream-
ers and wet flies in various colors and patterns, so that
the box looked like a miniature garden of flowers.

Strange place for a Hardy box, he thought. He put
the box back on the shelf and walked over to the fireplace. He took out his watch. It was just noon.

A door opened, and Juan Lopez came into the room.
He was a short, slightly pudgy man, and he moved
slowly across to where Ethan was standing. Lopez's
face was dark and lined and blotched with darker spots
from years of exposure to the sun. His nose was a large
beak that dominated his other features. His black hair
had no gray in it, and it was combed back from his face
and glistened with some kind of hair dressing. He had
almost no neck at all. He reminded Ethan of a sea turtle. The impression was strengthened by the watery
eyes, which Lopez dabbed now and then with a hand-
kerchief, for Ethan remembered watching a turtle lay-
ing her eggs on some faraway beach in the Pacific and
seeing her tears as she laid them. Jesús had told Ethan
about these tears. They were the result of black powder
grains that had damaged Lopez's tear ducts many years
ago. "Do not mistake these tears for tender emotion,"
Jesús had said.

Lopez was dressed expensively in traditional clothing, short black embroidered jacket, ruffled white shirt that was very clean, dark pants, and high black boots. He wore a red sash around his waist. At first glance it was hard for Ethan to believe that this man was dangerous, until he looked in the other man's small eyes. They were like obsidian.

"Buenas tardes, señor." Lopez did not offer to shake hands. His voice was deep and melodious with just a trace of rasp, just enough to make it distinctive. "You have come with my old *compadre,* I understand. He tells me you are a serious man and that he respects you. You are therefore welcome, although it is not often that I entertain Nord Americanos. It is because I remember the old wars, you see."

"Buenas tardes, Señor Lopez. I am grateful for your hospitality, and I understand about the old days. Jesús has told me."

"Yes. He was there, too. Your Spanish is not bad. When you learn to say your R's properly, you may be able to pass for a peon." Lopez said this without any trace of humor. "Well, what brings you here, *señor?"*

"Business."

"Business is a good thing, Señor Hardin." He dabbed at his eyes and then stared at Ethan as if evaluating him. "I have heard of you. They say you have not accepted the results of the war between your states, that you are still a rebel and that you have killed forty men, not including Indians. Many of them soldiers from the gringo army. Is this true?"

"Close enough."

"Yes. Well, regardless of the precise number, it is an impressive score. Please, sit down. We will have a little talk. Now, tell me, what is this business you spoke about?"

"I have heard you have your hand in most everything that goes on around the border, so I thought you might be interested in hiring on another gun."

"It's possible. I can always use another good man. But I am reluctant to hire one who is still fighting a lost war. Such people take unnecessary chances because they are always angry. It is not good for business. Besides, I must speak plainly to you. I do not like gringos, and my men do not like them either."

"I understand that kind of feeling. I once rode with a fella who was half Commanche and half nigger. I didn't care for either side of his family tree. But he was a good man in a scrap, and we worked well together until the Yankees hung him. Point is, I'm just looking to do a little business, not get adopted. Besides, I have some information that you might find interesting."

"Yes? What is this information?"

Ethan paused, as if trying to decide how much to reveal. "I was up in Tucson last week," he said finally, "drinking in a cantina with some Yankee soldiers. We got to talking, and they let it slip that pretty soon they'd be taking the payroll to some of the forts along the border. They were grumbling about it because the last patrol that went out got attacked and everyone got killed and the money stolen. Maybe you heard about that." Ethan smiled at Lopez as if to suggest that Lopez might know more than just the fact of the attack, but Lopez's expression betrayed nothing.

"Yes, I have heard of that."

"Apparently, the Apaches did it. Well, those boys weren't too happy about having to go, because they didn't think they had enough men to make it safely, especially after the last attack. But the fort is undermanned right now and they can't spare any more men. No more than a half a dozen. That's a tempting target.

A handful of men could bushwhack that patrol somewhere in the mountains and then slide back over the border and let the Apaches take the blame again."

"When is this going to happen?"

"Next week."

"And if I were interested in such a project, why would I need a gringo *pistolero*?"

"You wouldn't. But I brought you the information. That might be worth something."

"I see. Well, *señor,* I must tell you that what you have said is somewhat interesting to me. I have often thought about similar projects. In fact, things of this nature have been proposed to me before. But I do not think it is in my line. You seem like a serious man, and Jesús has vouched for you, so I will explain my thinking to you. As you can see, I have a very comfortable arrangement here. The Mexican authorities do not bother me, and I do not bother them. In fact, many of them are on my payroll. I go one way; they look the other. It is convenient for both of us. In some cases they are even customers for the horses and cattle that I acquire in Texas and elsewhere. So, it is simply a matter of gathering from one place and selling to another. Now and then my men are forced to exchange a few shots with the gringo ranchers, but these little skirmishes are nothing to speak of usually. Both sides start shooting and then both go quickly in opposite directions, my men leaving with the cattle and the ranchers leaving with their lives. Of course, I am not sentimental about killing someone, but I do not regard it as an essential aspect of the business. Merely something that happens now and then. Do you see?"

"I suppose so."

"Good. What you propose is a different matter. It makes killing a necessity. That puts my men in some jeopardy. And stealing from the Yankee army could disturb the comfortable arrangements I have with my friends in the government here. It might even bring your Yankee soldiers down here, and that would be unfortunate. So one must weigh the costs and benefits of such a project, and also put the calculation in the context of the existing business. If one is already wealthy from a comparatively safe business of gathering in one market and selling in another, why fight your army?"

"What you say is reasonable."

"Of course. I have given it a great deal of thought. And I have been in this business for many years. I understand what I am doing. Now then, what would you say to having a glass of wine?"

"I would say I'd prefer tequila."

"*Bueno.* Tequila it is. I will join you." Lopez rang a small bell that was sitting on the table, and the Indian woman came into the room. "Lupe, a bottle of tequila and two glasses, *por favor.*"

"*Sí, patrón,*" said the woman. She returned in a moment with the drinks. Lopez poured out the tequila and then offered Ethan a cigar, which he accepted. Both men lit up and sat back in their chairs.

"Lupe is an interesting case," said Lopez after he had taken a few sips. "She is a Paiute. A very poor tribe, as you might know, that lives in the desert in the Utah territory. Diggers, they are sometimes called because they subsist on roots and little else. I acquired her when she was just a small girl. Her father sold her to me in exchange for an ax. He was very pleased, because getting children was easy for him but getting an ax was difficult. This little incident illustrates my point. I could have simply shot her father and taken the girl. But why? An ax was nothing to me, but everything to the father. It is simply a matter of making what you gringos call a deal. We both went away satisfied. Sometimes, of course, we would have to kill an Indian or two in order to acquire captives. But that was rare. Usually we could reason our way through the transaction and end up with both sides quite happy. As for the slaves we acquired, they soon learned that a tortilla and some frijoles are infinitely preferable to roots. And when we sold them down in Hermosillo or Mexico City or wherever the market was strongest, they had the opportunity to become Christians. Very good. Food and the promise of heaven. And for me, a reasonable profit with no unpleasantness, do you see?"

"I understand. But they were still slaves, someone's property."

"Theoretically, yes. But I have come to understand that this whole idea of property is nothing more than a joke, a fraud. I learned this from the Utes, who were my partners in the slave trade in those days. The Utes are a thoughtful people, and like many of the Indians of the north they do not look at things the way a white man does. For example, they do not believe in the concept of property. How can a man own the earth or even a small part of it, they would ask? The earth is eternal and man's life is no more significant than the yip of a coyote. How can the temporary own the eternal? It is absurd. To think otherwise is nothing but vanity. And, of course, if you take these poetical ideas to their logical conclusion, you realize that, if there is no such thing as property, there are no such things as property rights. And, if there are no such things as property rights, there can be no such thing as theft. You cannot steal what belongs to no one. Such a thing is a logical impossibility. A paradox.

"What a sense of relief and freedom I achieved when I realized this! Before that I was occasionally troubled by conscience, for I was young and I had been raised by a pious mother who had not thought these things through and merely accepted the conventional morality. For a time I especially worried about the business of slavery. But when I thought more about it, I realized that is was the greatest joke of all, for how can another man be property? The fact that you exchange some money for a man does not change the fact that that same man can simply get up and run away someday. Man has free will, after all. And where does that leave the supposed property owner? You see? The slavery business proves my point that property does not exist. Acquiring and then selling slaves was therefore merely a fraud, which is not a sin, but only a trick which the clever play on the gullible. Do you see?"

"I think I do."

"Of course I am a man of property, in a sense, but I do not think of any of this as belonging to me. I am simply using it while I am here on the earth. Anyway, I felt this huge sense of peace once I saw the light, thanks to my friends the Utes."

"Well, if everything you say is true, how come these Indians raise such a ruckus when the white man comes in and grabs their territory?"

Lopez smiled and gestured with his hands to indicate his acceptance of human frailty. "You are not surprised by inconsistency, are you? Few people are truly logical in their thinking, especially when their own interests are threatened. That is why most people are sheep, not wolves. But to a rational man it is clear that there is no such thing as theft and that what matters is being powerful, for the powerful go where they want to go and do what they want to do. With a clear conscience. It is in the nature of things. More tequila?"

"Yes, thanks."

"I got this shipment from a teamster who was taking it to Santa Fe. He did not agree with my ideas about property, and we had to shoot him, unfortunately. But it is quite good tequila, I think."

"Yes. Very smooth."

"Well, it is good to discuss these things. Philosophy is one of my passions, along with beautiful women and fishing. I tell you all this because you seem to be a thoughtful man, and I want to explain to you why I have no interest in stealing Army payrolls. Having to kill that many soldiers as a necessary part of the business would be troubling to me. At my age, I do not need such trouble. I am starting to think about my prospects for heaven, and so I will avoid that kind of business. Killing people is a sin unless it is necessary."

"I understand. What you say makes perfect sense."

"Naturally."

Ethan sat thinking for a moment, as though trying to come up with an alternative plan. "I take it, then," he said finally, "that since you are not interested in this project, you would have no objection if I did it myself. I can get some men to help me easy enough."

Lopez shrugged. "It means nothing to me, *señor*. I wish you luck." Lopez studied Ethan for a moment as though trying to come to a decision about him. "Even though I am not interested in doing this job, I do have a suggestion for you, *señor*," he said finally. "About this project. Would you care to hear it?"

"Of course."

Lopez leaned back and put his fingers together. He looked like a college professor about to embark on a lecture. His small black eyes darted back and forth as he considered what he would say.

"Here is the situation, as I see it," he said. "Suppose you are successful in stealing the payroll. You then have money. That is a good thing and the object of the exercise. But suppose that money is traceable? Suppose it consists of new bank notes. That is not so good, because it would be very hard to spend without attracting notice. This is possible, no?"

"Yes, I suppose so."

"Well, the problem then becomes, how do you make this traceable money, which is in a sense soiled, clean again? One way, of course, would be to leave the territory. Go to somewhere in the East or perhaps Europe. That could work. But you would always be worried about the other men in your gang. Where would they go and what would they do with their share of the money? If only one were apprehended with the cash, he could betray you and the authorities could track you down."

"That is always one of the risks."

"Yes. True. But suppose there were a way to take this dirty money and immediately make it clean again. Baptize it, so to speak. This would be better because then you could divide the clean money with your associates, and everyone would be safe regardless of where they went after that."

Ethan leaned forward in his chair. It was not necessary for him to feign interest or excitement. "How could that be done?"

"It is not difficult. After the raid you bring the money here. I will then sell you a herd of cattle in exchange for the money. You then drive the cattle back across the border and resell them. I then have the traceable money, but it is easy for me to dispose of it here. I can give a little to my vaqueros, who will naturally then exchange it for tequila or women, but I will retain the rest. You, meanwhile, will have become a respectable cattleman. Very neat. Of course, since there is a big price on your head, you might need an agent to make the sale for you, but that is easily arranged. I can put you in touch with the right people."

Ethan stiffened. "Who told you there was a bounty on me?"

"Oh, I naturally assumed it. Also, Jesús gave me

this." Lopez unfolded the wanted poster and passed it to Ethan. "Five thousand dollars is a nice round sum, *señor.* It is perhaps fortunate for you that I am not in the business of collecting bounties. But that is not my line. I dislike the Tejano police especially. So do not be alarmed."

Ethan folded the poster and put it in his pocket. He relaxed and smiled at Lopez. "Yes, it is a good thing you're not in that business. I'd hate to have to shoot my way out of here."

"I agree entirely. You would not make it, but you would do some damage along the way. Perhaps to someone I care about, such as myself. So, *señor,* what do you think of this idea of the cattle?"

"I think it's a very good idea, Señor Lopez. Very good. But do you have that many cattle available?"

Lopez smiled. His expression showed that he felt he was dealing with an amateur, but an amateur that had some promise. "Probably. But if not, it is merely a matter of going to Texas or New Mexico to get them, *señor.* It all depends on how much money you acquire in the original business with the Army. I may need to add to my inventory to cover the transaction, but that is easy enough to do."

"So you steal cattle in Texas, bring them here, and then sell them to me in exchange for the dollars."

"Precisely. Of course I would sell them to you for slightly more than the market price, which will compensate me for my troubles and motivate me to sell them to you rather than to my friends here. But that slight premium should not bother you, *señor,* because they will have cost you nothing beyond a few bullets. So if you steal one hundred thousand dollars and then clear ninety thousand dollars when you sell the cattle, you will still be far ahead, and you can think of the ten thousand dollars as insurance against the possibility of having the money traced. And who knows, perhaps the prices in the Northern markets will go up during the time it takes to complete this transaction, so that you will therefore make a trading profit. This is always a possibility in fluctuating markets."

"Those cattle will have Texas brands."

"Brands can be changed, *señor*. That would be part of the service I would provide to you in exchange for the premium price. And even if someone should learn where you acquired the cattle, do not forget that Americans consider the theft of Mexican beef as perfectly legitimate. Many businessmen acquire their herds this way, and often they know that these Mexican cattle originally came from Texas. Having been stolen once, they can be stolen again without concern for the original owner. It is quite respectable."

"How about bills of sale? Wouldn't I need them in order to resell in the markets? In order to prove that I actually own the cattle?"

"Sometimes these are necessary. But they are merely pieces of paper that can be forged. Well, what do you say?"

Ethan thought for a minute, as if trying to get the mechanics of the transaction straight in his mind. "Something doesn't quite make sense to me. I understand the idea of giving the cash a baptism. But why go to the work of trailing a herd of cattle? Why don't you just buy the money from me? At a discount, of course."

"I could, but I would not make as much money. Suppose you brought me one hundred thousand dollars and I bought it from you for, say, ninety thousand dollars in Mexican silver dollars. You would have clean money, and I would make about ten percent, and my capital would increase from ninety thousand to one hundred thousand. But suppose I keep my ninety thousand in my vault and instead sell you ninety thousand dollars worth of cattle at more than the market price, say one hundred thousand. In that case, my cash goes from ninety thousand to one hundred ninety thousand, in one quick transaction. And my profit is infinite, since the cattle cost me nothing. You see? You end up with ninety thousand in either case. And you are clean. The advantage to me is that I can do one big transaction at one time, instead of having to sell the cattle in smaller lots. That would take time and therefore cost money."

Ethan grinned and shook his head in admiration. "Pretty damned clever."

"Of course. It is my idea."

"There is just one hitch, though."

"What is that?"

"Well, let's say the payroll does amount to something like one hundred thousand. Bringing that much money down here could be a mighty big temptation. You might just decide to take the money and keep your cattle."

Lopez smiled slyly and nodded at Ethan.

"*Bueno,* Señor Hardin. Of course I could. And if you had not said this, I would not have wanted to do business with you, because that would have proved you are a fool. But look at the situation from my point of view. I do not think that you would surrender the money without a fight. You would have a gang of men with you who would also fight to protect their interests. Of course, I would outnumber you, but still there would be bloodshed. I do not go out of my way to pick fights with Tejano *pistoleros.* Besides, as I have told you, that is not my line. Why should I risk a gun battle to steal the money from you when I can safely steal the cattle from the Tejanos and sell them to you? I end up with the same amount of money either way. Of course, you are correct to identify this risk. But I would hope that we could do business in a civilized manner. Still, it is something that you must consider before you agree to this transaction. To be honest, *señor,* it does not matter much to me whether you want to do it or not. I will be happy regardless."

"How soon would you need to know whether I would want to do this?"

"I do not need to know. If you do the business with the Army, just come back here. Then, when we know how much you have cleared, we will know how many cattle you will need in exchange. If we have to gather a few, you can wait here until the gathering is complete. You can always hide the money somewhere in the desert while you are waiting, in the event that you are still slightly mistrustful. If it were me, I would certainly do that. Then when the herd is assembled, you can retrieve the money and we will make the exchange. Very simple, very clean. On the other hand, if you decide not to do the robbery at all, then so be it. I can always find other markets for Tejano beef, which I intend to continue gathering regardless of what you decide."

Ethan nodded. "Señor Lopez, I think we've got a deal."

"Good." Lopez stood up to signal that the meeting was over. "And now, Señor Hardin, you must excuse me. I have some other people I must see this afternoon."

"I understand. Besides, if I'm going to put this plan into motion, I'd better get back to the border. I'll need some time to get the men together. I'm going to ask Jesús if he wants to join me. Assuming you have no objections."

"None whatever. He is restless, I think. The cantina business is steady, but dull. He could use a little variety. But you should know, *señor,* he shoots very badly."

"Yes, he told me that."

"I'm not surprised. Jesús is an honest man. Well, good-bye, *señor.* I wish you luck."

Ethan went outside. The sunlight was especially bright after the darkness of the hacienda. Ethan could just make out Jesús standing by the fountain talking to a fat woman. Jesús looked up when Ethan came out, and came immediately over to him.

"Well, *señor?* Things went well?"

"Things went well, Jesús."

"You are smiling. That is good."

"Yep, I think I just figured out the answers to a couple of problems. Now, what do you say we get the hell out of here."

"*Bueno, señor. Bueno.*"

Sixteen

They rode hard until they reached the spring where Ethan had camped the night before. They stopped there to water the animals before setting out to the lower elevations and the desert.

"So, *señor*, perhaps you will tell me now why you were smiling. Have you decided whether Juan Lopez was involved in the robbery of the Army payroll?"

"He was involved all right, but not directly. He didn't steal the money, but he ended up with it. Whoever took it was worried that the bills could be traced, so he traded the money to Lopez for some cattle and then drove those cattle back across the border and sold them."

"Apaches?" Jesús considered the possibility. "No, I do not think so. Juan Lopez used to deal with the Indians of the north, but he never worked with Apaches. No Mexican likes them, *señor*."

"I agree. Besides, it isn't the Apaches' style. Whoever did this kept the money and left the Army horses in Black Tail Canyon. Apaches would be more likely to do things the other way around. They would have been after the horses and weapons and probably wouldn't have paid much attention to anything else."

"And so, *señor,* what are your ideas?"

"Had to be white men who were used to dealing with cattle. Someone whose ranch was close to the border so that they could claim the cows they got from Lopez were rustled Mexican beef. That way no one would question how they came by them."

"The Curtains."

"Maybe. But do you think the Curtains were smart enough to come up with a deal like this, and do you think Juan Lopez would be willing to work with them?"

"It seems unlikely. But the Army horses were found on the Curtains's land."

"I figure they were planted there. I don't think the Curtains even knew they were there. They were put there so that people would think the Curtains were involved. That was a kind of fallback alibi in case the Army decided the Apaches were not involved after all. And now that the Curtains are all dead, there's no way to prove they weren't involved somehow."

"Yes, that is too bad."

"Well, it's too bad for the Curtains, but in a funny kind of way, it helps us. Who, after all, had the most reason to get rid of the Curtains? The man who actually pulled the raid. And who organized the attack on the Curtains and made sure they were all killed? Sam Shelby."

"Yes. He is a very respectable man and therefore capable of big ideas like this. What's more, he is a foreigner, which would make him more *simpático* for Juan Lopez. That makes sense. But who shot Tomás, if not the Curtains?"

"I don't know. It might have been one of Shelby's men. Tomás could have stumbled across the horses when Ellis or maybe Rourke was just getting them penned up in that canyon. Or it might have been one of the Curtains looking to pick up some easy cash. I'm not sure we'll ever find out for sure."

"Perhaps not, although I would like to know. I would like to put a bullet into that man, whoever he is, for Tomás's sake. But this Shelby. He is the man with the beautiful wife, is he not?" Jesús looked at Ethan and grinned. "Perhaps that is why you were smiling when you left Juan Lopez, *señor.*"

"You have a devious mind, Jesús."

"Perhaps, but it would be convenient if the husband were a thief and a murderer, would it not?"

"Can't say, Jesús. If you were a woman, how would you feel about the man who came and arrested your husband and had him hung?"

"It would depend how I felt about this husband, *señor,* and about the man who arrested him. I might be grateful. I will tell you a quick story. My Rosa was once married to a bad *hombre.* He was a gambler and small-time thief. One day I was drinking in the cantina and he came after me with a machete for no reason beyond I was talking to Rosa—in a polite way, I assure you. So I was forced to shoot this man. He was standing very close to me at the time, and even I could not miss. We buried him down by the river. You know the rest, I think. I ended up with Rosa and the cantina, both."

"A happy ending."

"Yes, in general, although I had to buy his interest in the cantina from Rosa. She is difficult when it comes to business. But my advice to you is not to worry too much about this problem. Women are sometimes complicated in the way they think about things. Of course, I understand that this is difficult advice to follow, because I know that this woman is very interesting to you, *señor.* I can tell from the way you look when the subject comes up. You are a very good actor most of the time, but when the subject is this woman, you are very bad. I have noticed this."

"Well, there's no sense lying about it, Jesús. She has been on my mind. And it seems to me it complicates things, if Shelby is really the one we are after."

"Maybe, *señor.* But as I have tried to say, maybe it simplifies them."

"I guess we'll find out. Now let's get going. I need to get up to Tucson to see the Army. There are a few more things I need to check before I can be sure about Shelby. So keep all this under your hat."

"Of course, *señor.* I have a very large hat when it comes to secrets of this kind. But I would ask you one last thing, *señor.* When you go after the men who did this, I want to go with you. I still have Tomás's shooting to think about. And also, I must tell you that I have enjoyed these last few days. I feel as though I have recovered something of my past. A man can get stale sitting in a cantina."

"That's a deal, Jesús. I'll stop in Tubac and pick you up when I get back from Tucson. Then, if things work out the way I think they will, we'll go on over to Verity and see what's what."

Two days later they reached Tubac. It was just sunset when they arrived. Jesús went in to see Rosa, and Ethan took the animals to the livery stable and unpacked. Wentworth's bay was in one of the stalls.

"A man came for that horse you brought here last week, *señor,*" said the livery man.

"Really? What'd he look like?"

"He was a small man, *señor.* He had eyes like a weasel. His manner was very impolite."

Rourke, thought Ethan. *Well, that puts him on the alert.*

"Where'd he go, do you know?"

"No, *señor.* He took the horse and left."

"How long ago?"

"This afternoon, *señor.*"

Ethan went to the cantina. It was crowded. Wentworth's men were sitting at one of the tables, and Jesús was at the other with Wentworth, himself.

"Ah, Ethan Jaeger," said Wentworth. "Back from your wanderings. This is good luck, I must say. Happy to see you." Wentworth stood up and offered Ethan a limp handshake. "Take a pew, please, and have a drink. This tequila grows on you, I assure you. Jesús tells me you were hunting mountain lions in Mexico. How did it go? Any luck?"

"Some. How'd you make out in Verity?"

"Pretty well. That is good country over there. Just the sort of thing my people are looking for, although the Apaches are still making a nuisance of themselves, as you know. But that is temporary. The Army will settle them sooner or later. I met your friend Shelby. It seems he might be interested in selling his ranch."

"Oh?"

"Yes. But I tell you, if that fellow's the son of an earl, then I'm the Archbishop of Canterbury. Oh, he pulls it off well enough for the uninformed, but he's lacking in the subtleties, which is where the difference always lies, you see. I've seen this sort of thing dozens of times. Some jumped-up son of a brewer or a Scotch mine owner wants to be a gentleman, but they can't do it, you see. No subtlety. Well, there you are."

"I thought he said he was Irish."

"That's what he claims. Anglo-Irish, you know. The

aristocracy. Oh, he's Irish for sure, but nothing more than a bog trotter. If he didn't spend the first years of his life digging peat and saying Hail Marys, I'll boil my head. Fellow positively reeks of cabbage and potatoes, which, by the way, he calls 'praties.' Well, no one but a peasant calls them 'praties.' Big mistake. Saw through it immediately. You can take the Irishman out of the bog but you can't take the bog out of the Irishman. Ha, ha. Said nothing, though. No skin off my nose. Beautiful wife, though. Isn't she, just. My God, this is a wonderful country. Fellow arrives in steerage and then comes out here and claims he's the son of an earl and runs off with the prettiest woman I've ever laid eyes on with a father who's a wine grower to boot. Bloody hell, it's marvelous. I may move here myself. Tell everyone I'm the Czar of Russia. No one would bat an eye. Ha, ha.

"Oh, and we went out shooting one day. Fellow couldn't hit a flying cow. Well, that shows you, doesn't it? Of course, in all fairness to this fellow Shelby, the Prince of Wales can't shoot either. Too fat. Spoils his gun mounting. Still, a gentleman should be able to shoot well, I believe.

"Had dinner with him and his wife that night. Charming. Happened to mention that I knew you, Ethan, and she positively blushed at the sound of your name. Yes, it's true. 'Well, well,' thinks I. 'These writing fellows are downy birds. This one, anyway.' I told them, though, that I didn't think you were really a newspaperman. Figured you for an Army man on the sly or a gunfighter or something more romantic. Thought it might do you a bit of good to be more mysterious, you see. Anyway, she asked after you very touchingly, and I decided to put all carnal thoughts away as far as she was concerned. One knows when one is destined to run second in a two-horse race.

"As a matter of interest, her husband didn't notice her reaction. Too drunk. Fellow's a bit of a swine, I would say. But that's an arranged marriage if I ever saw one, and I have seen plenty. Beauty for money. Simple trade. Happens all the time. Well, Jesús, speaking of dinner, what's on the menu tonight? *Menudo? Chile rellenos?* Something spicy, I'll warrant. I have become positively fond of the Mexican food. I shall hate to leave here. Indeed I shall."

Ethan considered what Wentworth had said. It confirmed much of what he already thought about Shelby. And as for Wentworth's suggestion that Ethan wasn't who he appeared to be, it wouldn't do much harm at this stage. Rourke already knew that Ellis was missing and, having discovered his horse in Tubac, he was smart enough to figure out what probably happened. And it was pretty clear that Rourke was working with Shelby. Ellis had said that they suspected Ethan was a lawman, which was why Ellis trailed him and tried to ambush him in the mountains. The time for aliases and cover stories was nearly over. They were getting close to the end game. And as far as Danielle Shelby's blushes were concerned, well, he could not afford to think about that. Not yet, anyway.

"How did you come here?" asked Ethan. "Did you stop at Pete Kitchen's on the way back?"

"No, we came through the mountains. I wanted to see them firsthand, you know. Thought maybe we'd run into an Apache or two. That was an amazing shot Pete Kitchen made, wasn't it? Potted that fellow from a good three hundred yards. Well, that's what I call good shooting. Anyway, there were enough of us to come through the pass without too much worry. One of Shelby's men guided us. Another bog trotter. Rourke, I think his name is. Unfortunate-looking man, but he seemed to know his business. But we had no trouble.

Came across the remains of someone who hadn't been so lucky. Down in one of the canyons. Not much left of him, poor fellow. Rourke said he was probably a miner that ran into the Apaches. Well, that's the way it happens, I suppose. Too bad, but there it is."

Yes, thought Ethan. *Too bad.* And now he was sure that Rourke, and therefore Shelby, would be waiting for him somewhere.

Ethan left for Tucson early the next morning. He did not take Priam or any of his packs, because he wanted to travel fast.

"Good-bye again, Ethan," said Wentworth. "I expect we'll meet again soon. If I buy a ranch over in Verity, who can say, maybe we'll be neighbors." Wentworth winked and laughed.

"I would like that," said Ethan.

"Oh, I understand you. Indeed I do."

Ethan traveled hard. The road north seemed to be deserted, but even so he did not want to risk spending the night in some dry camp along the trail. He reached town about sunset and found a hotel near the fort. In the morning he would see Captain Wilkes.

Wilkes was at his desk going through a mound of papers when Ethan came in.

"Ah, Mr. Jaeger or whoever you are. Good to see you." He stood up and shook hands with Ethan.

"Hello, Captain."

"Well, we got your signals. That worked out pretty well, I think."

"Yes. Very well. I appreciate your help on this."

"Not at all. Sit down and have a cup of coffee. It's pretty good today. Almost can't see the bottom of the cup. Well, then, what's the news? Any luck in finding out about this robbery?"

"I've got a pretty good idea about how it happened, but before I get into that, I wonder if you were able to get the information I asked for."

Wilkes shuffled through his papers. "Yep. I've got the stuff right here." He studied the papers for a minute. "All right. First off, here's the answer to the telegram we sent General Chamberlain. Seems like he remembers you."

"Yes, he was my teacher at Bowdoin College before the war." Ethan read the telegram. "Dear Ethan, How good to hear from you again. I hope you are prospering. In answer to your question, the 15th Texas regiment was not against me at Little Round Top. It was the 15th Alabama, William Oates commanding. The 15th Texas may have been in reserve, but I never encountered them. I am not even sure that there was such a regiment, since the accounts of the battle I have read do not mention them. Write soon and tell me why you wanted this information. Are you writing a book? My kindest regards to Maria. Someday, perhaps, I will have the pleasure of meeting her. J. Chamberlain."

"He spared no expense on that telegram," said Wilkes.

"No. He is not the sort of man who would chop his sentences just to save a few pennies."

"Who is Maria?"

"She was my wife. I haven't written to Chamberlain in years, so he doesn't know. She died."

"I see."

Ethan nodded grimly. "Wish I did. Well, that's the first question."

"Here are the other two. Both of these came through

the British embassy in Washington." Wilkes read the first. " 'The 7th earl of Roscommon had only one son, who inherited, and eight daughters.' Good God, what a bouquet. 'The present earl has no children.' Does that mean anything to you?"

"Yes." Wentworth had been right about that part of it, Ethan thought. He was not at all surprised.

"And here's the other message: 'The Heavy Brigade consisted of the Scots Greys and the Inniskillings. There is no record of a Samuel Shelby in either regiment.' "

"That figures," said Ethan.

"Well, that's it. Is it useful?"

"Yes, it pretty much confirms my ideas."

"What's the business about Samuel Shelby? Isn't he that rancher down in Verity?"

"Yep. He's our man."

"Really! So it wasn't the Apaches. I didn't think so. What's the story on Shelby? I mean, what makes you think he's involved?"

"Shelby's one of these men who's made himself up as he's gone along. Far as I can see, there's nothing about his story that's true. These telegrams confirm that. Says he's the son of a lord, which he isn't. Said he was with the 15th Texas at Little Round Top, and no such regiment existed. Not at the fight, anyway. Said he was with the Heavy Brigade at Balaclava, but there's no record of it. That's what these messages tell us. I met him down there and I spent some time with him, and the rest of his story is just as false."

"Yes. I see. But there are plenty of men out here with made-up identities." Wilkes smiled at Ethan knowingly.

"I suppose. But everything points to him. The whole scheme is based on the cattle rustling that goes on back and forth across the border from here to Texas. No one on either side pays much attention to it. You told me that when we first met."

"Yes, I remember."

"So Shelby could go down there and claim to be rustling Mexican beef and nobody would think anything of it. In fact, they'd think it was pretty clever. But actually he was paying for those cattle with stolen money. I went down there and saw Juan Lopez, myself."

"That old bandit. Was he in on it too?"

"Only in the sense that he sold Shelby the cattle for the payroll money. Shelby then drove the cattle north again and sold them."

Wilkes sat back in his chair. He shook his head as the mechanics of the deal fell into place. "I see it. Lovely bit of irony. Fellow claims to be a rustler in order to cover his crimes."

"Yes. And who knows, maybe that's how Shelby actually got started. Maybe he used to be an honest rustler who got into money troubles and took this way out. Or maybe he's been at this game for years. Maybe his sales in the Northern markets will roughly coincide with some big robberies throughout the Southwest. Or he could have been working with Lopez all these years stealing Texas cattle and driving them through Mexico and selling them up north where he could get a better price. Then maybe he came up with this idea. I don't know all the details yet, but I know damn well he did it."

"How do we prove it?"

"Well, he had at least two other fellas working with him. Men named Ellis and Rourke. I figure they were involved in the attack on the patrol. And Rourke sent Ellis after me to try to ambush me in the mountains. I got that out of Ellis before he passed on."

Wilkes raised his eyebrows and looked at Ethan over his reading glasses. "Died of natural causes, did he?"

"He had an accident. But anyway, that gives us more than enough to arrest Rourke. Conspiracy and attempted murder. I figure I'll pick him up and have a chat with him. He seems like a pretty tough nut, but I believe he'll crack eventually. I'll stake the son of a bitch out on an anthill, pour some honey on his pecker, and stand by while he thinks things over. Couple of hours of that and I believe he'll see the light."

Wilkes whistled. "You're a hard man, Mr. Jaeger."

"I don't like being shot at, Captain."

"That's understandable. But you know the Army can't officially be involved in something like that."

"I wouldn't expect it, Captain. But once I have Rourke's cooperation, I'll bring him in and turn what's left of him over to the sheriff, and you can work it out how best to proceed from there. My job'll be done. Till then, though, I'd like to keep our arrangement about the heliograph just the way it is. Might come in handy if I have to send for the cavalry."

"Of course. I'll have our signalmen watching Mount Wrightson same as always. What do you think our chances are of recovering the money?"

"Pretty slim, I would think, but that's something we'll have to deal with after we get the case buttoned up."

Wilkes nodded. "Well, at least we know it wasn't the Apaches this time. That in itself is good intelligence. And Mr. Jaeger, this seems like a damned good piece of work. If this Shelby was responsible for killing my men, I'll make goddam sure he hangs even if he didn't do the actual shooting. Yuma prison's way too good for him."

"Thank you, Captain. Let's hope it turns out that way."

Seventeen

The next evening when Ethan arrived at Jesús's cantina, the dog Nariz was lying in the dust outside the door. He was tied to the hitching post. The dog recognized Ethan and wagged his tail a few times, but did not bother to get up.

"Sleeping one off, Nariz? Well, don't let me disturb you."

Ethan tied Rangeley to the hitching post and stepped over the dog and went inside. There were a few teamsters eating dinner, and at the other table Sweet Jimmy O'Brian was sitting with a bottle in front of him. The bottle was half empty. Jesús was behind the bar and he nodded at Ethan, but did not say anything. He glanced toward O'Brian as if to put Ethan on the alert. Ethan went over to O'Brian's table.

"Hello, Marshal," he said. O'Brian looked up. His eyes were red and there were dark circles below them. His bald head was glistening from sweat, and he smelled like the inside of a chicken coop.

"What? Oh, it's you. Jaeger, right? I remember you. The newspaperman."

"That's right. What brings you here?"

"Oh, I was hired on to ride shotgun for those teamsters. Seems they were worried about the Apaches between here and Verity. Didn't see any, though."

"Staying long?"

"As long as this bottle lasts. Going back then."

"Tonight? What about the Apaches?"

"Ain't no Apaches around here to speak of. 'Sides, they don't like to fight at night, much. A man knows what he's doing will travel at night." O'Brian's words were slurred and he seemed angry. A few more drinks and he would turn mean, if someone gave him the chance. Ethan thought about his next move. Running into O'Brian might present an opportunity. He had been wondering how he was going to get Rourke alone. It would be difficult to go to the Double S and arrest him, but if he could lure him out to the trail somehow, things might go more easily. He knew what Rourke would most likely do if he had the chance, and that knowledge gave Ethan something of an edge. It was a long shot, but worth trying.

"Well, then," said Ethan in a friendly tone. "I'll probably see you over there in a couple of days. There's something I want to talk over with that foreman from the Double S, Rourke."

"Yeah? What might that be?" O'Brian's eyes were not focusing.

"Private matter, Marshal."

"Private, huh?"

"That's right."

"What'd he do? Steal one of your girlfriends?"

"Like I said. It's between him and me."

"Well, I expect he'll be around when you want him."

"I imagine. If you see him before I do, you can give him my regards. Tell him I'll be looking for him."

"I doubt he'll sleep once he hears that." O'Brian grinned, but there was no humor in it.

"You said you just came by the southern trail, right? And you didn't see any Apaches."

"No Apaches. No sense going through the mountains. More likely to run into them there. If you're going over to Verity, you'd be best off taking the southern trail." Ethan noticed that O'Brian seemed able to concentrate as he said this.

"Thanks for the advice, Marshal. I'll see you later."

Ethan went to his room, and in a few minutes there was a knock on his door. It was Jesús.

"Good evening, *señor.* I am glad to see you back. I hope your trip to Tucson was useful."

"Yes. Very. Now look, Jesús, there's something we need to talk over. You know that fella O'Brian?"

"Yes. He is a bad man, *señor.* He is the kind of man one often meets in a cantina."

"You're right about that. But here's the situation. He's in pretty tight with Rourke and Shelby. I don't know if he was involved in the robbery, but he was there at the Curtain ranch when they cleaned them out, so nothing would surprise me. He's headed back to Verity, and I tipped him that I was coming there to look for Rourke. Rourke suspects that I'm a lawman, and he's probably figured out that I took care of Ellis."

Jesús's eyes grew wide. "That is not good, *señor.* This man Rourke will run away."

"I doubt it. If he runs, he'll know I'll be following. It would make more sense for him to set up an ambush somewhere along the trail. If he gets rid of me, he and Shelby can go on as before. I figure that's what he'll try."

Jesús nodded sorrowfully. "I see what you are planning, *señor.* You are baiting the trap with yourself. I think you must be tired of living."

"I agree, it's risky. But it would be even more risky to go into Verity and try to pluck him out of there. I need to get him alone so I can squeeze a confession out of him. That's really the only way I can prove that Shelby is responsible for the payroll. Do you see?"

"All too well, *señor.*"

"I tell you this because you said you wanted to go with me. I don't think that's such a good idea now."

Jesús thought about it and then shook his head. "You are wrong about that, *señor.* It is even a better idea now, because you should not be alone in this. I will not let you do this by yourself." Jesús said this with no trace of reluctance or trepidation. "I must go with you."

Ethan looked at the other man gratefully and with affection. "You're sure? You know what may happen."

"Yes, *señor.* It is because I know what may happen that I must go."

Ethan smiled and patted Jesus on the shoulder.

"Gracias, amigo. Now, tell me about the southern trail. If you were going to set up an ambush, where would you do it?"

Jesús thought for a minute. "Well, *señor,* for our purposes the southern trail is much better than the mountains. In the mountains, you know, there are many, many places to hide. But the southern trail does not have so many. Between here and Pete Kitchen's the country is flat, so I do not think they would try anything there. Once you turn east from Pete Kitchen's the country begins to climb, but it is still open." Jesús tried to picture the trail in his mind. He was silent for a minute as he thought. "Yes, I know where they will try it, *señor,*" he said suddenly. "About ten miles outside of Verity there is a canyon. The trail is narrow through there with cliffs on both sides. It is a perfect spot for such a thing. There are many big rocks to hide behind on both sides. Yes, *señor,* if it were me, that is where I would place the ambush."

"Good," said Ethan. "That makes sense. Now, we'll need to give O'Brian some time to get back to Verity. He said he was going to head back tonight. So if we leave the day after tomorrow, the timing should be about right."

"What happens if O'Brian forgets? He is very drunk. He may not remember to tell Rourke."

"It's possible. In that case we'll keep on going to Verity, and I'll have to come up with another way to smoke Rourke out. But I have a feeling O'Brian wasn't as drunk as he let on. It wouldn't surprise me at all if he showed up in that canyon along with Rourke. Time'll tell."

"Bueno, señor. It is a good plan, with the only exception being that we are not the ones setting up the ambush. We are the ones walking into it. Other than that, it is a masterpiece." Jesús smiled ruefully.

"I know. But if you're right about that canyon, I think maybe those fellas are going to learn something," Ethan said grimly. "Now, what do you say we have some dinner?"

"Bueno, señor. Rosa has made some very fine *chile rellenos."*

"Good. I'll go put Rangeley in the livery stable, and then we'll eat."

The two men went out into the main room of the cantina. O'Brian was gone, and the bottle on the table was empty.

"Madre mia," said Jesus. "He left without paying."

Ethan laughed. "Not surprising. But don't worry, Jesús. We'll get it out of him a couple of days from now. One way or the other."

*   *   *

Over dinner they worked out some of the details of the plan. Jesús remembered that there was a grove of cottonwoods at the entrance of the canyon, and that the trees ran all the way through the canyon alongside a small spring creek. The canyon was not very long, perhaps two hundred yards, but the road through it curved to the right at the entrance, so that it would be possible to get very close to the canyon before actually entering it.

"They will be able to see us coming from some distance, *señor,* because they will undoubtedly put a lookout on the cliff above. But once we are close, we will be screened by the trees and by the curving of the road."

"That's good. In fact, that's perfect, because I have an idea about how to get them to show themselves, and those trees will come in handy. You remember that you said we would be using ourselves to bait the trap."

"Yes, *señor.* It is the uncomfortable part of the plan. They will be hidden and we will be exposed, unfortunately."

"Maybe not. Is there anyone in Tubac who could make a couple of man-sized piñatas?"

"Man-sized piñatas? But what . . . Ah, yes." Jesus grinned. "I see. Yes, that is a good idea, *señor.* Very good. That would be a surprise, no? We put the piñata men on the horses and send them through the canyon, and we follow on foot, hiding behind the rocks and trees. Then when they shoot the piñatas, we shoot them. Yes?"

"That's more or less the idea, although it's important to take Rourke alive if we can. Can it be done? The piñatas, I mean."

"Maybe. The time is short. But it is possible. No, wait, *señor.* I have another idea." He jumped up from the table. "Come with me. I will show you something."

They went outside to a small shed behind the cantina. Jesús opened the door and gestured for Ethan to look inside. "Let me introduce you to José and Pedro, *señor.*"

Hanging on a hook on the wall were two figures dressed in elaborate festival costumes. They were realistic in every detail except that instead of human faces they had skulls. There were black circles painted around their empty eye sockets, and their skeletal hands were crossed in front of them.

"They look a little undernourished, Jesús."

"Yes. We use them for the Day of the Dead celebration. We parade them through the streets and go to the cemetery with gifts for the departed. It is a very happy occasion. But you see, *señor,* they are full-sized. If we put hats on them and add a little padding and cover up their bony hands and change their clothes to something less festive, they would look like real people from a distance, no?"

"Yes, they would. And maybe we could borrow a little rouge from Rosa, just to freshen them up some."

"Of course. Rosa's collection of cosmetics has grown over the years. Unfortunately, these things are increasingly necessary. So that could be done easily."

"Jesús, I think this will work just fine." Ethan was staring at the figures, and they were grinning back at him. "Those aren't really what's left of José and Pedro, are they?"

"Oh, no, *señor.* They are made of papier-mâché. If they get shot to pieces, it is no problem. We can fix them up afterwards. It would be much easier to repair them than to repair ourselves, I think. But there is just one last thing, *señor.* How will this man Rourke and perhaps O'Brian know that it is you coming through the canyon? There will be two of us, and that might make them hesitate."

"Well, like you said, they will be watching for us, and they'll probably be using binoculars, so they'll be able to identify us before we get to that grove of trees, which is where we'll make the switch. Then we'll send Rangeley through the canyon first, with your horse following. Rourke and Shelby and O'Brian all know that Rangeley had his ear shot off, so it figures that they'll assume that the first rider is me. They won't wonder that I have someone with me. And I doubt they'd care much about shooting this extra man even though they don't know who he is."

"Yes. If they are the ones who ambushed the Army and also Tomás, they are not the kind to worry about shooting one more man. Even a stranger. But what about the danger to the horses, *señor?*"

"It's a risk. But when they ambushed the Army, they didn't hit any of the animals. They are good shots."

"I suppose that is a good thing, although it seems strange to say it. I am fond of my horse and would not want him injured. And as for this matter of your own horse's ear, his misfortune turns out to be a help to us. Perhaps that shows that things always happen for the best."

"You believe that, Jesús?"

"Not really, *señor.*"

"Me either. Well, boys," said Ethan to the figures on the wall, "you're hired. No need to thank me. I have a feeling you're going to earn your wages."

The next day they made their preparations, so that on the following morning they were ready to leave around sunup. Jesús came from his rooms behind the cantina dressed in his traveling clothes. He had two bandoliers of rifle bullets crossed over his chest, and he was holding his Winchester. He had his pistol on his belt, which was also filled with bullets, and he was wearing his second or third best hat.

"*Bueno,* Jesús. You look like a bad *hombre.*"

"Yes, *señor.* It feels good. Like the old days. But I had forgotten how heavy these bullets can be. Still, it is better to have too many than not enough."

"Yeah, we don't want to end up throwing rocks at these fellas."

They packed José and Pedro on Priam and covered them with a tarp. They had already dressed them in clothes similar to the ones they were wearing. Ethan packed his shotgun and extra ammunition on Priam and put his Henry rifle in Rangeley's saddle scabbard. He checked the loads in his Schofields and slipped his derringer in his pants pocket.

"Well, are you ready, Jesús?"

"Yes, but there is just one thing I would like to ask you, *señor.* . . ."

"Yeah, I figured. Why not. Bring him along. Maybe he'll bite Rourke on the ass and save us the trouble of shooting him."

Jesús grinned. "Yes, and who knows, maybe the sight of his master dressed in the old way will remind him of what he used to be."

Jesús went around to the back of the cantina and untied Nariz from the tree where Rosa had put him the night before. The dog sprinted around the side and ran off into the distance, heading south.

"He knows where we are going, *señor.* You see?"

"Your faith is a wonderful thing, Jesús. Well, let's get going."

They got to Pete Kitchen's ranch around noon, and they stopped long enough to water the animals and have a quick lunch.

"Any more trouble with the Apaches, Pete?" asked Ethan.

"Nope. That fella last week must've been alone, like I thought."

"I don't suppose you saw Sweet Jimmy O'Brian come through here the other night."

"Well, as a matter of fact I did. I found him sprawled out front there under that tree yesterday morning. Seems he was on a spree up in Tubac, and was only able to make it this far before he passed out. He didn't stay long enough to exchange pleasantries, though. Ducked his head in the water trough and then headed east. Seemed like there was something on his mind."

Ethan nodded and winked at Jesús.

"You know something I don't know?" said Kitchen.

"I doubt it, Pete. Well, thanks for the lunch. We'll see you next time around."

"By the way, Jesús," said Kitchen. "I saw your dog go by a while ago. He took the road to the east."

Jesús nodded with satisfaction. "You see, *señor?*" he said to Ethan.

They headed east. Soon they crossed the Santa Cruz River. From there the road began to climb gradually into the meadows that lay at the base of the foothills. There were a few yuccas and mesquite trees scattered here and there, but Jesús had been right about the terrain. There was no good place for an ambush in this stretch of the road. Even the grass-covered foothills offered little cover. Just a few rocks and small trees. An Apache could hide himself there, thought Ethan, but a white man wouldn't try it. Not when there was a better place farther along.

As they rode, they could see the twin peaks of the Santa Ritas in the distance to the north. They looked like pyramids, thought Ethan. They were green from their covering of trees except at the top, where the gray rock was barren. He wondered whether he had been wrong in taking this approach. Maybe they should have circled through that pass and come into Verity that way and avoided the potential ambush. But it was too late to worry about that now.

In less than two hours they came to a broad meadow. From there they could see a set of red cliffs about one mile away. The cliffs were on both sides of the road, and the mountains rose sharply behind them. There would be no way to go around that canyon. The only way led right through it. At the base of the canyon, they could see the grove of trees that Jesús had remembered. They stopped, and Ethan took out his field glasses and surveyed the trail and the tops of both cliffs.

"Can you see anything, *señor?*"

"Nothing out of the ordinary." He could see the little stream that bordered the trail and the cottonwoods that grew alongside. The cottonwoods had lost most of their leaves, and they stood like skeletons in the bright sunlight. Here and there on the cliffs Ethan could see small flashes of light. He assumed these came from the sun glancing off the minerals imbedded in the red rock. Perhaps one of these flashes came from the reflection of field glasses that were watching them, but he could not tell for sure. The cliffs were perhaps one hundred yards high, and Ethan figured that Rourke and maybe the others would not risk a shot from that height and angle. If they were there, they were inside the canyon somewhere. He and Jesús could make it safely to the grove of trees at the entrance to the canyon.

"Perhaps we should make a dash at those trees, *señor.*"

"It's tempting. But that'd give us away. We don't

want them to think we're suspicious. I'm afraid we're just going to have to walk on up there. I think we'll be all right."

Ethan took one last look at the grove of trees at the canyon mouth. Suddenly he saw some movement around the trees, and he narrowed his eyes to try to determine what it was.

"Nariz," he said.

"Nariz! *Bueno.* I told you, *señor.* If there were men in that grove of trees, he would be barking like the fiend of hell. But I hear nothing."

"No, he seems like he's just sniffing around. Probably smells a mouse."

"Or a rat, *señor.*"

"Maybe. Well, let's go."

They rode slowly toward the trees. Ethan pulled his Henry from the saddle scabbard and chambered a round. He put the hammer down to half-cock. Jesús did the same. Ethan noticed Rangeley getting nervous. Maybe he smelled the other horses up ahead somewhere. He tossed his head and showed his teeth and nickered softly. Ethan turned and looked at Priam. The mule squinted back at him; his ears were twitching.

"Something's up," said Ethan.

Ethan felt the tension rising in him as they approached the trees. He kept scanning the tops of the cliffs, but he could see no movement. He could see the dog now in the grove. He was hunting around the base of the cottonwoods, smelling the ground like a bird dog that knows there are quail nearby. Now and then he would lift his head and sniff the breeze. But he did not seem alarmed. Just interested.

Finally, they reached the grove. The trees were thick in there and even though they had no leaves, the overhanging branches hid Ethan and Jesús from the top of the cliff, which was looming directly above. The cliff on the other side was screened by the wall of the nearer rocks. They were safe for the moment. The dog came over and lay down on his belly next to Jesús's horse.

"Bravo, Nariz," Jesús whispered. "You are back." He smiled at Ethan, but said nothing.

They dismounted and tethered Priam to a tree, and then quickly unpacked the two manikins. They placed them on their horses and tied their legs to the stirrups and their hands to the reins. They stuck crucifixes made of sticks down the manikins' backs and across their shoulders to hold them upright, and then put their hats on the grinning skulls and tied them under the bony chins with string. They placed their neckerchiefs around the throats. Up close the effect was hideous.

"You know," said Ethan. "If I saw these boys coming after me, I believe I'd go the other way. Well, that's as good as it's going to get. Let's send 'em through."

They led the two horses out of the grove to the corner of the canyon mouth. Ethan paused a moment and looked at Rangeley. He stroked the horse's nose and whispered in his one ear. "Now you take care of yourself, old amigo. Don't waste any time getting through there." He looked at Jesús. "You ready? You know where to go when the shooting starts?" Jesús nodded.

Ethan slapped Rangeley on the rump and yelled. The horse bolted into the canyon with Jesus's horse following at a run. Nariz streaked after them. Ethan then darted around the corner. He pressed his back against the wall of the cliff, and Jesús crept behind him. From that place they could see into the length of the canyon. The two horses were dashing down the trail, and the two manikins were swaying side to side, though they stayed upright.

Those boys can't ride a lick, thought Ethan. *But they look real enough.*

When the horses were about fifty yards away, Ethan

saw two men, one on either side of the trail, stand up and raise their rifles. Sweet Jimmy O'Brian was on the left, standing alongside the little stream, and Rourke was on the right, half hidden by a boulder. O'Brian fired first, and the head of the first manikin flew off, hat and all, but the rider stayed upright still and the horse kept going. Then Rourke fired at the second rider. Apparently the bullet passed through the manikin. Ethan shouted to Jesús, "Go," and Jesús ran to the other side of the trail and jumped into the weeds alongside the little stream. Simultaneously Ethan pulled his hammer back to full cock, raised his rifle in one smooth motion, and shot Sweet Jimmy just as O'Brian had turned and spotted Ethan, so that the shot took him squarely in the face, about midway between his hat brim and his nose. O'Brian's hat flew off, along with a chunk of his forehead. The force of the shot knocked him flat on his back, and he landed in the watercress at streamside and was still. By this time the horses were nearly through the canyon. The dog had passed them, and was now just a dot in the distance. As soon as he shot O'Brian, Ethan turned to look for Rourke. He saw the other man standing behind the rock about forty yards away. Rourke seemed stunned momentarily, and Ethan chambered another round and fired, but Rourke had ducked behind the rock in time and the bullet ricocheted off the cliff face behind him.

"You got him spotted, Jesús? He's behind that rock in front of me."

"*Sí, señor.* I see where he is."

Jesús began to creep along the stream. He had some trees for cover, but he was exposed now and then.

"Keep your head down, Jesús," yelled Ethan. The other man flattened and began to crawl. Thirty or more yards, and he would be even with the rock where Rourke was hiding. The rock was just barely big enough to protect Rourke, and Ethan could see the man now and then shifting his position behind it. The trail behind him was open, so he would not be able to run. He was trapped.

"Rourke!" yelled Ethan. "Give it up. I want you alive. Just come out from behind there and you'll be all right!"

"Go to hell, ya bastard," said Rourke. "Bastard" came out "bahsturd." *Irishman,* thought Ethan. *Well, that figures.* Ethan stayed alongside the wall of the cliff. There was enough cover there, and he could still see Rourke's rock, and he could see Jesús crawling down the gully by the stream on the other side of the trail.

Slowly Jesús crawled toward a spot opposite Rourke.

"Keep it down, Jesús!" yelled Ethan. "I'll tell you when you're in position! Then find yourself a tree and get behind it."

Jesús kept crawling. When he was at a slight angle from Rourke, Ethan yelled again. "That's good enough, Jesús! Get behind a cottonwood! You'll be able to see Rourke!"

There were a few yards between the gully where Jesús was crawling and a large cottonwood. Ethan could see Jesús gather himself for the quick dash to the tree. He rose up on his haunches and then launched himself in a dive toward the cottonwood. Just as he was landing there was a shot. Ethan did not see where it came from. He hadn't been watching Rourke for that instant. Jesús yelled as he hit the ground, and he landed behind the tree and lay facedown and did not move.

"Jesús! Jesús!" yelled Ethan. "Are you hit?" But there was no answer, and Jesús was not moving.

"Son of a bitch," said Ethan. "Son of a bitch!"

Then he noticed movement behind Rourke's rock. The other man was trying to run away down the canyon. He was crouched over but moving quickly, zigzagging down the trail.

"Rourke!" yelled Ethan. "Stop or you're a dead man!" The other man kept running. He got up from his crouch then and started to sprint, still weaving to spoil Ethan's shot. Ethan felt the rage taking over. It felt like acid in his mouth, and he lost all thought of taking the other man alive. His peripheral vision disappeared. All he could see was Rourke sprinting away, and he raised his rifle and fired. The shot kicked up some dust at Rourke's feet, but he kept going. Ethan levered in another shell and his field of vision narrowed even more and he fired again. The shot took Rourke in the back, and he threw his hands up and his body arched backward and he pitched forward on his face, creating a small dust cloud when he fell. Ethan levered in another shell and fired again. He could see the shot take effect, for Rourke's body flinched and shuddered. Ethan levered in still another shell and fired again, and again the shot went home, this time throwing Rourke's left arm into the air momentarily before it flopped back into the dust. Ethan started walking toward the body in the road levering in another shell and firing again in blind rage. The shot knocked Rourke's hat about twenty feet up the road. Ethan got within ten yards, then pulled his Schofield and shot Rourke in the back twice more. And then he stopped. Rourke was a bloody mess.

"I think you got him," said a voice from halfway up the cliff. "So put down those guns."

It was Shelby. He was standing in a crevice about twenty yards up the cliff. He was pointing a rifle at Ethan's chest.

"I said put down those guns."

Ethan bent down slightly and laid his rifle and his pistol on the ground.

"Now the other pistol. Put it on the ground."

Ethan did it. He watched as Shelby moved slowly down the narrow path of the cliff all the while keeping the rifle pointed at Ethan. He could see there was rage in Shelby's eyes, too, the same rage that Ethan had felt when he saw Jesús get hit. It must have been Shelby who shot him.

"You just killed a couple of good men, Jaeger," said Shelby. He was still moving slowly down the cliff side. "Now, before I deal with you, I want to know who the hell you are and what you know."

Ethan said nothing. He thought about the derringer in his pocket, but the range was still too great. Shelby would have to be within ten yards at least before a derringer would be reliable.

"I said who the hell are you and what do you know? What's your game?" Ethan noticed that in his anger Shelby's brogue had grown thicker. All the years of trying to eradicate his accent had been forgotten in the stress of the moment. Ethan's hands were at his side. He was watching as Shelby moved ever closer, and he was wondering how fast he could get the small gun out of his pocket and fire. He would have to make some quick movement and hope that Shelby's first shot would miss. If that happened, Shelby was a dead man. If it didn't, Ethan was.

"Ah, you're a lawman, sure. I knew you were no newspaperman."

"How could you tell?" said Ethan. He was hoping conversation might distract the man.

"Never mind about that," said Shelby. "I want to know what you know and who the hell you are. With the Army, are you?"

"Why would that matter to you? Unless you had something to do with that payroll."

"Ah, you're a sharp one. Let's not worry about what I've been up to. Let's talk about what you've been doing and who else knows about it."

By this time Shelby had reached the bottom of the cliff and he was walking slowly toward Ethan. When he got to within five yards, he stopped.

"Well," he said. "It looks like you're not going to tell me, so there's no sense in prolonging this." He started to raise his rifle, and Ethan dove to the side and reached frantically into his pocket, but before he could grab his derringer, there was a shot. Ethan looked up at Shelby and saw the other man's stunned expression, and then he saw the blood forming on Shelby's shirt-front. Shelby looked down and dropped his rifle and grabbed at his shirt and tore it open and stared at the wound in his abdomen. He looked at Ethan quizzically, but then his knees buckled, and he fell in a heap and rolled over on his back and died.

"Bueno, señor!" called the voice from the other side of the road.

Ethan stood up. His knees were trembling and he was still shocked by what had so suddenly happened. Jesús was scrambling through the gully toward him.

"Are you all right, my friend?' said Jesús. He came up and put his hand on Ethan's shoulder.

"Yeah, I guess so. What about you? I thought they got you."

"No, *señor*. When I dove to the tree, I hit my head on a root and it stunned me for a moment. I only awoke in time to see you shooting Rourke, and then this man Shelby had you trapped, and I was very fearful that he would shoot you from his place on the cliff. I was about ready to shoot at him, but then he started moving toward you, and I was afraid that if I shot I would miss.

And so I waited, *señor.*" Jesus smiled contritely. "I waited until he stood still."

Ethan exhaled and nodded. "I understand, Jesús."

"I hope my waiting did not cause you too much fearfulness."

"No, Jesús. It was all right. Just fine. You saved me. I could never have gotten my derringer out in time. *Gracias, amigo. Gracias.*"

Jesus nodded and smiled. "I am glad I did not need all these bullets, *señor.*" He slipped off his bandoliers and let them drop. "If I had, we would have been in trouble. Well, what do we do now, *señor?*"

"I guess we'd better round up the horses. I hope they didn't run to Verity when the shooting started. Then we'll pack these fellas up and take them back to Tubac, I suppose. We can keep them there until the Army or the sheriff come for them."

"Yes. *Madre mia!* I have just had a terrible thought, *señor.* What if there had been other men with them. Here we are standing in the middle of the canyon. They could have killed us easily."

Ethan looked around suddenly and then laughed ruefully. "You know, you're right. But I guess if there were others, we wouldn't be here talking about it. Let's see if we can find those horses."

"And Nariz, *señor.* Do not forget him."

"No. He was a big help today."

"I knew he would be. One does not ever completely forget one's past."

"That's true, Jesús. That's true."

The horses had run only a half a mile or so beyond the canyon. They had stopped then, and were grazing peacefully when Ethan and Jesús walked up to them. Neither horse had been hit by the gunfire. The two manikins were still on their backs, but they were leaning to the side, like drunks about to fall, and they were each torn in several places. One had lost his head and, with it, Ethan's hat.

"I guess my hat has a few more holes in it," said Ethan. "Time for a new one, I suppose."

"Yes, and José and Pedro also look a little worse for their adventure. But they can be repaired. And what a story they will have to tell the other residents of the cemetery! They will be the stars of the next Day of the Dead."

They looked around for Nariz, but he was gone. Jesús whistled and called, but he did not appear. "I do not think he was injured, *señor*. He was running too fast. I must tell you a secret about him. He is a little gun-shy. He does not like the noise."

"He'll turn up."

"Oh, yes. He always does, after he has had time to investigate his own ideas for a while."

They rode back to the canyon. They gathered up the three bodies, and wrapped them in the tarp and tied them on to Priam. He did not seem to mind the weight or the smell of the blood. The work was grisly, but doing it gave both men a little time to recover from the shock of the fight. And when they were finished, they sat under a cottonwood and rested their backs against the tree. Jesús got out some cigars and a small flask of tequila. "To settle us, *señor*," he said. Ethan gratefully took a pull on the flask, and then another one. They lit the cigars and sat in the quiet and listened to the little stream and the birds that had resumed their chirping after the noise of the battle. Ethan was very tired. It seemed that all his strength had drained out of him.

"I have been thinking, *señor*, and I have a suggestion for you," said Jesús after a while. "Why don't you let me take these men back to Tubac. You should go to Verity and see this woman who has been in your thoughts."

"I'm not sure I want to, Jesús. We just killed her husband."

"Of course. But perhaps the news will be less shocking coming from you. And as for killing her husband, I have been thinking about that, too. You did not do it. Your conscience is clear, and so is the way to the future. And if you look at it objectively, his death was an accident."

Ethan looked at Jesús. "What do you mean, an accident?"

"Yes, it's true, *señor*. After all, I did the shooting and any time I actually hit something, it is the same as an accident. You could tell her this. Or something similar. It was a mistake that happened when we were ambushed by these men. Perhaps you could say that he was trying to help us and was killed by mistake. There is at least some truth in that, *señor*. Not much, but it will make things easier, I think."

"Your mind grows more and more devious, Jesús."

"No, *señor*. The man is dead now. There is no sense letting his ghost corrupt the future. What can it matter? It is simply to protect this woman. And yourself."

"I don't think I can do that, Jesús. I really don't think I can."

"Well, it is your decision, of course, *señor*. But you have time to think about it. The ride from here to Verity is several hours. That is enough time to think and decide. Whatever you decide, I will support you, *señor*. But please, *señor*, take my advice and go there now. I will take these men back to Tubac. I will send Tomás to Tucson to see the Army and to tell them what has happened. It is not necessary for you to do this with me."

"I don't know."

Jesús put his arm around Ethan. "Go, Señor Knight," he said gently. "Go and rescue the fair lady."

Ethan looked at Jesús. "I'm not sure that's who needs rescuing, Jesús."

"All the more reason to go, my friend."

THE LAST GUNFIGHTER SERIES BY
WILLIAM W. JOHNSTONE

THE EAGLES SERIES BY
WILLIAM W. JOHNSTONE

THE MOUNTAIN MAN SERIES BY
WILLIAM W. JOHNSTONE